BIG RED

Damien Larkin

DANCING LEMUR PRESS, L.L.C.
Pikeville, North Carolina
www.dancinglemurpress.com

Library of Congress Cataloging-in-Publication Data:
Names: Larkin, Damien, author.
Title: Big red / Damien Larkin.
Description: Pikeville, North Carolina : Dancing Lemur
Press, L.L.C., [2019]
Identifiers: LCCN 2018055682 (print) | LCCN 2018057963
(ebook) | ISBN
    9781939844613 (ebook) | ISBN 9781939844606 (pbk.
: alk. paper)
Subjects: | GSAFD: Science fiction.
Classification: LCC PR6112.A746 (ebook) | LCC PR6112.
A746 B54 2019 (print) |
    DDC 823/.92--dc23

Dedication

"In loving memory of Niamh Kennedy. Breathe easy, angel."

At first, I thought the piercing white light that bore down on me flowed from the sparks of an electric buzz saw. A relentless, slicing agony carved through my brain, tearing through flesh and bone, mind and memory. My skull felt as though it was being split in half. But I heard no high-pitched scream of a saw and, from an involuntary muscle spasm in my arm, I found I wasn't restrained.

It took a moment for me to realise sparks weren't raining fiery kisses onto my face and the light above me remained as constant as a laser. I hadn't blinked in what seemed like an eternity, so upon forcing my eyelids shut and reopening them again, my senses burst to life. I rolled over and lifted a shaking hand to rub my throbbing temples. Through my blurry vision, I could make out the polished marble floors of the room. Beside the leg of the folding cot, I spied cracks on the floor and vaguely recalled noting those same cracks the first time I had climbed onto this hard mattress a year before.

Dazed, I perceived another needle of fire being strategically inserted into my brain, causing incomprehensible pain. I let out a roar as my eyes teared up, and I struggled for breath. I gasped, trying to suck in sweet, unrecycled air, and another harsh pain surged through my chest, temporarily forcing me to forget the buzz saw slicing its way through my skull.

In response, a firm, gloved hand gripped my

shoulder and eased me back onto the mattress. A masked figure blocked the painful light glaring down on me, and cold, gloved hands prodded at my head and body. I tried to speak but screams and whimpers escaped. I sensed the cool tears running down my face and squeezed my eyes closed to stop them.

That only made things worse.

In the darkness of my mind, figures emerged and disappeared. They looked like faded silhouettes of people I had known and grown to like—or at least endured—but I couldn't see their faces. It started slow at first, just one or two shadows emerging long enough to mimic a humorous incident from long hours of training, but as the pain in my chest intensified, the silhouettes rushed faster and faster, eager to reach their climax. Days, weeks, and months sped past in a heartbeat, each image more vivid and detailed than the last, until that final moment, and I knew why I was screaming.

I bolted upright in the cot, knocking the doctor away from me. With eyes wide open, I remembered my wound. I saw the stunned doctors shouting for an orderly over the high-pitched ringing in my eardrums. Panicking, I grabbed at my chest to stop the blood from oozing out of my wound. My trembling hand touched the dark green T-shirt that we all wore, but to my surprise, I didn't feel the gaping hole that should have been there. I pulled up my T-shirt to see my pale, hairless skin untouched by blood, not burned flesh. I prodded at myself in disbelief, expecting a barb of pain to shoot through the area where I thought had been operated on, but I felt nothing. The pain in my head and chest retreated, as did the ringing in my ears. It was then that I noted the screaming and shouting around me.

Two pairs of sturdy hands eased me back onto the cot mattress again, and still struggling to make sense of my jumbled thoughts, I offered no resistance. Lying back on the soft pillow, I moved my head from side to side as the doctor completed her checks. She looked vaguely familiar, even behind the mask, and something told me she was trustworthy.

All around me were rows of cots with dozens of uniformed soldiers in various states of agonised shock. Some fought with the orderlies, roaring and screaming incoherently, and others were curled up in the foetal position, numb from what they had experienced. Cries of pain and bitter sobs of regret echoed throughout the room, a testament to the horror we had survived.

A light shone into my eyes. Looking up, I saw the red-haired doctor standing over me, studying me in-depth. This time, the light caused no pain, so I let her do what she needed. After a moment, she pulled down her face mask and, with a clinical expression, spoke to me.

"Do you remember where you are?"

I didn't. The room was familiar. I knew I had been here a year before, but a fog draped itself over my memory. I was positive I could navigate the halls of this place but had no idea of its purpose or what we were doing here.

"Yes," I lied, surprised to hear my voice so hoarse.

I must have been screaming non-stop from the moment I regained consciousness. As if reading my mind, she reached behind her to a small, metallic trolley and pulling out a plastic container with a flexible straw, uncapped it, and handed it to me. My quivering hands accepted it. Parched, I sucked on the straw. The cool water made its way down my aching throat to spread instant relief throughout my body.

"What's the last thing you remember happening?" she asked, scrutinising my every movement.

Although it sounded like a typical question to be

ticked off a medical checklist, I got the impression that the doctor had no idea what we'd been through and was genuinely confounded by our pain-filled outbursts.

"I got shot," I groaned and tapped at my chest.

For a moment, the pain was real again. Searing, hot flames engulfed my torso and ate away at my innards, but as soon as I patted myself, it faded. A part of me wondered if it had really happened, if it was part of a twisted nightmare or a side effect of the treatment, but the memory felt so real. I couldn't remember the exact circumstances, but I recalled being lodged into a shaft or confined space with two or three others when I got hit.

"I need you to focus your mind and try to remember. Did anyone else make it? Is anyone else alive up there?"

Up where?

I could see snippets of a firefight and older memories of training and patrols but nothing else sprang to mind. Sensing the urgency of her question, I focused on that image of the shaft and studied it for tell-tale clues. At least three others were there, but from the shouts and sounds of explosions that hung outside the boundaries of my memory, there had to be more. I remembered being terrified to the core. Although the adrenaline kept me moving, my hands had trembled as I held my weapon. The sound of intense hand-to-hand combat echoed from all around us, and the screams of the dying grew closer as an unseen enemy approached.

"Think," she said, rubbing my shoulder gently with a cold hand. "Did anyone else make it out alive?"

Trying to focus, I shifted in the cot and looked around. Surely there had to be someone in the room who could answer that better than me. To my right, I thought the soldier occupying the cot looked comatose, but then I saw his eyes. Huge and mesmerizing, they drew me in. A vague familiarity hung about him. His feet dangled, unmoving, off the edge of the cot, and his large hands rested on his chest. His smooth, ebony skin betrayed not a single scratch or mark, but those dark eyes gazed deep into mine, as if to communicate with me. His lips moved slowly as he mouthed something. Too drained and disorientated to make the effort of whispering back, I furrowed my brow and shook my head at him to show that I didn't understand. Without blinking, he moved his lips more concisely and whispered something with a raspy voice that terrified me to the core.

"Kill them all."

The doctor turned at the sudden utterance. While waving for another orderly, she began checking the traumatised soldier.

"We have another one," she shouted over the din of cries and screams.

Once she made sure someone tended to him, she returned her attention to me. She signalled for a drip and, without any warning, jabbed a needle into my arm. Unable to resist, I watched the transparent fluid flow from the drip into my body. Behind me there was a clash and clang of a trolley falling over and the grunts and shouts of what sounded like a scuffle.

"We need security in here now," a harsh voice shouted from somewhere in the room. "They've totally lost it. They need to be restrained and sedated until we know exactly what happened."

"They need compassion," the red-haired doctor above me fired back in anger. "They're our girls and boys, and God only knows what they've gone through. Restrain them if you have to, sedate them if necessary, but don't treat them like the enemy."

It was good to know someone was on our side, whoever they were. Whoever *we* were for that matter.

BIG RED

The doctor returned her attention to me and, placing a hand on my wrist, checked my pulse.

"Feeling better?" she asked.

I was. Whatever was in that drip was making me float. All the pain and fear that had crashed through my skull evaporated. The screams of agony dwindled to soft background noise. It was like being back in a womb.

"Focus on my voice," she said, and I did. "I need you to think very, very hard. I know whatever you experienced was traumatic, but there are people still up there. Your people. I need you to remember exactly what happened. You said you got shot. Who shot you?"

I replayed the memory in my head again, but I couldn't see anyone. I was doing something with my left hand while holding a rifle or a gun in my right.

"I don't know. I didn't see them."

"Were you on the base when you got shot?"

I thought about it as hard as I could.

"What base?"

She patted me on the arm again and looked around her. Raising her right hand, she shook it vigorously at someone. After a few moments, a bearded man, with his face mask wrapped around his chin approached. He ignored me as he spoke with the red-haired doctor.

"I don't know how to explain it," she whispered, turning her back on me as if that would drown out her words. "Something must have happened during the transfer procedure. All of the simulations we ran never indicated the possibility of this level of memory fragmentation."

The bearded man turned to look at me and saw me staring up at him. He forced a smile before returning his attention to the doctor.

"It may be a temporary side-effect from them coming back so soon. This one seems far more lucid than the rest. Maybe they need time to recuperate. Check the records. They've been through a lot in the last year. That would take its toll even on veteran soldiers."

"Maybe," the red-haired doctor continued, "but right now, we don't have time. We need to find out what happened. I want you to supervise the rest. I'll take this one and see if we can jog his memory. Call Doctor Ling and get her down here, too."

"Okay, Doctor," the bearded man said. Without another word, he turned and walked away.

"Orderlies," the doctor called out and beckoned them over. She must have signalled something to them when I wasn't watching because one of the orderlies made his way to an empty patient trolley, which he dragged to my cot.

"We're going to move you, Corporal Luglin."

That didn't sound like my name.

Two hands eased themselves under my head and back, and another pair of hands gripped under my combat boots. With a three count, they hoisted me onto the trolley. One of the orderlies grabbed the drip and attached it to the trolley. Without warning, they strapped restraints around my wrists, ankles, and waist, pulling them tight to confirm they were secure. Then they began manoeuvring me between the rows of distressed soldiers. Confused at the name, I reached a weak hand under my T-shirt and pulled out a pair of dog tags resting on my chest.

"Loughlin," I said, correcting the doctor as she led the trolley towards our destination, "pronounced Lock-Linn. I'm Irish."

"My apologies," she said, half turning her head as she led the way.

My fingers continued toying with the dog tags.

"Darren Loughlin," I said aloud to no one in particular. That sounded familiar. The dog tags also confirmed my serial number, blood type, religion, and nationality.

The orderlies wheeled me past another two-dozen screaming, shouting, and horrified soldiers before pushing me through double doors into a side room. They inserted my trolley carefully between two rows of computer screens and strange-looking medical equipment. Without prompting, one of them hoisted my head rest as the orderlies prepared me for whatever was to come next.

The taller of the two male orderlies rubbed a cool gel onto my temples before sticking on some sort of miniature suction cups, and the smaller one attached what looked like a blood pressure cuff tightly around my right arm. While he did it, the smaller orderly kept glancing at me strangely. Like the soldier who had lain in the cot to my right, he looked as if he was trying to communicate something to me, but I had no idea of what.

The doctor called the taller orderly over to the monitors, and the moment their backs were turned, the smaller orderly leaned forward, pretending to check my drip. As quick as a flash, he pressed something small and cold into the palm of my right hand. I instinctively wrapped my hand around it to conceal the object from view and shifted my weight to hide it underneath my right thigh. Even though I only held it for a few seconds, a part of me already knew what it was. I had held it a hundred times before and knew it was dangerous.

"Stall them for as long as possible," he muttered under his breath. "When it's time, you'll know. *Salient.*"

I opened my mouth to speak, but he had already turned and headed towards the doctor.

"Wait outside," the doctor said to the orderlies when the double doors swung open again.

A tall Asian woman burst through the doors with a look of concern plastered over her face. She wore a long, neatly pressed black skirt and a white blouse. Several long beady ornaments dangled from her neck. She greeted the doctor with a nod before looking towards me. Smoothing her skirt and careful not to bump into the nearby computer monitors glaring down at me, she took a seat and pulled out paper files and a tablet device from her bag.

"Mr. Loughlin, how are you today?" she asked, trying to maintain eye contact as she leafed through several pages.

"I've been better," I groaned back. My throat still hurt, but I was glad I didn't sound as hoarse as I did earlier.

"My name is Doctor Ling," she said, extending a friendly hand to shake mine. I raised my right hand and waggled it against the restraints to show I was unable to reciprocate. Undeterred, she stood, leaned over me at an awkward angle, and gripped my hand. Resisting the urge to break eye contact and take advantage of the view that her loose blouse would undoubtedly present, I smiled back politely.

"I'm the head psychologist for the program, and I'd like to touch base with you about your condition."

"My schedule's clear."

"Great," she said, and flashed her wrist as she pushed a few renegade strands of hair behind her ear. "You've probably witnessed a lot of alarming things here since you've returned. It must be confusing for you, but rest assured, you're in good hands."

I felt safe, but then again, that could have been the drugs they were pumping into me.

"Do you know where you are?"

I thought hard about it. Although I recognised the room I woke up in and a few of the faces, I couldn't place myself. I shook my head.

13

"That's okay. It's normal considering what you've been through. I have full confidence that your memories will return in due process. We just need to give them a jump start."

She picked up the tablet device and became engrossed by something of interest. Distracted, she forced herself back to the present and placed the tablet on the chair beside her.

"We're going to try something a bit different, if that's okay with you?" Doctor Ling asked. I nodded my consent to proceed. "I'm sure it must be frustrating trying to remember where you are and what's happened to you and your colleagues, so I want you to push all of that from your mind. For the moment, we'll push aside the MOF, EISEN, Mars, and the program, and start with the basics."

"Mars?"

I looked at her as if she had two heads.

"Yes, Mars. We'll focus on that later. To start: Can you tell me what today's date is?"

I was still baffled by that "Mars" utterance but decided to play along. I tried to focus my jumbled mind to find any record or reminder of what the date could be.

"Twenty-fourth of...March..."

"Very good," Doctor Ling said, and smiled as she made a note on her tablet. "Do you remember what year it is?"

"2018."

That didn't sound right, but a voice inside me told me it was.

"Correct again," she said, scribbling. "And how long has your assignment lasted?"

A voice on the inside told me this was a trick question. A voice that protected me when danger was near.

"From your perspective or mine?" I asked, unable

to mask a victorious smile at spotting her trick question.

"Your perspective is the one that matters," she said with a wink.

"Thirteen months from my point of view."

"Great. This is great, Darren. Your ability to recall these details shows that you haven't suffered any permanent damage. It may take time, but if we start slow, it won't be long before you'll feel as right as rain."

She was right. I wasn't sure how, but the more I spoke, the more I felt as though the fractured pieces of my life were slowly reassembling. Images flashed through my mind, but it felt more like a laptop updating its software. It started at one percent and moved gradually upwards as my life and memories began downloading. It was a strange sensation inherently knowing but not able to access or recall specific things at will.

"Okay, next," the doctor continued. "I want you to tell me how you joined the program. Focus on what your life was like before and how you came to join. We'll get to the bigger stuff in time."

"Hopefully not too much time," I said before laughing. "I'm pretty sure I have somewhere I need to be. Okay, here goes..."

There's nothing important about me, nothing that marks me as anything different from anyone else you know. I'm that person you barely notice on your way to work, that familiar face in the office whose name you don't know. I'm liked and I'm happy, but I've never been special.

I grew up in a suburb of Dublin, Ireland and spent most of my life there. It was a nice area; it had its rough spots, but I liked it. At school, I passed tests and did my homework, but my scores didn't indicate I was gifted or anything.

Growing up, I was a typical teenage boy who chased girls, got into fights, and had fun with my friends, but no matter what I got myself into, I never brought trouble to my mother's door. She knew I was no angel, but I think she knew that I was smart enough to never get caught.

At seventeen, I joined the Reserve Defence Forces— Ireland's version of the British Territorial Army or the American National Guard. As a neutral country, it wasn't as though there was any chance we'd ever see any action, but when one of my buddies told me he enlisted, I decided to check it out.

That probably ranks as one of the best decisions I ever made. From the moment they marched us around the parade square, I was hooked. It wasn't just the assault rifles and uniforms, it was the camaraderie, the discipline, the notion that for once I was giving back to the country I loved so much. They also had cheap, tax-free beer. That helped, too.

I spent seven years in the Reserves. Although exhausting and a lot of times boring, I enjoyed it. Seven years later, only myself and two others remained out of a training platoon once thirty-three people strong, so we asked for our discharge papers and left.

I wasn't sure where to go next and bounced between jobs, working and partying—sometimes doing both simultaneously. That is, until I met Louise. We hit it off straight away. She was fiery, intelligent, and ambitious. She was so ambitious that when we moved in together and had a daughter a few years later, I committed to staying at home to raise Kat.

It was on another average day when I got the call that would change my life. I had picked up Kat from play school and was watching her race around the room, still exhausted from my birthday celebrations a few days earlier, when my phone buzzed.

I didn't recognise the number, but thinking it was Louise calling from another number, I answered.

"Oi! Oi! Governor!" a voice with a mock-English accent greeted me.

I recognized the joker on the other end of the line as Rory and laughed, greeting my ex-army comrade.

As Kat ran about, content like only a child could be, I dived into it with Rory. We talked like the old friends that we were and caught up quickly.

I was glad to hear he had stuck with his career in the British Army and had recently returned from a deployment to Afghanistan as a logistics officer. He shared colourful stories about his time over there before asking what I had been up to. I didn't have much to share, so that didn't take too long. At this point, Kat got upset with a doll that made the mistake of refusing to obey her will. Sensing a tidal wave of temper tantrums, I was bringing our talk to a friendly conclusion when Rory said the innocent words that would cost me a portion of my life and a head-full of jumbled, fractured memories.

"Ever wish you could get paid to play with guns and blow stuff up on the weekends again?"

"Hell yeah," I responded enthusiastically. "I'd give my left arm to re-live those days, but I don't have the time between work, Kat, and Louise's job. If only, eh?"

"That's why I called you, brother," Rory continued. His infectious enthusiasm leaked through the phone. "The EU is putting together a new program for ex-service personnel. It's in beta-phase at this stage, and it's strictly hush-hush and invite-only, but they're looking for people with skills to do some flexible work. You interested?"

It sounded too good to be true and, in my experience, if it sounded too good to be true, it usually was.

"Yeah, man, it sounds great, but I'm sure those types of things are for ex-full timers. As tempting as it is, I have to look after Kat, and there's no way I could get time off work. The weekends are way too busy."

"That's the thing—" Rory laughed, and excitement built in his voice. "It's totally unlike anything before. It doesn't matter what your skill level is. As long as you served and you pass the tests, you're in. I'm telling you, brother, if you do one weekend a month, that works out as the equivalent of a few weeks of pay now. Imagine having more time with Louise and Kat for doing something you'd be good at and not having to work at that dead-end job."

As sales pitches went, his was pretty damn good.

"There has to be a catch, though," I pressed. "What does it involve?"

Rory laughed again.

"The catch works in your favour, my friend. I got posted to it recently as a liaison officer. It's a European initiative to create a part time, flexible body of troops that can aid the civil power in times of emergency and free up duties for front line personnel. The British are overseeing it so far, but with everything going on with them and to keep it fair and equal, the EU has pushed for quotas from different nationalities to apply, and they need more Irish and Europeans. Since it's invite-only, consider this yours. You just need to pass the tests and you're in."

I was sold. I spoke with Rory for a few more minutes, squeezing as much information as possible out of him before letting him go. Barely a few minutes passed after hanging up when an application pinged straight into my phone's email inbox.

Louise encouraged me to go for it. The very next day, I got a response on my application. The assessment stage was set for the coming Saturday morning, which was short notice, but Louise being Louise managed to book me a cheap flight to London on Friday night, stay in a nice hotel, and then fly back early on Sunday, all as an additional birthday present. I made plans with Rory to go out for drinks afterwards, so everything wrapped up well.

Screw my job. They could get by without me for one weekend.

I'm not going to go into too much detail about the flight over. Suffice it to say, I'm not the biggest fan of airplanes, but it was uneventful and thankfully my plane didn't smash into the Irish Sea in a giant ball of flames.

Assessment day dawned. After showering, shaving, and getting changed into my freshly pressed suit, I hailed a London cab and arrived fifteen minutes early at the address for the interview. It was a mundane office block smack bang in the centre of London with nothing indicating it as being affiliated with the military. My heart pounded as I re-read the email, fearing I had the wrong address, but everything checked out.

Composing myself, I approached the revolving door and greeted the receptionist. Dressed in a black uniform that made him look more like a security guard, he unexpectedly flashed a disarming smile and, after taking my name, held up a leather-bound tablet and rose from his seat to study it. For a moment, I thought he was trying to take my picture, but he turned it around to show me a photo of myself, which was accompanied with additional information. It struck me as strange, since I'd never sent them my picture, but I didn't say anything.

He directed me towards a solitary door to the right of the reception desk and buzzed me in. I opened the solid, reinforced door. On the other side, two heavily armed men clad entirely in black greeted me. At that point, I wondered if I'd fallen victim to an elaborate kidnapping scam, but realising I wasn't worth that much to anyone, I flashed them a nervous smile.

They thoroughly patted me down and ran me through a metal detector. Despite the fact I wasn't carrying a weapon of any kind, I relaxed immediately when they found nothing incriminating on me and followed one of the guards as he escorted me down a long, well-lit corridor. At the end, we reached a lift. The guard punched in a code and then led me into it.

"Don't be nervous," he said as the lift doors slammed closed.

"Thanks. Can I..."

"I'm not authorised to answer questions. But you look as though you're about to crap yourself. Pull it together. You'll do fine."

Strangely enough, an armed guard telling me I looked as if I was about to void my bowels did reassure my fraying nerves. I took a deep breath and told myself I could do this. I had nothing to lose. Or so I thought.

We descended several floors before the lift doors creaked open and the guard gestured for me to step out. I nodded my thanks and stepped out into an illuminated, sterile-looking corridor. A tall and thin man with an immaculate suit and greasy, slicked-back black hair nodded politely at me.

"Mr. Loughlin," he said, extending his hand and firmly shaking mine, "I'm glad you could make it. Shall we?"

He gestured to my left, and we walked and chatted politely about London and the weather. What followed next was four hours of non-stop gruelling psychometric, physical, and mental testing. It wasn't as bad as I expected, though, because although I get a bit jittery, I excel at interviews.

The questions themselves were nothing unusual and gave no hint about the actual program or my expected duties. It was standard stuff: talking about myself, my life, my time in the Reserves, what I would do in this or that situation, how I would resolve a certain series of problems, and so forth. Once you've heard one set of interview questions, you've heard them all. The written test was next, which didn't seem any different from tests I'd done in school. Most of the questions were straightforward problem-solving, while others were similar to that of a personality test, like the ones Louise had gotten me to do online.

The physical side of the assessment was the thing I was afraid might let me down. I wouldn't class myself as unfit, but I'd let myself go a little. It had been hard to find a proper balance between working, looking after Kat, and the million other things I had to do every day.

For this part of the test, the slicked-back hair man, who never gave me his name, led me into a changing room and handed me a green Army-style uniform. The camouflage patterns weren't Irish or British, or any other nation's colourings that I recognised, but I pulled them on all the same. After donning the trousers, T-shirt, shirt, and combat boots, they led me into a waiting area, where I got a first glimpse of my soon-to-be-comrades. Everyone appeared nervous, so taking advantage of that, I cracked a few jokes to lighten the mood. I could tell it was well received; sometimes people need someone to break the ice before they know it's okay to let their guard down. Thinking about it now, although I didn't know them at the time, that was the first time I spoke to Tazz, Smack, and Big Mo.

They led us to a large exercise hall filled with all sorts of equipment and training gear. They ordered us to remove our shirts and attached heart rate monitors to our chests and suction cup devices to our temples. Then we began group exercises. It was excruciating, but I held my own, as did everyone else.

After giving us all water, one of the doctors led us back to the waiting room and told us we'd be called upon one at a time to discuss whether we'd made it to the next round. A few minutes later, they called my name. I said my goodbyes to everyone and exited the room. I remember thinking at the time that they were a nice bunch of people and I hoped that if I got through, I'd see them again. I was escorted into a nearby office where a bureaucrat in a suit and a cheap haircut looked me up and down with bored indifference.

"Congratulations, Mr. Loughlin. You've passed. We'd like to offer you a position in the program."

I was stunned. I had expected there to be at least another round of interviews or assessments, but, after replaying his words over in my mind, there was no way I could be misinterpreting him.

"Thank you, sir," I said, trying my best to contain my excitement. "I'm grateful for this opportunity.

When do I start?"

"Soon," he replied dryly. "You'll need to sign some paperwork first, followed by a mandatory blood test. Once everything is signed, you'll be briefed on all relevant information. Please follow the nurse outside."

He waved at the door for me to leave. Without another glance, he returned to something far more interesting than me buried in his paper work. Smiling, I left the room as Tazz walked in, nodding as she gave me a cheery wink and a smile. The nurse silently led me back down the corridor towards the lift I had emerged from earlier, but we took a left through another set of reinforced, security code-protected doors. As the doors opened, I was surprised to see at least two or three dozen uniformed applicants already queued up in a line by the wall ahead of me. I didn't recognise any of them from the waiting room, but it made sense that they'd have multiple, smaller assessment groups all on the same day. The nurse motioned for me to join the line and, after disappearing for a moment, returned with a clipboard and at least a hundred pages of a document attached to it. The writing was extra small; it looked as though I had the guts of a compressed encyclopaedia to read through and the queue edged forward at a quick pace.

Several more interviewees from my own assessment group fell into line, flashing me victorious smiles as I tried to speed read through the document. Unfortunately, I'm not fluent in legalese, but from skimming through some of the pages, it seemed to be about protecting the program from liability in the event of injury. I could understand the logic to that, but I felt a bit uneasy at signing something that I hadn't had the time to read through properly.

The top of the queue stopped at the entrance to an open set of doors. By the time I reached the top, I'd barely gotten through the first few pages when an authoritative "Next!" called from the room.

Still trying to race through the document, I stepped forward and found myself in a large, open hall with dozens of green, foldout cots. A sterile room with gleaming white walls and dozens of large, luminous lights glared down at us, illuminating every aspect of the hall. Already, at least thirty or forty uniformed applicants were sprawled on or sitting on the cots with dozens of scurrying orderlies racing around, pushing trolleys laden with equipment back and forth. I noted three other sets of double doors along the far wall and wondered if more groups were in there, too.

At the head of the room sat three doctors working from a folding table, surrounded by stacks of paperwork. I eagerly approached them, hoping they could answer a few questions.

"Name?" a tall, bearded doctor asked.

"Loughlin, Darren, Sir."

Without looking up at me, he handed me a ball point pen.

"Please sign the areas highlighted with stickers," he said.

I looked back at the clipboard in my hands and noted four stickers at the edges of the document, showing where I had to sign.

"That's the thing, sir. I haven't had a chance to read everything before I sign—"

He sighed loudly and rubbed his face in annoyance. "Christ, there's always one," he growled through his hands.

I thought his frustration was a bit extreme considering I only had a few questions before I signed my life away. Beside him, a red-haired doctor with cool eyes looked up at me.

"Mr. Loughlin, my name is Doctor Lucas. Allow me to be blunt. You are fully entitled to read every word of that document, but if you haven't read it by now, we'll have to stop the queue completely and wait for you to go through it line by line before proceeding. That means everyone else out there in the corridor will have to wait until you're done and everyone else in here will have to sit there, unable to leave. Would you really like that to be the first impression your future colleagues have of you?"

That hit home a bit. I suddenly felt the eyes of all my future comrades staring up at me, judging me. They probably weren't, but I still didn't want to be *that guy.*

"I swore an oath, Mr. Loughlin, to do no harm," she continued, "you have my word as a doctor that there's nothing illegal in that document. It's a standard waiver to cover the program from liability in the event of injury. If you were to be injured, that document states that we'll cover the full cost of any medical expenses or loss of earnings. It is entirely your choice, though. Would you like to step aside and read this document or would you like to proceed?"

All three of the doctors looked at me with a combination of frustration and pleading. Against my better judgment, I conceded. Resting the clipboard on their table, I quickly signed my name on all the relevant spaces. If you couldn't trust a doctor, who could you trust?

Relieved, the doctor thanked me and signalled for an orderly to lead me away, before calling for the next applicant to come in. The masked orderly led me through the maze of cots before selecting an empty one and ordered me to take my shirt off and sit down. Despite being self-conscious about how sweat-stained my T-shirt underneath would be from the earlier workout, I did as I was told.

Gesturing to a nearby nurse pushing around a trolley, he gave her my name. She checked her clipboard, rummaged around in a plastic box, and pulled out a small plastic bag with my name labelled on it. The orderly took it from her, pulled out a set of dog tags, and told me to put them on. I remember thinking how weird it was that they already had a set of dog tags made for me when I'd just signed up, but I pushed that out of my mind, too.

With everyone settled, the orderlies eventually made their way around the room and one-by-one took blood samples from us before giving us separate inoculations. I was a bit wary of being injected with something containing an unknown substance, but a neighbour asked the burning question of what it was. The orderly advised it was a backup injection to reinforce our immune systems and it was perfectly fine, but that the side-effects sometimes resulted in drowsiness or temporary disorientation; hence the cots.

When it came to my turn, I didn't even ask and presented my arm. I looked around to see those who had gone before me were mostly lying back on the cots, looking around or fidgeting to get comfortable. Sure enough, a minute or two after the injection, my mind went hazy, and I decided it was best to lay back, too. My head swam, but I hoped the powerful white light above my cot would be enough to keep me conscious. I didn't want to be known as the guy who made a fuss about paperwork and then passed out.

It wasn't to be, though. Even with the light shining down on me, my eyelids grew heavier and my brain drifted away. I didn't fight it and remember thinking that everything would be fine when I woke up in a few minutes.

"**A**nd that brings us to right now," I concluded, glancing over at Doctor Ling.

My head felt a lot better. Although the calming euphoria of the drugs they were pumping into my body affected me, my mind was starting to focus. I could recall most of my memories from prior to the job interview and snippets of what happened after, although in certain places they were a bit fuzzy. Apart from a few grainy images of a firefight, I couldn't recall what had happened to me yesterday or the day before.

Doctor Ling finished scribbling her notes before looking back up at me.

"So, what happened next?"

"I woke up on Phobos."

"And what happened after you woke up?"

"That was thirteen months ago," I stated, ignoring her question.

Turning away from her, I focused my attention on the doctor gazing intently at the monitors at the end of the room.

"I thought you looked familiar. No, 'trustworthy' was what I was thinking when I first woke up. You look similar to the doctor who told me I had nothing to worry about when I signed that damn contract a year ago."

Doctor Lucas turned away from her work to look at me. I could see a flash of remorse cut across her cool exterior, but her lips remained firmly shut as she looked in my direction. I don't know why, but a surge

27

of hostility rose in me. It felt like something left over from weeks of dwelling, like when you have a fight with your partner and it goes on for so long that you forget what the actual tiff was about.

"I remember lying down in a room similar to the one I woke up in, after an interview a year ago. Tell me doctor, how long has it been for you since I lost consciousness?"

"There's no need for this," she replied, trying to maintain her professional composure. "You've already been briefed. You know exactly how this works. We're on the same side. Right now, civilians are counting on us. We don't have time for games."

"Answer the question or I stop talking. I want to hear you say it. I laid down on that cot over a year ago. How long ago was that for you?" I hissed at her.

The doctor shifted her weight before taking a few steps towards the foot of my trolley and folding her arms. "Okay, fine. You and everyone else were unconscious for exactly seventeen minutes. You were supposed to serve a twelve-month tour of duty and be rotated back after sixty minutes, my time. Instead, according to the Compression Matrix logs, you were gone for thirteen months and you were back in a quarter of the recommended time. On top of that, the exact minute that we received the compression signal, we lost contact with every one of our off-world colonies. Every single one has gone dark."

She turned, walked towards the double doors leading to the room that I'd woken up in, and threw them open. Outside, I could still hear the cries and groans of my comrades, although it had quietened down considerably. With steel in her voice, she turned to face me while gesturing towards the noise outside.

"Three quarters of your fellow soldiers haven't returned and those who have show evidence of Post-Traumatic Stress Disorder from gunshot wounds, stabbings, and dismembered limbs, indicating an extremely violent confrontation. Only two of you are lucid enough to speak, so we must focus on the task at hand. We need to know what happened up there or everything we've worked for and sacrificed for is over. Do you understand?"

"Okay, that's enough," Doctor Ling interjected, holding her hand up to silence the doctor. She returned her attention to me and patted me reassuringly on the hand.

"I'm glad it's coming back to you, Darren. I really am. I know the last year hasn't been easy for you, and you have every right to be angry. Let's continue to take this nice and slow. We'll figure this out together, shall we?"

I ignored Doctor Lucas and returned my attention to Doctor Ling, nodding my consent. As I shifted in the trolley to get comfortable, I felt the cylinder the orderly had slipped me nestled underneath my right thigh. For a moment, I saw a flash of what it could be used for and, stretching my muscles as a pretext, looked around at the monitors on my left and right, wondering if it would work on one of them. No rush, though. I still hadn't received the signal yet—whatever it was supposed to be.

"Fine," I continued, "so, I woke up in Asaph Hall Research Station, on Phobos..."

I remember blinking my eyes a few times and wondering if the whole interview had been a dream. It took a few seconds for my memories to load up and my brain to switch back on before I bolted upright in the cot. For a moment, I feared I had been the only one who passed out, but while peering groggily around the room, I noticed the rest of my comrades were still comatose.

It struck me as odd that all of us had been rendered unconscious by the inoculation, but that was quickly overshadowed by the realisation that we were no longer in the same room. We were in the exact same order, but everything appeared completely different. Those sterile, white walls were now grey; the large luminous lights now dim and much smaller; and our standard-issue folding cots replaced with medical beds.

I contemplated waking someone up when a door at the top-right of the room whooshed open. Dressed like a surgeon in blue scrubs, a man strolled in, whistling quietly, and headed towards a desk at the head of the room. He grabbed a chart and turned to exit. That's when he must've spied me out of the corner of his eye, because he dropped the chart to the ground and jumped back in fright. Then he let out a laugh, half in shock, half trying to catch his breath.

"You scared the living hell out of me," he said as he stood straight again. "I'm glad you're awake, though. We were wondering when you sleepy heads would rise and shine."

"Where am I?" I groaned, desperate for a caffeine fix to force my brain cells to activate. "Were we out for long?"

The surgeon patted his chart and inhaled loudly through his teeth, as if contemplating how to answer.

"You know what? I'm gonna let the higher-ups go through all that with you. Hang tight and someone will be with you shortly."

I watched him leave, too tired to press the matter, and took a seat back on my bed. Several of my new colleagues began to stir from our unexpected slumber. By the time anyone came for us, we were all awake, grouchy, and hungry. I hoped we hadn't been asleep too long. The email said that the entire assessment would be completed by 4pm, but we had gotten our injections at around 3pm. I was looking forward to sharing my good news with Rory later over a few well-deserved beers.

The door opened and a small but stocky female soldier entered. She stood a few paces from the door and glanced around the room at all of us. She wore the same green uniform, although hers was far neater, pressed, and ironed. Without even seeing her sergeant's rank markings, the hard jaw and scowl she wore easily marked her as a senior non-commissioned officer.

"All right, everyone on your feet. Let's go," she called out. "Move it. Follow the lights on the floor."

Anyone who had still been lazing on their beds immediately jumped to their feet and, like a zombie horde from an '80s horror, we lumbered towards the door. The corridor outside was far brighter, and it took a minute for my eyes to adjust. Like the room, it was plain and grey, giving no indication of even what floor we were on.

As the sergeant had stated, small green lights

flashed along the sides of the floor, like waves gently lapping against the beach, ushering us in the right direction. Small chatter broke out as we walked, but I kept to myself, hoping they would feed and dismiss us so I could call Louise and tell her I was okay.

After about twenty meters, the head of the group stopped at two reinforced doors that refused to open. The sergeant shoved her way through until she reached the front of the group. She ran a swipe card over a plastic scanner to the right, and the doors shot open, revealing another length of corridor ahead with multiple doors.

"Follow the lights," the sergeant roared at us again.

As we filed out and continued along the corridor, someone dared to ask the sergeant when we would be dismissed, only to be told in graphic and colourful language to shut it or risk having a boot forcibly inserted in a place where boots weren't designed to go.

A few of us snickered, but no one dared to ask anything else and continued towards the end of the corridor. Another set of reinforced doors automatically opened, revealing a large auditorium. Rows and rows of seats started at the front of a raised stage at the far-end of the room and worked their way back, each row increasing in height. I was tempted to risk taking a seat somewhere in the back row, but unwilling to break ranks, I followed the green lights flashing us closer to the stage. It took a few minutes for the auditorium to fill up, and I noted that far more people than just my group were present. With a quick glance, it looked as though there were over two hundred of us, with seating capacity for at least a hundred more.

While awaiting further instructions, I studied the rest of the room, hoping for tell-tale clues as to our location. When I first entered the building, I went down a few levels in the elevator, so I figured they moved us to another level after we lost consciousness, but that struck me as a bit unnecessary. The other door in the room looked to be situated to the right-hand side of the stage, which also appeared suspiciously devoid of markings. The walls to the left and right of the auditorium were also grey and bare, except for the ten metre partitions on the left wall, which looked as though they were sealed over windows. The stage held two podiums on each side and a row of fold out chairs neatly lined up against the wall in the centre.

"On your feet," the sergeant called from somewhere behind us, and we did as we were told. The door to the right of the stage slid open. An officer in a strange green, formal dress uniform strolled out, followed by a doctor clad in blue scrubs and a nervous-looking man in brown slacks and a white lab coat. The officer made his way to the podium on our left while the other two men took their seats. The officer leafed through a few files in front of him before grabbing the microphone and adjusting it towards his mouth.

"Be seated," he commanded in a posh, well-spoken voice. I guessed him to be in his late fifties, possibly early sixties, with a worn and creased face, but his body language was rigid as a statue. He struck me as someone who, despite appearance, was far fitter than any one of us. He removed his black beret to reveal wisps of snow-white hair wrapped around a balding crown, raised his hand towards the back row, and waited. It took a few moments but the doors opened to rows of black-clad, masked soldiers sporting strange assault rifles. They formed a protective cordon around the stage and filed along the back row. That was the first time I remember having a bad feeling about what I had signed up for.

"Good morning," he began and tried his best to force a smile. The auditorium reciprocated halfheartedly, probably because it was the afternoon. Then it struck me—had we slept all day and night? Was it Sunday already? I hoped Louise wasn't worried about me.

"Thank you all for being here," the officer continued. "My name is Brigadier-General Sir Walter Penford, commanding officer of this installation and formally of Her Majesty's Irish Guard. I am sure many of you will have questions with regards to your assignment and the circumstances surrounding your involvement in the program. To that end, I would like to present Doctor Bradley Milton, who will answer any questions better suited to his role."

The doctor fidgeted nervously in his chair, appearing unsure of whether to approach the podium on the right-hand side or stay seated. He waved his hand at us, but a look from the brigadier-general confirmed he was to take his spot. Grabbing his suitcase, he stumbled forward before sheepishly mumbling a hello into his own microphone.

"There is no easy way to say this, but I believe a demonstration would be apt to allow you all to grasp our current situation," the brigadier-general said.

He reached into this pocket, pulled out a small rectangular box, not unlike a television remote control, pointed it at the left wall, and pressed a button. We all turned to study the wall for this demonstration, but nothing happened. The room remained deathly silent as we continued watching. After a few more moments, we returned our confused attention back to the podium.

"You need to press and hold the button, sir," Doctor Milton whispered loudly, while covering the microphone with his hand. The brigadier-general continued fumbling with the remote, forcing the doctor to leave his podium and point out the relevant button. The general mumbled something inaudible under his breath but, finding the correct button, raised his hand again and pressed it.

Again, we turned our attention to the left wall and waited. A few seconds later, I thought the general still hadn't figured out how to operate the device and was about to turn away when I saw a flicker of light and movement. A crack had appeared at the bottom of the partition, allowing a small line of dull light through. I realised I was correct in thinking that the partitions were giant, sealed-over windows and the brigadier-general was in the process of raising the external shutters upwards to look outside.

At that moment, what I thought was my worst concern at the time crept to life. Instead of sunshine, a dim blackness seeped through, meaning I had lost most of, if not all, of my Saturday. I shook my head in frustration that I'd missed an opportunity to get drunk with Rory and wondered why the general was wasting his time showing us a window view. I was about to look away again when something else caught my eye.

As the shutters inched upwards, a handful of sparkling lights on a black velvet background came into view. Twinkling softly, I realised these were stars, but they were nothing in comparison to what took up the view through the middle windows. Large, ominous, swirling red and brown colours danced and weaved before us, drowning out everything else and drawing us in. A collective gasp sounded at the sight of the vivid and mesmerising beauty that looked close enough to touch. By the time the shutters reached to the top of the windows, we were transfixed by the sight of the stunning tapestry that lay before us.

"Mars," the brigadier-general said in a triumphant tone. "It is my pleasure to welcome each of you to Asaph Hall Research Station on Phobos."

A few heartbeats of silence stretched during which

I found myself torn between the breath-taking sight in front of me and trying to contemplate the general's choice of words. What the hell was a 'Phobos'?

"That's some sight," someone in the first row said aloud. "Sir, is that Augmented Reality or a hologram or something? It looks so real."

The brigadier-general cleared his throat before answering.

"It is real."

That made us all return our attention to the podium. The swirling vivid mass that danced outside our window still awed me, but a lump of ice formed in my stomach at the brigadier's words. His face was stern and serious; he didn't strike me as someone who joked or even had a sense of humour. Forgetting ourselves, everyone spoke at once, demanding answers and clarification, which prompted the black-clad soldiers to take a simultaneous step towards us in warning. The chatter died off instantly. The brigadier-general held up his hand to maintain silence for a few more seconds before answering.

"It is best to get this dealt with now, quickly and concisely. As I have said, we are in Asaph Hall Research Station on Phobos, one of the two moons orbiting Mars. Each of you signed a contract for a year-long tour of duty with the Unified Earth Armed Forces and will be sub-contracted out to the Mars Occupation Force..."

That was it. That's where I blurred out. I shook my confused head as the general continued jabbering on and wondered what type of mad house I had stumbled into. Of course, it was too good to be true. No wonder the doctor hadn't wanted me to read the contract; I had signed up for some sort of social or psychological study. Something like the Stamford Prison Experiment but with little green men and interplanetary colonisation. Still, I nodded along and hoped they weren't going to stiff me on the pay.

The brigadier-general continued for some time, outlining basic details about the program and the colonies on Mars, but from the faces of disbelief and confusion surrounding me, it didn't look as though many people bought it. Eventually, the general opened the floor to questions on the condition we put our hands in the air to ask and stood when talking. Every single hand went up. The brigadier-general selected a tall, wiry soldier from the front to start. He asked what I'm pretty sure was the burning question on everyone's minds.

"Sir, respectfully... Is this a joke?"

"No. This isn't a joke. You are currently on Phobos awaiting deployment to Mars."

The general looked around the room, and I did my best to stretch my hand as high as possible. I knew better than to provoke an officer, but this was all a bit outlandish, so I decided to chance it. He selected me, and I snapped to attention.

"Thank you, sir," I started, trying to look as serious as possible. "No seriously, sir. Is this a joke?"

That drew muted laughs from the crowd, but the general didn't seem too happy. He glared at me, so I took my seat and waited for his response.

"No," he replied firmly. "This is not a joke. I will not field any more questions on the subject of this being a joke."

About half the hands in the auditorium dropped, to even more muffled chuckles.

"Silence!" the sergeant called out from the back of the room.

The brigadier-general selected another soldier who stood to speak.

"Thank you, sir. My question isn't specifically about Mars but about the human colonisation effort and our knowledge of the Solar System." The soldier paused as several groans erupted at him for killing our fun.

The general nodded at him to continue.

"Sir, have we discovered any Klingons on Uranus?"

The room exploded in laughter. It was probably the worst thing you could do in the presence of a senior officer, but it was worth it, and we didn't care about the consequences. If they were going to pitch us a story about humans on Mars, so be it, but we were going to have our fun, too. That soldier—Smithy—became a legend after that.

"Enough!" the brigadier-general roared into the microphone. The room fell silent. "I had hoped that so-called professionals would maintain a certain level of dignity and decorum and accept the word of a senior officer, but it seems we shall have to escalate matters."

The general mumbled "bring him in" as he stepped away from the microphone and gestured at the surgeon in blue scrubs seated behind him. The surgeon stood and hastily exited through the doors. We remained silent and watched the doors with intent, wondering what else they could show to convince us that we were no longer on Earth. After a minute or two, we got our answer, and no one was smiling anymore.

"Allow me to present a captured Insectoid hostile, one of the non-human species currently residing on Mars."

Despite a lifetime of memories, there's very few that resonate with you enough that you can remember every single detail. Not just the image, but the sight, the smell, the feeling, every aspect of that moment. Up until that point, holding Kat for the first time or the time I got head-butted by the lead singer of a trash metal band for drunkenly climbing onto the stage to steal his microphone ranked up there. But seeing that thing for the first time seared itself into my brain forever.

It was more wide than tall but still looked the height of an average person. Flanked by six guards, this spider-demon from hell barely squeezed through the corridor and now stood passive on the stage, with chains held by the guards pulling at it from all directions to keep it steady. Its torso and head appeared human; I could easily make out an ugly nose, mouth, and deep, black eyes, but that's where the similarities ended. Eight crooked, scalpel-tipped legs clicked on the stage floor with even the slightest of movements, adding to its insidious horror.

A few seconds after they escorted it in, the room fell silent. It was as if we all held our breaths collectively, unsure if exhaling might set it off on a murderous rampage. In slow, controlled movements, it looked around the auditorium, studying us as we gaped at it. Those strange black eyes probed us and made us unsure of who it was looking at specifically.

It opened its mouth and let out a series of high-pitched shrieks that echoed and bounced around the room. A crash and bang sounded from the front row and from somewhere behind me as two soldiers fainted in shock. Guards rushed forward to administer first aid, while the rest of us stared in awe at the devilish specimen in front of us.

"Thank you," the general said, nodding at the guards. "Get that thing out of here."

The massive creature shrieked again, and I got the impression it was baffled by why we were all so fascinatedly horrified by it, but the guards tugged on its chains and dragged it back the way they had come. We started breathing again as soon as the door slammed shut.

We returned our attention to the brigadier-general, who remained poised at the podium with a smug smile plastered across his face as he patted

Doctor Milton on the back. Doctor Milton looked overly pleased with himself, too, as he scribbled furiously into a notebook in his hand. He smiled in glee at our stunned reactions. Although we were still shocked by what we had witnessed, every hand in the room went up again. This time, however, no one joked.

"Sir, what is our mission on Mars?"

"To provide security and defence to the five human colonies on Mars and to render any services, as needed, to protect and defend the property and personnel of MARSCORP and the civilian population."

"Sir, how did we get to Phobos?"

"I'll answer that," Doctor Milton jumped in. "Your consciousness was downloaded via a complex procedure that..."

"The specific details are classified," the brigadier-general interrupted and gave the doctor a stern look.

"Um, yes. I can't go into specifics, but your consciousness was downloaded, compressed, and sent via a series of nano-relays between Earth and here. Your consciousness was then downloaded into cloned versions of your own bodies."

"So, we're clones?" a soldier shouted incredulously from the back row. The brigadier general glared at her until she stood and repeated her question.

"No," the doctor carried on, "well, not in the sense that you think. We do not have the level of technology to make a copy of a human mind, but we can transfer it. These bodies, gestated in under forty-eight hours, are exact replicas of your own, right down to old injuries, tattoos, traumas, genetic memories, and reflexes.

"So, our real bodies are back on Earth? What happens to these bodies when we leave?"

"Yes. Your real bodies are exactly where you left them. After your term of duty, you'll be sent back approximately one hour after you lost consciousness.

You'll have your memories intact, but one hour will have passed in, what you would term as, real time. Since these bodies can only be used by your consciousness, they'll be placed into cold storage or kept for scientific and research purposes."

"What's today's date? Is it the same as back on Earth or—"

"Classified," the general cut across the young soldier.

"Do we, I mean, the Unified Earth Armed Forces have spaceships?"

"Yes, but they have no relevance to your mission."

"How does the fleet travel, sir? Like, do we have engines that can go faster than light speed or warp drive or what?"

The general looked as though he was going to ignore the question, but Doctor Milton leaned forward with a smile to answer.

"Neither. We haven't developed FTL drives or warp speed or anything like that. We have improved our engine designs considerably from what you might see in the media, but it takes months for a manned journey to Mars and under two years to reach Jupiter. For longer range missions, we use Sleeper Ships. We're hoping what we used to bring you here today can eventually be Earth's answer to interstellar travel, but it's still in its infancy."

"Are we at war?" another voice called out.

The room fell silent once more, and all stares turned to the brigadier-general.

"Okay, that is enough," he replied firmly. "My role was to ease you into the realisation of your circumstances, and I have done that adequately. You will be fully briefed once you reach your units in New Berlin. Sergeant, you know the drill."

"Atten-shun," the sergeant called out.

Still trying to comprehend everything we had been

told, we rose to our feet. We watched the brigadier-general return a salute from the sergeant before exiting the room, flanked by the doctor and surgeon. As soon as they left, the green, flickering lights flittered on and directed us towards the doors behind them.

"Come on you Terran knuckle-draggers, it's time to get you Mars bound," screeched the sergeant. "Follow the lights to the hanger bay. Move it."

I took one last look at the planet, seemingly within hands reach from outside the massive windows, and got the feeling this was going to be a long day. Followed by a long week. Followed by a long year. And what the hell was a 'Terran?'

"It means 'human from Earth' or somethin' like that," someone answered matter-of-factly as we strapped ourselves into the seats aboard the troop transport. "Terra's like the Greek or Latin word for 'Earth' or some shit."

At least that answered that.

Despite my preoccupation with the giant spider-like alien, I had entered the hangar bay hoping to find evidence of this being an elaborate ruse, but nothing indicated so. The transport vessels looked real enough. As I stepped aboard my assigned craft, I considered the amount of effort needed to build several dozen mock spaceships and create such a realistic, giant insect costume. It seemed a bit out there to test a bunch of average twenty-something year olds, but it was a lot more believable than humanity having colonised Mars and somehow keeping it hidden from Wikileaks.

Being a nervous flier, I wasn't happy at the prospect of hurtling through space towards an alien-infested planet, but I gritted my teeth, triple checked my seat straps, and tried to look as unconcerned as possible. The transport had a maximum occupancy of fifty, with twenty-five seats on either side facing one another. Not wanting to embarrass myself in front of my new colleagues, I focused my mind and thought about Louise and Kat. Despite my concerns about being a clone, abducted for a year, and stranded on a planet full of life forms pulled straight from my worst nightmares, thinking about them still centred me.

After a few minutes, red lights flashed in our compartment, and the doors slammed shut. I gripped the armrests as the sound of the engines warming up increased and kept my jaw clenched to stop myself from whining when the transport jolted to life.

I was seated towards the top of the compartment and although there were no windows, the pilots had left the door to the cockpit open. Despite my better judgement, I leaned forward and watched as the transport rose and inched towards the opening hangar bay door. A burst of static from the intercoms around the compartment caused me to jolt from my seat (or would have, had I not been strapped in) before the pilot started speaking.

"This is... uggghhhh... Captain Lockhart speaking... I... uggghhhh... will be piloting MOF Atmospheric Troop Transport Vehicle... uggghhhh... seven-niner-seven... uggghhhh... Our destination today is New Berlin—Spaceport... uggghhhh... Expected flight time is approximately... uggghhhh... twenty-six minutes... uggghhhh... Weather conditions are favourable... uggghhhh... It's a lovely minus twenty-six degrees out and there's a... uggghhhh... storm with winds of approximately one hundred and fifty kilometres per hour heading in from our north-west that I'm hoping we can avoid... uggghhhh... please stay strapped in at all times, follow all instructions from our... uggghhhh... air hostesses, and thank you again for flying Mars Air."

"Is this guy taking the piss or what?" someone exclaimed incredulously, but no one replied.

Those of us who could leaned forward and watched as the transport approached the hangar bay doors and slammed into the vastness of space. My stomach churned as the twinkling blackness enveloped the cockpit window, but soon enough our destination shimmered into view. Hoping to distract myself, I turned to make small talk with whoever sat beside me when the pilot strutted out from the cockpit. A grin was plastered across his greasy, bearded face.

In my mind I had pictured our pilot as a clear-cut Captain America type in a well-pressed uniform, with the distinction meaning the difference between a safe landing and being splattered across the Martian landscape. Instead, Captain Lockhart looked like a cross between a hippy and a drugged-up Hells Angel. We debated it afterwards, but I still think he was drunk at the time.

"First time on Mars?" he shouted even though there was no discernible noise coming from the engines, or any noise for that matter. A few of my new colleagues mumbled a yes, while shooting confused looks at one another.

"You're gonna love it," he said before erupting into a semi-hysterical, semi-sinister laugh. "It's great. It's really great. If you love sand, the colour red, and being shot at, then it's definitely the place for you."

"Eh, sir? Who's flying the plane?" I blurted out.

I certainly didn't want to draw his crazed attention, but I struggle enough with normal planes and felt I needed the reassurance of a non-inebriated pilot before I could relax into the concept of space travel.

"What?" he roared and turned his left ear to face me.

"The plane, sir. This transport. If you're here, who's flying it?"

"Flying it? Oh, Cheech is up there. Ain't that right, Cheech?"

A reply didn't come, and my heart sank. If our pilot was in the middle of a psychotic episode, that was it. Forget about the pay. Game over. Darren wants out.

"Cheech? You all right in there?"

After a prolonged silence, there was, thankfully,

a grumble of an answer from the cockpit. I breathed a sigh of relief and tried to avert my eyes from the captain, hoping he wouldn't latch on.

"There she is," he yelled in excitement as Mars drew alarmingly closer to the cockpit window. "The Red Planet. Big Red. Old...Marsie."

He raised his hands in triumph, as if expecting us to cheer, but we were too busy trying to avoid eye contact with him. Taking the hint, he lowered his arms and looked embarrassed.

"Anyway," he continued, more quietly, "I wanted to see if anyone here likes classical music. It's a tradition to blast out sweet tunes for the new arrivals. Anyone?"

After a few moments a recruit from the back of the compartment raised his hand.

"Eh, yeah. I do, I guess. Have you any Bach or..."

"I can do you one better," Captain Lockhart said, baring his crooked yellow teeth in a twisted smile. "How about a nice little number called 'Song 2' by Blur?"

He didn't wait for an answer and quickly disappeared into the cockpit. Seconds later, the compartment blasted to life with music.

"WOO-HOO!"

I've always liked that song. As far as musical accompaniment to smashing through the Martian atmosphere, swerving from an apocalyptic hurricane, and seeing a different planet for the first time goes, it was a pretty good choice. What I didn't enjoy was that it was so loud that it felt as if my ears were bleeding, and it played in a continuous loop. But the main thing was, we made it to the New Berlin spaceport with barely any scratches and hardly anyone threw up.

Although we approached from the sky, I didn't get a good look at the New Berlin colony. Against the red backdrop of the Martian landscape, the black and grey buildings blended in, making it hard to distinguish any of them. Maybe that was the point. The spaceport didn't look busy. From what little I could see, there didn't appear to be any other sign of traffic. We landed on a circular, lit-up landing pad. After a few seconds, the transport wobbled as we began our descent into the hangar bay. It grew dark when the landing pad sealed up over us, and we waited nervously for the order to disembark.

When the transport stopped, the captain switched off the music and swaggered out into the compartment.

"Thank you for flying Mars Air," he said with a cheesy grin. He looked around at us as if expecting us to laugh, but we remained silent.

"Okay, okay," he grumbled, disappointed with his audience. "You can unstrap yourselves, but before you leave, reach down beneath your seats and pull on your facemasks. There's an earth-like atmosphere in here, but the air can be a thinner than you're used to this close to the launch pad. Now, skedaddle! Bullet trains are waiting for you outside the bay. It's time to get you boys and girls out of those Terran greens and into some nice, fresh Red'n'Blacks."

Unstrapping ourselves, we nodded our thanks to the captain for not killing us and fastened on the facemasks. They weren't anything too sophisticated, just plastic and rubber masks that nestled tightly over the mouth and nose and were attached to a small canister sling. Without any other equipment to pick up or unpack, we stood and waited for the door to open.

As soon as it did, we winced from the sudden rush of cold air into the compartment. For a terrifying second, I thought it was the prelude to an explosive decompression. Instead, the stocky sergeant greeted us with her own breathing mask on, which did little to filter her disdain for us.

"Get your asses off that transport! Move it! Move it! Move it!" she shrieked.

We jumped off one at time. Following a small corridor of flashing green lights across the hangar bay floor, we bolted towards a nearby exit. As I ran, I glanced around the hangar bay and noticed that it looked identical to the one on Asaph Hall, but my hopes were dashed that this could be an overly-complicated hoax when I saw the row-upon-row of strange-looking crafts and vehicles. Far more people were present here, too, going about their chores, dressed in red and black uniforms, and wearing breathing masks. Finally, we came to more faded graffiti covering the walls that looked worn with time.

In short, the New Berlin hangar bay looked like a dump.

Once through the exit doors, we found ourselves at what looked like a tube station. We were met by angry-looking, red-and-black-clad non-commissioned officers and guards who screeched at us to fall into five rows. After the sergeant came through the door and sealed it behind her, they ordered us to take our breathing masks off. The air was stale, dry, and possessed an oily tang, but it was breathable. We remained in our rows on the platform, facing away from the tube track and awaiting further instructions.

The sergeant ignored us and walked up to one of the other sergeants who extended a hand.

"Bowers, you old dog, how in the hell are you keeping?" she asked with a grin as she adjusted her black beret.

"I'm fine, Watford. How are you? I haven't seen you since..."

"Forward Base Zulu."

Although I was supposed to keep my eyes straightforward, fixed on an imaginary point on the wall, I couldn't help risking a glance at the two sergeants and noticed a flicker of sadness and anger at the mention of this Zulu place.

"Right. That was a long time ago. What has you in Terran greens?"

"I'm rotating home at the end of the month. It's easy street on Asaph Hall till I get shipped back to Terra," Sergeant Watford said.

"Wow. Twenty years nearly done. Congratulations, Sergeant. I got two years left on mine."

"Hopefully it'll fly by for you. Are you taking these Hollows?"

"Just to the Shoe. They're Hopkins' problem after that. How'd they take the news? They look calm enough to me.

"Better than expected. They're still fairly doped up, though. Should be medicated long enough to get 'em into the Rigs."

I didn't feel doped up at that point, but after thinking about it, despite my worries, I *was* taking the news of my abduction and forcible relocation to another planet remarkably well. While I wondered if I was so high that I didn't even realise it, Sergeant Bowers took a few steps forward and studied us closely.

"They look human, don't they? Stubble, sweat, eye blinks. Beats me why they don't create one universal Hollow template body and stick 'em in that."

"The head shrinkers reckon they'd have a meltdown if they woke up in a body they didn't recognise. Last thing we need is even more crazy people on Big Red." As she finished speaking, a hissing noise approached from behind us and ground to a halt. The sergeants said goodbye to one another.

Without so much as a look in our direction, Sergeant Watford strapped on her breathing mask and headed back towards the hangar bay.

"Listen up, you Hollow pieces of Terran scum! On my order, about turn, fall out, and find the nearest seat. No talking. Wait for further instructions. Fall... out!"

We executed a precision one-hundred-and-eighty-degree about turn in unison, which was interesting considering we had never drilled together before, and clambered onto the bullet train. It looked a lot like a standard train, except all the seats had seatbelts and straps and the walls were plastered with faded notices recommending against standing without a harness. Thankfully, we were the only ones on the transport, so we all found a seat.

It took a few seconds after the train lurched forward before I understood why it wasn't recommended to stand up. I've been on plenty of trains in my time, but this was like riding on the back of a bullet. It took ten seconds for it to reach what I assumed was top speed, and by that stage, we were all tilting back against the sudden velocity. I could guess at how fast we were travelling, but even under Captain Lockhart's suicidal piloting skills, I had never felt this level of acceleration. Within five minutes, the transport slowed down and came to a halt at another identical platform.

Outside, five individual rows of red-and-black uniformed corporals, sergeants, and officers waited for us. They were flanked by at least a dozen heavily-armed masked guards with leashed German shepherds. It looked more like a welcome party for concentration camp detainees than new recruits.

Sergeant Bowers ordered us out and, after forming us back into five rows, saluted at a tall, lean man who I guessed to be our new commanding officer. After talking quietly together, the sergeant saluted again and left. Another sergeant immediately replaced him.

"Okay, listen up," the new sergeant called out, "my name is Sergeant Hopkins. Welcome to the MOF

Operations Centre. You are now members of the Mars Occupation Force and have been assigned to Third Brigade, Second Battalion, A Company. Listen for your names to be called out and fall into your platoons. You will be given proper uniforms, assigned billets, and receive briefings. Your training begins today."

Without further delay, the various platoon commanders roared out our names, each trying to shout louder than their counterparts. With five platoons, it was nearly impossible to distinguish your own name over the competing shouts, but I strained my ears while my gaze raced back and forth between the mouths of the platoon commanders, desperate not to miss my cue. Thankfully, I heard my name and darted over to one platoon while trying to avoid the annoyed glares of the corporals. It took a few minutes to separate us, and then they marched us off the platform and down a nearby passageway.

Wherever this Operations Centre was, I got the impression we were somewhere in the basement. The flickering lights and smooth concrete walls looked old and worn, reminding me of a bunker you'd see in a World War II movie. We marched to the sound of our boot steps echoing throughout the dim corridor before reaching a set of reinforced doors. After opening it, the corridor ahead looked eerily similar to Asaph Hall with the grey metal walls and the flickering green lights guiding us to our destination. Since we were number one platoon, we were the first to be dropped off. Our corporals led us into a medium-sized room divided into five distinct areas crammed with bunk beds.

Having stayed in various military installations, camps, and barracks in my past life, I'd developed theories about the best locations to sleep in situations like this. You don't want to position yourself too close to the entrance, to avoid being picked for mindless duties. It's best to place yourself somewhere near the back, but not necessarily beside the toilets and showers, so as to not be awoken every time someone gets up in the middle of the night.

Seeing as how I now found myself in the number one section of number one platoon, I feared I had a year of sleeping by the door and being the first picked to run errands, deliver messages, or form night pickets. I was relieved when the corporal ordered myself and the other nine members of One Section towards the end of the room, close to but not directly beside the toilets and showers.

I tried to move to the front of the pack to select the best bunk, but my comrades had the same idea, and it broke into a free-for-all. I managed to seize a well-positioned bunk in the corner of our enclave and stuck my hand on the top bunk to claim it. A split second later, a second hand slammed down.

"I'll take the top, if you don't mind," a Northern Irish accent said behind me.

Maybe it was an Irish thing, but anything said in a Northern Irish accent always sounded like a threat to me.

I faced my competitor and eyed him up and down. As much as I like to consider myself an easy-going and friendly person, first impressions count. Knowing we had to spend a year together, I couldn't take the risk of being seen as a doormat.

"The top bunk suits me just fine," I said, studying him.

He didn't make any move to push past me, but my right hand was free, and I reckoned I could stop him if needs be.

"Are we gonna have a problem here?" he replied.

I didn't detect any flash of hostility or any indication he was planning on taking a swing at me, but I readied myself all the same.

"Not if you take the bottom bunk, bud," I said, trying to overemphasise my Dublin accent and wishing it sounded half as menacing as his.

We continued glaring at each other for another second or two before he whipped his hand away and a smile cut across his face.

"Aye, you're all right for a Dub," he said, patting me on the shoulder and climbing onto the bottom bunk. "I reckon we can be mates."

"You're all right for a Nordie," I said, victoriously heaving myself onto my bunk.

And with that brief exchange, an interplanetary friendship was born.

The double doors flew open with enough force to dent the walls and snap me out of my train of thought. An angry officer in Terran colours burst through, flanked by two guards. Homing in on the doctor, he marched directly up to her.

"Doctor Lucas," he roared, "I want a situation report. Now."

Doctor Lucas tore herself away from her monitors. She leafed through some papers, selected one, and handed it to the officer. Without taking his glare off her, he snatched the paper out of her hand and slapped it back onto the consoles.

"Sir, this isn't the best time..." Doctor Ling interjected.

She stood up from her chair and approached the officer. He tore his gaze off Doctor Lucas long enough to shoot the psychologist a sharp look, silencing her.

"Not good enough," the officer shouted back. His face burned red, and his peppered moustache bounced wildly with every syllable. "Everything except the damn Lunar colonies have gone dark. I want answers now. Not five minutes from now. Not an hour from now. Release the patient to my custody for interrogation."

"Sir, with all due respect, you cannot interrogate him in his present state. He can barely remember his own name, let alone what happened to him."

Without responding, the officer turned to face me, and I noted his lieutenant-general rank insignia and his name-tag. 'Barrymore' sounded vaguely familiar. My right hand instinctively pulled to salute but was stopped short by the restraints. I let it flop back down.

"You," he growled at me, "name and rank, soldier."

"Loughlin, Darren, Corporal. Third Brigade, Second Battalion, Mars Occupation Force, sir," I choked out.

"Report, Corporal. I want to know what happened up there."

"We were in a firefight, sir. I got shot. I'm not sure what happened to everyone else, sir."

I didn't think it was possible, but his face glowed an even darker shade of red. If he were a cartoon, steam would've burst from his ears and his head would've exploded. Still feeling loopy from whatever they were giving me, I bit the inside of my cheek to stop myself from laughing at that thought.

"That's not good enough, soldier. I asked you a question and I want an answer. What happened in New Berlin and why can't we communicate with it? Where are the rest of your team?"

"This will do no good," Doctor Ling pleaded, stepping between the general and my trolley. "They've all experienced something traumatic, possibly due to an issue with the compression signal. We're lucky he's talking at all. If we prod him too hard and too soon, it could push him over the edge. As he is my patient, I will not allow you to question him without my consent and until I determine he's ready."

The general kept glaring at me as if expecting me to answer, but I didn't have anything new to tell him. I was in the dark as much as the colonies were, apparently. He finally broke eye contact and focused his attention on Doctor Ling.

"He's a military asset in a crisis situation," the lieutenant-general barked, but much of the sting had leaked from his voice.

"Look at his brain activity," Doctor Lucas called out, pointing to one of the monitors in front of her. It looked like swirling piles of gibberish to me, but they caught the general's eye.

"His brain activity is through the roof," she continued. "It could be symptoms of a botched compression download or possible pattern degradation, but the fact that's he's talking is a miracle. Look at this." She directed the general's attention to another screen with an image of a human brain in black and white. "See these? This indicates no trauma to the memory or language centres of the brain, so in theory, he should be able to answer your questions when he recovers, but there are too many variables at play to say when that will be. It could be an hour, a day, a week. They were the first test batch to survive compression travel and the first group to return. We're in new territory here, sir."

"He is coming around, sir," Doctor Ling continued, eager to hammer the point home. "A few minutes ago, he didn't even know his own name. Now he can recall everything about waking up on Phobos and arriving at New Berlin. I just need more time with him."

The lieutenant-general remained silent for a few moments before responding.

"Okay, Doctor. You can have your time. For now. The other one lost consciousness, so make this one your main priority, unless you come across any other promising candidates."

"I will, sir," the doctor said gratefully. "We're coming up to the first incident in his records, so if the patient can recall that correctly, it will show that he hasn't fully blocked all traumatic memories."

"Very good," the general grumbled in a far quieter tone than his initial outbursts. He turned to leave and shot me a fleeting glance as his guards reached for the doors.

"Barrymore," I mumbled. "I think I knew a Barrymore back in New Berlin. He looked a bit like you."

I don't know why I said it, but as soon as I did, I knew it was a mistake. A father searching for a lost son was a potent force in any situation. Throw in that father's military rank, access to firearms, and the ability to have me interrogated around the clock and that didn't spell a relaxing Saturday for this poor Terran.

Doctor Ling again ran interception and made sure to stand between me and the general. "Sir, you have my word. As soon as he gives us anything at all, you will be notified immediately."

The general looked past the doctor to give me one last hard stare before he nodded and exited. Sighing loudly, Doctor Ling mouthed something to Doctor Lucas and, flashing her a quick smile, retook her seat beside me.

"I'm sorry about that," she said, while resting one hand under her chin and squeezing my hand with her free one. "I know the last thing you want to deal with is everyone shouting at you after everything you've been through."

"That's okay, Doctor," I replied as she let go of my hand. "I know it's not your fault. What's the 'incident' you mentioned earlier, though?"

She exhaled through her teeth as her lips grew tight and her forehead crinkled up in concern. After a moment of silence, she reached onto the chair beside her, picked up her tablet, and began swiping furiously until she found what she was looking for.

"You all had a rough time up there. I can see that from your reports," she said, accidently flashing a glimpse of the report at me but without enough time for me to study its contents. "Let's continue from where we were. If you recall the incident, we can talk

57

about it further if you'd like. Does that sound fair?"

"Okay, cool."

"Great. So, you were assigned billets, you made contact with Andrew 'Nordie' Pritchett, and you were about to get your first briefing about your overall mission, responsibilities, and duties. What was that like?"

I had barely relaxed onto my bunk when the corporals returned, wheeling containers with our new Martian uniforms to replace the Terran colours. The uniform was the exact same style, except we were to wear red-and-black khaki. Still uncertain of one another, we turned our backs and stripped out of our old uniforms and slipped into our new ones. That was the first time I noticed that I was wearing black boxers, not the Mickey Mouse ones I had put on in the hotel. Remembering I was a cloned version of myself, I double checked everything was okay down there when I was sure no one else was looking. Crisis averted; everything looked fine.

I stashed the bag of toiletries they had supplied me with on my bunk and fell into rows with the rest of my platoon. We marched out the door and moved to the far end of the corridor. The rest of the platoons fell into step as we marched past. Then we entered another auditorium exactly like the one on Asaph Hall, but this one didn't have the massive windows on the left wall. Plenty of armed forces replicated designs of their military installations, so this wasn't unusual, but the part of my brain that found this whole scenario fantastical was desperately searching for evidence that this was all a massive psychological test.

We took our seats, and our new commanding officer Colonel Jack Wellesley—or "Mad Jack" as we later found out he was informally known as—introduced himself. When I first saw him on the platform as we arrived, I got the impression he was a bit of a hard nose, but after a few minutes, that changed. He was soft spoken, clear, and direct. Despite the fact that he was probably the type of officer who wanted things to go exactly his way at all times, he struck me as a fairly likeable person with the potential of being a good leader. At least, those were my first impressions.

We greeted Mad Jack far more enthusiastically than we had the brigadier-general, and he went on to tell us that the purpose of the brief was to explain everything once and for all about our mission; its relevance, purpose, and what was expected of us. I respected the way he openly told us that a lot of what we were about to hear was counter-intuitive and what we were going to learn actively went against everything we were taught in school and what the media rammed down our throats. After a brief preamble, he started the speech that would forever change my life.

At first it sounded like a bad science fiction novel—Nazis colonising Mars, making pacts with the hostiles. Then there was the Allied invasion in 1954 following the 1952 Washington UFO incident. It was a lot to take in. I wondered how the folks back home would react if the truth ever came out. Not only did some Nazis escape the war, but they emigrated and were the first to colonise Mars.

Although maintaining his composure, Mad Jack grew visibly animated as he walked us through the historical side of things, but his pace slowed as he explained the political set-up. We learned that New Berlin fell under the jurisdiction of the European powers and was officially administered by the European Interstellar Space Exploration Network or EISEN, making us the EISEN division of the UEAF, which in turn subcontracted us out to the MOF.

From the way the colonel explained things, the

chances of us ever being caught up in battle with the natives was relatively low since New Berlin was situated so far from the front lines. Our role for the next twelve months would be confined to providing security to the colony, escorting transports, and undertaking patrols of the surrounding area, freeing the full-time personnel to be shipped to the Forward Bases on the borders.

Lastly, we learned that if anything happened to us here, resulting in our deaths, we wouldn't wake up at home. A murmur erupted throughout the auditorium at that revelation. Up until this point, I assumed we were something similar to drones or computer game characters; if anything happened, we would wake up fine on Terra. This was a game changer.

After receiving all that information, I looked forward to getting some training in to distract my confused and weary mind. Unfortunately, the training did anything but.

Following the colonel's briefing, they led us to the company's training centre where I expected to find us thrown into a mix of marching, weapons drills, tactics, survival techniques, and standard indoctrination about the enemy that looked forward to killing us. Although I was right about the content, I had no idea about the process.

They led us, platoon by platoon, into rooms with these egg-shaped stations they referred to as 'Rigs.' They handed us each a set of one-piece body suits, sent us into locker rooms, and ordered us to get changed. Although the body suits looked personalised to each of us based on body weight and height, it was still a squeeze to get into mine. When I did, it felt strangely snug and warm, like having an extra layer of skin on. As everyone else did, I pulled the hood of the body suit up onto my head so that only my eyes, nose, and mouth were visible. They then led us to our individual Rigs and attached sensors to our hearts and foreheads before fastening on a visor that covered our eyes. Training began as soon as the visor slid into place.

It would be hard to explain what Rig training was like to someone who'd never experienced it before. I suppose the best definition would be a type of virtual reality, but everything looked so life-like and crisp it was hard to differentiate between that and the real world until the corporals removed the visor at the end.

The Rigs were comprised of thousands of hours of

training programmes that could run either individually or networked into your platoon or overall company. These programmes operated faster than real-time, meaning that for every hour that passed in the real world, five simulated hours would pass in training, with the trainee feeling every lingering second of it.

The first simulation involved stripping, assembling, and learning everything we could absorb about our primary weapon: the HK-17 Hybrid Assault Rifle. I recognised her as the weapons all the guards possessed. To say she was a beast would be an understatement. When the simulation began, I found myself fully clothed in my MOF uniform, kneeling over a HK-17 while one of the corporals rattled off endless facts about the weapon. I glanced to my right and left and saw my entire platoon, fully uniformed and kneeling in a line over their own weapons. Nordie met my glance. He nodded back at me with a confused shrug.

While the corporal spoke, I reached out my right hand and gently ran it over the cold, hard plastic exterior to feel the smooth, finely crafted barrel of the weapon. There was no doubt in my mind that it was real. We spent hours disassembling and reassembling it while the corporal continued to pace back and forth, listing the same statistics on a constant loop. The only time he stopped was to hunch down to assist someone or point out a mistake before he started back up again. This continued over and over until it got to the point that I didn't have to consciously think about it. My hands reacted like those of an experienced veteran, but it did take a few days to get to that level.

Apart from weapons drills, the simulations also taught us hand-to-hand combat, about the Exo-Suits we were required to wear while on duty, marching drills, and how to fight and survive in the barren

Martian terrain. The one exercise that profoundly affected us was the combat simulation at the end of the first week.

Having mastered the HK-17 and completed several intense sessions of simulated individual and group firing exercises, they deemed us competent enough to engage in simulated battles against the hostile aliens that infested Mars—the Insectoids. Like most of the training, these were based on real-world memories of soldiers before us and on up-to-date tactics and styles of fighting the enemy favoured. What freaked me out the most, and which the rest of the platoon later admitted to as well, was the personal nature of these exercises as well as the presence of, what we dubbed, "the Voice of God."

I had heard the Voice on the first day of training, but immediately dismissed it as a glitch or a delusion brought on by the visor's direct connection to my brain. It started as a minor whisper, something I couldn't quite make out, like someone talking in a room next door, and I ignored it as such. As we used the Rigs more and more, the Voice grew stronger, although it remained a whisper, blending softly into the background noise. From that point on, it grew in intensity and strength. Originally, I found it to be a source of annoyance, but as time moved on and the horrors of what I was being subjected to increasingly affected me, it became a source of strength, driving me harder to strive for victory, motivating me, pushing me to never give up.

During a Rig exercise, I found myself on the street where my house in Ireland stood, except everything was a burning ruin. The houses, the gardens, and the cars were engulfed in flames; there didn't seem to be a single building untouched by the devastation of war. Standing on the debris-filled road, dressed in my MOF uniform and gripping my HK-17, with panic overwhelming me, the Voice whispered loud enough for me to finally decipher its words.

"PROTECT TERRA."

Even though it was a whisper, I jumped in fear and spun around, expecting an enemy to appear from behind. Kat's voice called out for help from one of the nearby burning buildings, but I couldn't locate the direction her call came from. I rushed towards the nearest building when six Insectoids burst out of a blazing, smouldering house, jostling with one another. They froze when they saw me. Then, standing up on the hind two of their eight legs, they unleashed a barrage of hellish screams before charging. Hands trembling, I raised my weapon and squeezed the trigger to wound one of the beasts on the left but not before the other five were upon me. The scalpel-like points at the end of their legs were poised to strike from a multitude of directions. I let out a scream as their sharpened legs pierced through my flesh.

"PROTECT KAT. PROTECT TERRA."

In the blink of an eye, I found myself standing on the exact same spot as before while everything I called home continued to blaze and crumble. Again, I heard Kat's terrified pleas for assistance, and I moved around the debris, desperately trying to pinpoint her. Again, the six Insectoids burst out of the smouldering house and charged at me. This time, I readied myself. Per my training, I controlled my breathing, took careful aim, and fired. The first creature hit the ground with a violent slump as my bullet found its mark. It was quickly followed by the second one, but I was still too slow. The other four were upon me before I could fire. My last moments were of those snarling, horrible spider-like demons ripping through my flesh.

"TRY HARDER, DARREN. SHE NEEDS YOU. PROTECT TERRA."

"Kat!" I screamed when I reappeared in the same

spot. This time, I rushed forward as she called out to me. The desperation to find her increased. I closed the distance on the house the Insectoids were set to rush out of and fired controlled bursts as they raced out, dropping them one at a time. With all six of the enemy down, I raced over their twitching bodies into the burning building and called out to Kat, but I couldn't find her. I escaped the smouldering shell of a house, coughing wildly as the smoke seared my lungs, and spotted six more of those vile creatures scampering from another house. Kat continued to scream for me. I charged them angrily and fired my assault rifle, but after subduing two, I took too long to reload before one of them impaled me through the stomach.

"TERRA IS LIFE. YOU MUST PROTECT THEM ALL. PROTECT TERRA."

I fought them a thousand times, in and around every still-standing house in the estate. I butchered them and was mowed down more times than I cared to remember, but I grew stronger with every round. I learned, adapted, anticipated.

"THEY WANT TO KILL LOUISE AND KAT. PROTECT THEM. PROTECT TERRA."

I hunted them around the wasteland that used to be my home town. I fought them in sewers, abandoned shops, parks, and schools. Every time I killed one of them, I felt myself inching closer to Kat and Louise's terrified voices. I had to reach them. They needed me to protect them.

"THEY WANT TO KILL YOU, DARREN. KILL THEM FIRST. KILL THEM ALL. PROTECT TERRA."

I passed the ruins that had once been my mother's house and murderous rage filled me when one of the Insectoids deigned to emerge from the ash-laden pile of charred bricks and wood. It squealed in terror as I emptied my entire magazine, reducing it to a bloody pile of entrails. I took a few paces closer to inspect my work and saw a small nest with at least a dozen hand-size versions of the creatures inside it. Its offspring, no doubt. Without hesitation, I whipped out a plasma grenade, tossed it into the nest, and watched as the squalling runts vaporised. I felt a minor tinge of sadness at what I had done, but only as a fleeting afterthought.

"THEY DO NOT LOVE. THEY DO NOT FEEL. THEY ARE MINDLESS DRONES. KILL THEM ALL. PROTECT TERRA."

I trekked across the shattered ruins of my country, hunting them down wherever I could find them. It was a sombre reminder of how important my job was; how, if I failed, the enemies of Earth, of Terra, would take everything away from us. They would reduce Terra to nothing more than a funeral pyre for our species. I couldn't allow that to happen. With every fibre of my being, I had to prevent that. I had to protect Terra.

By the end of each Rig session, we were exhausted and mentally drained. Thankfully, we had plenty of lectures and classroom work in between Rig sessions, which gave us a break from the intensity of the things we experienced. The Rigs also trained your reflexes and physical body to complement what you experienced in the training simulations. I noticed my hands began to callous with the constant use of the HK-17, but it was still important that every one of those skills followed you back or else there would be no point to them. I still remember how quickly I took my HK-17 apart the first time I tried in the real world; I had hundreds of hours of memories to draw upon, even if I had only held it a few times in real life.

Although we ate, trained, showered, and slept together, it felt as though we were finally learning about one another in the group Rig sessions. It's remarkable to think how we were so distant from each other at the start, but as we watched each other die terrible, simulated deaths repeatedly, we drew closer and our determination hardened to not let it happen in the real world. I had felt the strain after the first couple of days, but I could also see it in the gaunt faces of my section. We became each other's crutches, supporting one another through those dark times.

I bonded quickly with Nordie. Maybe it was the fact that we shared an island or he had this dry wit that I liked, but he was a good dude with a positive attitude. Big Mo was cool, too. He hated being called by anything else other than his nickname, apparently because only his mother called him Mohammed when he was in trouble. He was a friendly giant of a man with a passion for conspiracy theories that never failed to entertain.

Jacque, our resident French girl, had the misfortune of being related to a famous French undersea explorer, which led to non-stop nautical themed jokes, but she took it in stride. She was quiet and artistic, spending what little free time she had sketching. She did make an effort to get to know us, but deep down I think she preferred spending her time alone.

Smack was the exact opposite of Jacque. She was loud, talkative, social, and bursting with energy. Although she could come across as ditsy in other social situations, it was as if she flipped a switch in training and became gung-ho in her enthusiasm and execution.

Lionel and Richie were two brothers, originally hailing from Nigeria but who had spent most of their lives in London. They were born-again Christians, but they weren't preachy and excelled at everything they put their hands to. They kept to themselves, however, and had an air about them that made them come across as anti-social. They pulled their weight and did what they had to for the section, though, so they were fine in my books.

Every platoon had a Rambo wannabe and ours was Intense Dan. Exceptionally friendly, he went out of his way to be likeable to the point that it came across like he was trying too hard. He earned his nickname from the way he took everything about our training and mission so seriously. On the rare instances when we had a few minutes to relax, we'd tell jokes or BS a bit, but Dan just wanted to focus on the mission. It was all he ever spoke about, but he was a good kid.

Everyone referred to me as 'Dub' because of my Dublin accent. It wasn't exactly the most original name but was far easier than Nordie's suggestion of "Free State Bastard."

Finally, there was Tazz. She was the glue that held us all together. From day one, Tazz became mother, sister, best friend, and Amazonian warrior queen to each of us. She knew what to say and what to do in every situation, oozing natural confidence and charisma, making her a no-brainer for Section Leader. If the MOF were a democracy, there's no doubt that she would have been voted in unanimously. Without prompting, she inspected our uniforms and made sure we were presentable every morning and was always on hand to help anyone in the section that needed anything. She talked BS with the boys, chatted with the girls, and even managed to coax a smile out of Lionel and Richie. We loved her. I don't mean that in a romantic or sexual way—although she was highly attractive and had an amazing personality, so I'm sure there were some fleeting thoughts—but she was everything a bunch of strangers trapped on an alien planet surrounded by enemies needed.

That's what made everything that followed so much harder.

After a month of training, we were cruising. The entire company had jelled together, and we no longer displayed that nervous uncertainty of new recruits. Months' worth of training simulations rammed into our heads made us confident, strong, and smart. Even Corporal Owens didn't seem to hate us that much. He took an interest in the battlefield training scenarios but was happy to leave the minor details to Tazz, which suited us just fine. Under her stewardship, we were the best section in the platoon, probably even all of A-Company.

To reward our efforts, the powers-that-be decided to give us a weekend pass to blow off some steam after we completed our last round of assessments. To move past recruit status and into active duty, each section had to complete an obstacle course, followed by a mock attack on an enemy position all while under live fire. We had completed exercises like this plenty of times in the Rigs, but this time, it was to take place outside of New Berlin. After being cooped up, we were finally going to see Mars.

On the day of the assessment, we were pumped and ready to go. Tazz had drilled us relentlessly and even spent what little free time she had working with us individually on areas that we needed to improve. Morale soared high as the rumours circulated that we would be given limited access to civilian-populated areas within the MOF installation. Most importantly, we were given permission to get drunk.

"This is some Alex Jones type shit when you think about it," Big Mo said as he pulled on his Exo-suit.

The room collectively groaned. As likeable as Big Mo was, his fascination with conspiracy theories never ended. More than anyone, he mulled over every snippet of information about our predicament to uncover the truth about our mission.

"I mean think about it, a bunch of random strangers, and no offense to anyone, not exactly rocket scientists or Special Forces types, get kidnapped, cloned, and brought to Mars. To do what? We're gonna be glorified security guards. How does that make sense?"

"Does anything the Illuminati do make sense, Mo?" Nordie quipped, flashing him a mock serious face.

We snickered at that. Big Mo loved blaming the Illuminati for everything.

"It doesn't matter the reason. We're here and we're going to do a kick ass job. We're unstoppable," Intense Dan uttered, far too serious this early in the morning.

"Dial it back, Dan," I chided. "Remember the rule? Not till we've all had our morning coffee."

"Protect Terra," he replied and thumped his fist loudly onto the reinforced metal chest plate of his Exo-suit.

Protect Terra. More than anything, the Voice of God whispered to us in the Rigs. Those words constantly lingered under every thought and deed. It became our mantra, our sole reason for waking up in the morning and training for eighteen hours a day with barely any rest. Of course, Big Mo spent hours trying to convince us it was a form of brain washing. Looking at it objectively, it was possible he was right. But apart from becoming stronger, more resilient, and sharper, we didn't seem affected by it in any negative way, so I tried not to dwell on it too much.

"Come on, you Terran muck-savages, let's get it together. One more walk in the park and then it's Jägerbombs till midnight," Tazz called out to us.

I ran the last set of diagnostics on my Exo-suit via the console on my left forearm before pressing the button to lock my helmet into place. I stretched my arms and legs and turned by body from side to side. Gripping my HK-17, I jumped from foot to foot and raised it up and down in quick controlled motions. My Exo-suit functioned perfectly with no lag or delay. Confident that I was ready to go, I slung my weapon and began helping Nordie with his diagnostics.

The Exo-suit was probably the second-most interesting kit we had next to the HK-17. Unlike the assault rifle, if this broke while we were outside, we were dead. When I first heard the term 'Exo-suit,' I had immediate connotations of high-powered, advanced armour giving increased strength and the ability to fly or leap over tall buildings. Unfortunately, it wasn't meant to be. It was basically a streamlined, armoured EVA (extravehicular activity) suit with a personalised life-support system and advanced tactical systems providing us with everything we needed to survive and fight on the surface of Mars.

Built with so called 'smart-fibres' or 'flexi-metal' as the higher-ups called it, the Exo-suit was far thinner than a standard EVA to allow increased mobility and movement. Thanks to its ingenious design, it was tough enough to withstand multiple gun shots and even low-powered explosions, although it still couldn't protect fully against the particle weapons Martian hostiles used. The helmet was made from reinforced, transparent 'smart-plastic,' giving a 180-degree field of vision without having to turn your whole body and had a built-in interface that we controlled with combinations of well-rehearsed eye blinks. Although it took a while to master, thanks to dozens of simulated hours in the Rigs we were naturals at operating it. Like second nature, I could easily pull up tons of information on the inner screen of my helmet, ranging from terrain topography and the location of my comrades to pin-pointing enemy positions using the MOF orbiting satellites.

"Come on, let's go," Corporal Owens shouted, urging us to finish our checks. Tazz gave us each a quick once-over before patting our helmets fiercely in pride.

"Section One, ready to move, Corporal," she shouted back, taking her place at the head of the line.

"Move 'em out, Recruit Singh."

"Section One, move out."

Tazz led us out of the platoon preparation room and through the maze of corridors towards the southern airlock. Behind us, we heard the hustle and bustle of the other sections falling in, eager to complete the assessment and begin two and a half days of freedom and debauchery. After reaching the airlock, Corporal Owens waited for us to file in before sealing the door behind him and typing something on his left arm console. I nervously blinked open my Exo-suit's life support status menu and confirmed my suit was fully sealed and contained ample oxygen supply.

"You've seen Big Red a million times, but welcome to the real deal," the corporal said and nodded towards the opening outer airlock doors.

We stood transfixed at the sight of the barren Martian scenery ahead of us. He was correct; we had trained in simulations based on dozens of sites on Mars, but this was real. It looked the same, but there was something more to this planet that the Rigs couldn't capture, a strange unknowable beauty.

Tazz led us out. Gripping my weapon, I felt my

boots crunch onto the dark red Martian soil, and a strange sensation settled over me. It reminded me of walking on a beach back on Terra but something about the colour, the unusual rock formations, the lonely desert that surrounded us, looked so alien but also so familiar.

We jogged out to the training course a couple of hundred metres away from the base and fell into position, awaiting the arrival of the remainder of A-Company. The top-brass emerged and gave us the standard speech about the important work we were doing and how it contributed to the safety and well-being of Terra. It was the same old, same old.

The assessment, while gruelling, was relatively straightforward. Each section had to run an obstacle course comprising of various walls, tunnels, traps and, well, obstacles, before meeting up at a certain point and launching an attack on an enemy position. Although it was technically a live fire drill, the only time the non-commissioned officers would be firing directly at us would be in a narrow strip of land that we had to crawl over. It was straightforward enough: keep your head down and you keep your head. After that, we needed to storm a hill, mock-shoot a few dummies, and that was it.

Of course, the powers-that-be decided at the last minute that every section would have to complete the course successfully under a time limit and the fastest section from each of the five platoons would be pitted against their counterparts to determine the best platoon. Me, Big Mo, and Nordie each shook our heads at one another at hearing that. With Tazz being Tazz, she would whip us into being the fastest, which meant we would have to complete the course a second time. Yay.

Being the first section of the first platoon, we had the disadvantage of going first without the chance to see other sections and learn from their mistakes. We broke up into our three section components: Alpha Team, Bravo Team, and the Fire Support Team. After readying ourselves, we waited for the order to commence. As predicted, from the minute the assessment commenced, Tazz began a combination of motivating us and shouting colourful profanities to keep us moving. We completed the course without a hitch and launched a textbook attack on the enemy position, finishing it with time to spare and setting a new record. For the moment.

As expected, we were the fastest section in our platoon. This pitted us against the champions of the other four platoons, two of who had beaten our time, which grated on Tazz. More determined than ever, she pulled us into a huddle to discuss tactics.

"Okay, we killed it out there, but we need to do better if we're gonna win this thing."

"Do we have to, Mom?" I couldn't help saying. "Can't we just go play with the other kids?"

"You and Nordie can play on the swings all weekend long after this, okay sweetie?" she said in her best mother voice before patting me forcefully on the helmet. "In the meantime, here's the game plan: We have the course locked down, but we need to shave seconds off the attack if we're gonna beat everyone else. We're losing too much time crawling up the hill, so Dub and Nordie, I want you both to veer off to the left and draw some of that fire away. I want them to think you're going to flank them by climbing around that rocky outcrop, but let them keep you pinned down. That should keep them distracted. Jacque, you and I will break off and climb over those rocks on the right. It will be tight, but if we can cross over, that'll save us at least an extra thirty seconds. Wait for my signal. Everyone else, proceed as normal. Got it?"

We grunted our approval and readied ourselves.

I wasn't fond of the idea of being used as bait to lure high-powered particle beams that could take my head clean off, but I trusted Tazz; it was a solid plan. And if we all kept our heads down, we could do this and win in style.

Although fully recovered from the first round of the course, I could tell we were off to a slower start. Tazz continued to shout encouragement and urged us on as we stormed over walls, scurried through tunnels, raced over winding dirt paths with potholes, and swung over open pits. By the time we reached the base of the hill to launch the attack, we were a few seconds behind our last time.

"Come on. Move it," Tazz urged as she hurled herself on the ground and began crawling up the hill.

As soon as we hit the Martian dirt, the particle weapons started firing over our heads and to either side of us. Chunks of rock and sand sprayed onto us, but we kept crawling, moving forward as fast as possible. With a series of eye blinks, I opened the display of the hill on my helmet visor, using the orbiting satellites to track our position against that of the enemy and to see how far we were from where Nordie and I were to bail out.

"It's that crop of rock up to the left," I shouted into my Exo-suit's communicator built into the helmet. We were all networked together and could quickly communicate with each other or our NCO's, but Nordie would know that was meant for him.

"I see it," he grunted between heavy breaths and veered off to the left. I quickly followed him. The intensity of the weapons fire increased the closer we got.

"Ready?"

"Aye."

"Roll!"

We rolled off the path towards the rocky outcrop

and managed to reach it without injury. In response, the energy beams began smacking the large boulder we were positioned behind, blowing off chunks and causing it to vibrate. I shot Nordie a concerned look, but we each stayed pressed up against the rock, aware that if we took the risk of venturing a glance, it could cost us our heads. If this were real life, I had no doubt we would have risked our lives trying to climb over the sea of jagged rocks to flank the enemy position, but Tazz had told us to draw their fire, and since our own weapons weren't loaded, there was little we could do.

From our vantage point I saw Tazz and Jacque reach the boulder on the right and as fast as lightning, Tazz hurled herself over and landed on the small pathway on the far side. Eager to keep the enemy focused on us, Nordie and I picked up loose stones and threw them to our left, hoping that the sudden motion would keep them distracted. I used my helmet's enhanced visual apparatus to zoom in on Jacque and could see the nervous look on her face as she prepared to move. I opened my mouth to shout encouragement, but she was already launching herself over the boulder. A particle beam sliced right through her head, and her lifeless body crashed into the ground.

I opened my mouth to shout in horror, but it all happened so quickly. Seeing Jacque shot but not being able to see how badly, Lionel instinctively lifted himself up to race over to her. In the split second it took him to pull himself up, another energy beam punched through his chest and cut him down.

A series of horrified roars and cries erupted across the communications network as I stood rooted to the spot, wanting to rush out and help but unable to take action.

"FREEZE!" a voice roared into our ears. Recognising the corporal, we all remained perfectly still, frozen and barely breathing.

I found myself looking from Jacque to Lionel, willing the moment to reset. In the Rigs, as soon as you were killed, you started back at an earlier point in the exercise and kept replaying it until you got it right. We'd all become so used to it. Now, two of my comrades were down, and it couldn't be undone. I zoomed in on Tazz and studied her. She stood perched on a jagged rocky outcrop, evidently ready to help pull Jacque over when the corporal screamed the order to freeze. As per standing orders, she remained in that uncomfortable position, but I could see the look of shock etched on her face.

"Tazz," I whispered, switching to a private channel with an eyeblink, "Tazz. It was an accident."

I received silence in response. Her lips were unmoving, so she wasn't communicating with anyone else. It was possible she was getting chatter from the NCO's or officers, but I knew her well enough. She would blame herself.

"Jasmine. Respond. It was an accident."

No response. I couldn't blame her; she was probably in shock.

After a few seconds, the Exo-suited medics arrived at the scene and began checking Lionel and Jacque. The officers came next, with an angry-looking Corporal Owens a step behind them. The medics lifted our comrades onto stretchers and left the obstacle course as we continued to watch in stunned silence.

"End exercise," an officer's simmering voice rang out.

The officers quickly surrounded Tazz and escorted her off the training course. Another sergeant took control and led the rest of us back to New Berlin.

"I don't want to remember this anymore," I groaned and looked away, feeling an overwhelming surge of emotions wash over me. Whatever drugs they had pumped into me were wearing off. The soft, cotton, cloud I floated on turned grey, dark, and menacing. A storm approached.

"It's okay to take a break, Darren. You're doing really well," Doctor Ling said in a reassuring tone.

I looked around the room, studying the monitors to avoid her gaze. It felt as if I had abruptly woken up from a strange, troubling sleep. Everything looked more detailed, and my thoughts were my own again; things had finally begun to make sense.

"I want to get out of here," I said more forcefully than I had intended. "Why am I strapped to this? Why can't I move my hands higher than my chest? You need to let me go. I want to get out."

"Why do you think we have you restrained?"

It was easier to remember things now. There was no one or two second delay to recall events that had happened recently enough.

"I thought I was shot. I panicked. But I'm okay now. You can let me go. I've earned that much, haven't I?"

Doctor Ling made a note of something on her pad and gave me a pleasant but firm look. Even though she spoke in a friendly, almost flirtatious manner, I realised that everything she was doing was a means to an end. Although, I'm sure a part of her cared for

79

me as a patient, she still had a mission to fulfil.

"Darren, you've been through a lot. You have my word that when I think you're not at risk of injuring yourself, I'll have these straps removed. Until then, they have to remain on for your own safety."

"I understand," I replied, trying to strike a more conciliatory tone. "Can I at least see my section? I'm their corporal. I need to see Section One. They're my responsibility."

Doctor Lucas turned in her swivel chair and, gesturing to Doctor Ling, pointed at one of the monitors and tapped on it. Doctor Ling picked up her tablet, flicked through a few screens, paused, and studied something intently. After a moment, she looked me right in the eye.

"Most of Section One are unaccounted for. You and Big Mo made it back. It's possible they're still up there. You and the rest could have been sent back to get reinforcements or to update EISEN Command. We don't know."

"I wouldn't abandon them. They must still be alive. Can I see Big Mo?"

"Unfortunately, Private Hassan was incoherent and lost consciousness after a few minutes. So far, you're the only one capable of saying more than one sentence on a continuous loop."

I slammed my fists into the bed at that. Just thinking about Tazz, Jacque, and Lionel had caused emotions to bubble to the surface. I hadn't been able to save them. My entire section could be slaughtered or in desperate trouble and I had no recollection as to what was happening. I didn't like the feeling of being a prisoner in my own mind, but enough memory fragments had emerged from the darkened recesses of my mind that I knew I wasn't going to like what was coming next.

From my perspective, I had spent months with

my section in the Rigs. We had bonded and grown close. When they died, I had a vague recollection of it being hard for a long time after that but grew used to it. Now, their deaths were new and fresh again. That pain of seeing people I had lived with and grown accustomed to cut down felt as raw as a reopened wound. And there was Tazz. I didn't want to think of what happened to her at all, as if ignoring it wouldn't make it true. Doctor Ling patted my hand sympathetically as I gazed off into space, torn between my desire to repress the pain and save my section. I sighed sadly. There was no real choice here. I had to keep remembering to find out what had happened to them.

"Shall we begin again?" she asked, looking at me with kind, puppy-dog eyes.

"Tazz is dead. She died shortly after the first incident. I think...I know things would have been better if she had been around. She would have reacted better during the attack."

There were no dressing downs. No reprimands. No being screamed at till it looked as though the officer's head would pop. Instead, they led the entire company back to base and sealed us into our platoon areas. We hadn't seen Tazz since they led her off the field. They had taken Richie, too, who was inconsolable. We all lay on our bunks or gathered into groups and discussed the morning's events in detail.

The majority consensus was that Tazz hadn't done anything wrong. She executed a plan that was risky but hadn't been explicitly forbidden. All of our training was based around following orders, thinking outside the box, and protecting Terra. It was an accident, pure and simple.

A vocal minority took the opposing view. They claimed Tazz had been reckless and put the lives of those under her command at risk for her own personal glory. I grew angry at that and ended up getting into a heated shouting match with Lego from Section Five, nearly to the point of coming to blows, but Nordie and Big Mo broke it up. We retreated to our own section area where four beds now lay unoccupied.

"Poor Richie," Smack sighed, while polishing her boots. Even in our grief, we still found ourselves unable to sit back and do nothing.

"Maybe they lied about that whole 'if you die on Big Red, you die on Terra' thing," Big Mo suggested as he disassembled his HK-17 for routine cleaning. "I mean, they have this ability to transfer our consciousness between planets, who's to say they can't copy it? We could be prototypes for an entire clone army or something. Think about it." He looked up from his task and made it a point to look each one of us in the eye, as if he had unlocked the secret mystery to our presence.

"I don't think it was a lie," Nordie said from his bunk beneath me. "If it was, then why not recruit Special Forces and have them as the clone army. They'd be far better than us. They wouldn't need as much training and would be less inclined to…"

He didn't need to say anything else.

After a few hours, Tazz returned, escorted by Corporal Owens. With her face gaunt and her eyes red and blotchy from crying, Tazz still seemed physically shaken from the experience. We dropped what we were doing and stood together to greet her in solidarity while the rest of the platoon gawked at her in silence. Without making eye contact or so much as a whisper, she pushed past us and took to her bunk. The corporal told us the funeral would take place after the medical staff released the bodies and Richie would be removed from active duty for the next few days to mourn the loss of his brother.

I could tell the corporal was seething with anger from the way his eyes bore through us, but he spoke in an unusually calm tone. To keep morale up, he informed us that the powers-that-be had decided that we were still to get our weekend passes and would be formally dismissed after lunch. He shot Tazz a final glare before exiting.

As soon as the door slammed shut, Smack leaped from her bunk and cautiously approached Tazz. She whispered softly to her, trying to get her to talk. After much cajoling, she managed to coax her out of her daze. The rest of us kept our distance, hoping Smack could convince Tazz that it wasn't her fault and we were here for her if she needed us, the same way that she had been there for us so many times.

The rest of the day floated past like a bad dream. We went to lunch, were addressed as a company by the officers, and were dismissed to enjoy our first dose of freedom in a month. Even with the deaths of Lionel and Jacque strongly on our minds, the thought of being able to have free time and blow off some steam lifted everyone's spirits, except for Tazz.

Although the MOF provided us with uniforms, toiletries, and food, they didn't provide us with civilian clothing, so once off duty, we changed into our MOF jump suits, which were far more comfortable than the standard uniform. They issued us with wristbands, each containing an allocation of Martian credits to spend, escorted us to the double doors leading to the civilian-populated area, and gave us our standing orders. Under penalty of disciplinary action, we were forbidden from discussing our mission with anyone outside of the MOF, how we got here, current Terran politics or political affairs, or—most unusually—the date. We were permitted to get drunk but were trusted to maintain the high standards of behaviour expected of MOF members, and to behave respectfully towards the local Mars-born population.

As soon as the lecture ended, Sergeant Hopkins opened the double doors, allowing us our first look at The Rec. The Rec was three separate levels packed with shops, restaurants, gyms, pubs, and people. It looked more like a massive shopping centre than a recreational area. After staring at grey, sterile walls for the last four weeks, it was a treat to see colour again. We stepped onto the polished floors. Careful not to bump into the constant flow of people moving back and forth, we approached the nearby balcony to study the various sights and sounds that swirled around us.

DAMIEN LARKIN

The first thing that struck me was the unmistakable smell of cigarette smoke. After breathing in recycled air for so long, I had gotten used to its stale smell, but the Rec area reeked of tobacco. Looking around, I saw at least two out of every three people were smoking, which struck me as highly unusual. My own country had banned smoking in indoor public places over a decade ago. Although plenty of countries hadn't followed this route yet, I thought it strange that, on a different planet without a liveable atmosphere, people were content to poison each other in close proximity. It could have been the ex-smoker in me talking, though. I was jealous of them. And tempted.

The company broke up into smaller groups to wander around and explore the pleasures of the Rec, but Section One hung back. Nordie and Big Mo took the lead in suggesting what to do, and I continued to take in the sights of the locals scurrying about their daily business. It was easy to spot the off-duty MOF personnel from the way they grouped together as opposed to the civilians who moved about or sat and talked in much smaller groups or on their own. They looked no different than us in appearance, but they had an outdated sense of fashion. Every one of the men wore suits and hats, while the women wore long, colourful dresses and shawls or blouses. It looked as though they were going to a gangsters and molls themed party.

With Tazz too distracted to take the initiative, it took longer than normal to reach a consensus, but we eventually agreed on food and drinks to start. Intense Dan led a one-man mission to invade a nearby eatery, seize control of a table and a few chairs, and establish a defensive parameter while the rest of us sauntered behind and studied the menus. Everything was in German and the staff either couldn't or wouldn't speak English, but I eventually managed to order sausage

85

and sauerkraut with a pint of German beer. It wasn't half bad. After my first taste of alcohol in well over a month, a second and a third quickly followed.

Our mood lifted a bit as we unwound, but Tazz remained uncharacteristically quiet, sipping on her wine and refusing to make eye contact or engage in conversation. It was completely understandable given the shock of the experience she had been through. I guessed that the reason she joined us instead of staying in her bunk was that having us around gave her some measure of security. Strength in numbers and all that.

"Maybe we're not even here," Big Mo said, steering the conversation back to his favourite subject, before pausing to take a sip of his water. "Maybe this is all one giant Rig exercise and we're all back home right now."

"On that note, I'm outta here, loves," Smack chirped. She finished her beer, gave us all a cheeky wink, and disappeared into the crowd, looking for something or someone a bit more upbeat.

"So, we're in a Rig, dreaming about being in Rigs on Mars, yeah?" Nordie replied.

"It makes perfect sense. It's all just an experiment. We're not really here. It's an elaborate simulation to see how we'd adapt to a massive change in environment. Doesn't it strike you as strange how well everyone's been coping with this? We're told we're on another planet and everyone's like 'okay, that's cool.' How exactly is that a normal response? Shouldn't we be a bit more pissed off?"

"If it's a simulation, then no one really dies," Tazz said, looking up from her near-empty glass.

As much as I wanted to reassure her, I didn't think this was the best direction to go.

"There's no evidence to show this is a simulation," I said, shooting Big Mo a look to change the subject.

"Sure, everyone's taking it well, but that's because they have us in training for eighteen hours a day. And of those eighteen hours, we spend three quarters of it in the Rigs. That's close to sixty hours of training a day. We don't have time to be angry."

"There's no evidence to show it isn't a simulation, either," he continued, "and I don't buy the line that everyone's too tired. Try to think about Kat and Louise. Do you feel angry? Sad? I bet you feel as I do when I think about my momma. Hollow. And everything else? Space travel? Interplanetary transportation? Aliens? Colonies on Mars? It's like a bad science fiction novel. And what's our role in all of this? Guard duty. We stand around for twelve months doing nothing. That reeks of some lame psychological study to me."

"The mission is the mission, regardless of what it is," Intense Dan chimed in, sounding like an army recruitment advert.

"This isn't helping," I said, ignoring Intense Dan and kicking Big Mo's boot under the table. I subtly nodded towards Tazz. "Even if you're right, we've no way of knowing. We're still here for eleven months, so let's get on with it as best we can."

Big Mo finally took the hint and dropped the topic. He leaned back in his chair and folded his arms. A casual air clung about him as he observed the passing human traffic.

"I'm off to see a man about a dog," Nordie said and, eyeing a MOF soldier nearby, rose from his seat and wandered over to him.

"What does everyone else want to do?" I asked. It was great getting out, but I was exhausted already and could hear my bunk calling out to me.

"I want to go home," Tazz whispered, looking at me with sorrowful eyes.

"I'll take you back to your bunk," I offered and stood up to escort her.

I knew that wasn't what she meant, but I struggled to find something else to say. The higher-ups had made it clear that whether we liked it or not, we were here for the full tour. We could choose to spend that time as members of the MOF or locked up in solitary confinement. There was no other option.

Still dazed, Tazz rose from her chair, and I nodded my goodbyes to Big Mo and Intense Dan. We wandered through the growing crowd of Martian residents eager to sell their wares to the new arrivals and made our way back to the corridor and towards our billets. I could hear drunken laughs coming from one of the other platoon rooms. The sickly-sweet smell of tobacco lingered in the air. I suppressed the urge to ask someone for a spare cigarette and thought back on Big Mo's comment.

It was true what he said about Louise and Kat. They were always on my mind, but for some reason I wasn't angry at being sent here against my will. I thought that strange, but, in my mind, it was as though I had accepted I couldn't do anything about it. Besides, from their point of view, I'd only be gone for a weekend, so what was the problem? I would be protecting Terra and the girls wouldn't know any differently, so I accepted this as a unique opportunity.

After reaching the billets, I dropped Tazz off at her bunk. She climbed in and wrapped the blanket around herself before curling into the foetal position. I slipped off her boots and hung her beret from a bolt in the bedframe after checking she had enough water.

"I just want to hold my daughter," Tazz whimpered as I turned to flop onto my own bunk.

I paused and returned my attention to her.

"I know, but you'll see her soon. You just need to be strong and try not to be too hard on yourself."

"That's the thing. I'm not too hard on myself. I feel nothing. I'm crying because that's what I would have done back on Terra, but these tears aren't real. I don't feel bad. Or good. I'm empty."

"It's normal to feel numb after such a—"

"You don't get it," Tazz shrieked. She rolled over in her bunk to face me. "I haven't felt a thing since I got here. Only anger at the Insectoids in the Rigs. That's it. I don't miss home, I don't hate it here, I don't even feel the connection to my own daughter. For nine months she grew in my body—the body back on Terra—but when I think about her, it's like a faded dream. What if those memories are fake? What if we've never even been to Terra and we were grown in damned test tubes here on Big Red?"

Her sudden outburst caught me off guard. Tazz had always been calm, cool, and collected. Everything about her body language and facial expressions were off from the norm. Even though she claimed not to feel emotions, she certainly looked and sounded emotional.

I tried to reason with her, reassure her, and be there for her, but she abruptly cut me off and rolled over as if to sleep. I made for my own bunk and was about to hoist my weary Terran-bones onto my hard but surprisingly comfortable mattress when Nordie appeared with a cheesy grin plastered across his face.

"You'd be surprised what you can buy off these space Nazis," he said with a triumphant smile and raised a clear, plastic bag containing pre-rolled joints.

"They grow weed on Mars?" I asked, gleefully surprised.

"Yeah, and it's legal, apparently." He selected one from the bag, pulled out a lighter, and nodded towards the nearby showers. "Shall we?"

I'm not big into recreational drugs. Sure, I like going for pints as much as the next person and I've certainly smoked plenty of weed in my time, but I've never done anything harder than that. I stopped smoking weed after Kat was born for no other reason than most of my friends had stopped, too. But I'm not going to lie, I didn't hesitate for a moment in deciding. When you've been abducted from your planet and forcibly conscripted into a covert military force tasked with keeping murderous aliens at bay, you should be allowed to smoke weed. That's my theory anyway.

We blazed up in the showers. Although it burned my lungs, it wasn't half bad. After a few drags, I was already feeling lightheaded and euphorically disjointed, so I eagerly accepted a hip flask of what Nordie called whiskey but was in fact *whisky*. That led to an in-depth discussion until we realised we were rambling on and repeating the word "whiskey" over and over between sporadic fits of laughter.

Giggling to ourselves, we stumbled back to our bunks. That's when I noted Tazz missing. She hadn't entered the shower area to head towards the toilets, so I figured she had made her way to the one at the far end of the room to avoid us. I was about to haul myself onto my bunk to sleep when a frantic recruit appeared from around the corner. I recognised Smithy from Section Two and was about to give him a big, cheery hug (it made sense at the time) when he cut me off.

"It's Tazz."

His face and tone were serious enough that I knew this wasn't a joke. We followed Smithy out of the platoon room and towards the changing areas.

"She totally wigged out," Smithy said as we raced down the corridors. "We were having a few sly drinks by the airlock when she walked right past us and locked herself in."

"Jaysus," Nordie panted, "did you call security?"

"Yep. And the NCO on duty. They said to keep her talking."

We rounded the corner and saw three other

recruits standing abound the reinforced airlock door, trying to calm down a clearly distressed Tazz. She had barricaded herself in. Gripped in her right hand was the unmistakable grey cylinder of a plasma grenade.

"W-will that door hold the blast?" I said as my heart began to sink.

"It should. It looks thick enough," one of the recruits replied. I recognised him from one of the other platoons but didn't know his name.

"What are we gonna do?" Nordie asked.

"Keep her talking."

I moved my way to the front of the small crowd and pressed on the intercom. "Tazz. What's going on? You need to open the airlock door. Let us in."

She shook her head but didn't respond. Her lips were moving quickly but silently. She was praying.

"How long till security gets here?" I asked Smithy.

"We called them five minutes ago. They said to hang tight." He shrugged.

I looked at Nordie and shuddered as a plan sprang to mind.

"Tazz," I said again, pressing down on the intercom, "if you let off that grenade, you risk killing us all. Think of your daughter. She's still your daughter. She's back home, waiting for you. Put down the grenade, open the doors, and let us in."

"She's not my daughter," Tazz choked out, looking right at me. "None of this is real. It's all a dream, and I have to wake up. I have to go home." She held the grenade aloft for all to see and extended her hand towards the nearby manual release. "You should all go," she sobbed.

Frantic, I faced everyone.

"Evacuate this area. Now! I don't know for sure if those doors can withstand the blast, but let's not be here to find out. Seal off all the bulkheads. I'll grab my Exo-suit and get to the external door through one of the other airlocks. The suit will be able to take the brunt of the blast if it comes to that."

Smithy and the two recruits nodded and ran off to start locking down the area, but Nordie remained behind.

"I'll keep her talking," he said firmly, making it evident that he couldn't be persuaded to move.

After giving him a nod, I raced back to the platoon changing area, ripped open my locker, and began pulling on my suit. In a battlefield situation, it was expected of you to have your suit on and all preliminary checks completed within two minutes. We drilled and rehearsed it so many times that it was second nature, but I wasn't sure if Tazz had two minutes. Hoping that she wouldn't risk Nordie by detonating the grenade, I would have mere seconds to get to her and re-seal the outer airlock before she risked exposure. Hoping to cut time, I donned my Exo-suit in forty-five seconds, skipping the checks and over-riding the system, and ran as quick as I could to the nearest airlock. We kept our suits in excellent condition, so I wasn't expecting any problems. Unfortunately, if there were any problems, I'd find out the moment my boots touched Martian soil.

I locked myself into the airlock and pulled at the manual release, all the while keeping an eye on the console on my left arm as the Exo-suit ran its own diagnostic checks. Everything turned green by the time the outer door swung open and I jumped out, ignoring the Martian sand crunching under my boots.

"Nordie, sit-rep," I shouted into the helmet mic after patching myself through to the local communications system.

"She's not listening," Nordie roared back. Panic leaked from his voice. "She's armed the grenade and is about to blow the external doors. I can't talk her out of it."

I spotted the airlock she was in up ahead. Just a few more seconds. That's all I needed. I could override the door mechanism long enough to get in and grab her. The drop in pressure might even subdue her, giving me a few precious seconds to secure the grenade.

"Tazz, it's Dub. I'm outside. Don't release the grenade. You'll kill me and Nordie," I said, hoping to appeal to the Section Leader in her.

"Dub," she said quietly. "You're not real. We're not real. It's all lies. You don't understand. But you will."

I was close. Just a few more seconds. A little longer, that's all I needed.

"Help me to understand, Jasmine. Talk to me."

I extended my hand to reach for the airlock when she spoke again.

"We have been here before, Dub. A thousand times. A million. We have always been here. You know what you have to do. You've done it before. Kill them all."

I gripped my hand on the airlock manual release and pulled myself up to the reinforced window in time to see Tazz turn and face me. She yanked at the emergency release and lifted her thumb from the plasma grenade. For a moment, our gazes locked, and I saw the old Tazz. That confident leader, our mother, sister, and Amazonian warrior queen combined. I let go of the external release as the door crashed open. Tazz stumbled forward as the pressure dropped, but she maintained her grip. There was no way I would reach her in time.

The blast enveloped her in a split second. I don't even remember what it looked like. One second, she was there, smiling, and the next I felt a sledgehammer to my chest and found myself on my back, gazing up at the swirling, fading Martian sky. Several alarms buzzed throughout my helmet, vying for my attention on the helmet screen. The communications network screamed to life with dozens of voices all shouting to be heard at the same time. Some of them called my name. I ignored them and remained staring up at the sky.

It would be dark soon. I wanted to lay there all night to see how dark Mars got. I wanted to see what a Martian sunrise was like. As on Terra, I figured it was always darkest before the light. But I had duties; I had to bury my friends. I had to mourn Tazz.

I slowly pulled myself up and called Nordie.

As soon as I reported back, I was stripped of my Exo-suit at gunpoint and detained by security, along with Nordie, Smithy, and two others. They questioned us individually. I gave them the less colourful version of events, hoping Nordie would do the same. After a few hours, Mad Jack made a rare appearance and thanked us for our efforts, advising us that we were free to go.

The official line was that Tazz had been struggling to adjust from day one and the accidental deaths of those under her command pushed her over the edge. We were all immediately given access to psychologists and grief counsellors, who reported that we were under severe mental strain and were ordered to have our Rig time reduced in favour of real-world training and exercises. Since we were no longer recruits and had duties ahead as opposed to continued training, this was a moot point.

We buried Tazz, Lionel, and Jacque as a company the very next day. It was a sombre event, designed to hammer home that this wasn't a game. If we died on Big Red, we died back on Terra. We were no different than any other soldier that donned the Red'n'Blacks.

Since we were still on our own time, we spent the remainder of the day after the funeral trying to put everything behind us and hunting for pleasures and distractions in the Rec. I found mine at the bottom of a pint glass and tried hard not to let the horror of what I had witnessed weigh me down. Even though the powers-that-be declared this a once off scenario, I got the impression that they were watching every one of us, so I kept my head down. When not indulging in pints, I either read or caught up on some well-deserved sleep.

At least two more people tried to kill themselves that weekend, and about a dozen more were arrested or interned on medical grounds. The higher-ups did what they could to sweep it under the rug and make out that these were isolated incidents with people who had cracked under the pressure. They pointed to the clear majority of us who continued to function properly as evidence that these incidents were nothing to worry about and that the MOF Leadership had made appropriate changes to the training programme to ensure that this would never happen again. I didn't buy what they said at all, but I didn't question it aloud, either.

After that weekend, we were each assigned daily duties—with our sections, in other sections, individually, or in smaller groups. My first official duty was to provide security for an engineering team descending into the catacombs for routine maintenance work. I donned my Exo-suit and, after completing my checks, left with my HK-17 to find the engineers waiting for me outside the Rec area.

As I marched towards the elevators, I ignored the stares of the Martian colonists and the snickers from the full-time MOF personnel calling me a 'Hollow.' After passing the security checks at the door leading from the Rec into the rest of New Berlin, I resisted the urge to stand in awe and look out the windows at the massive buildings that surrounded the part of the complex we stayed in. I hoped to study them better on my way back, so I pushed on, rounded a few corners, and found the two engineers.

They were American but spoke with an accent I

didn't recognise and shot me a look as if to say "about time." I greeted them politely and waited for them to pick up their tool kits.

"So, we're going to these catacombs," I said, trying to sound professional and confident. "Why do you need a military escort?"

They turned to look at one another before returning their attention to me.

"You must be a noob," one of them laughed, "when did you rotate in from Terra?"

"Over a month ago."

They laughed at that and slapped each other on the shoulders.

"Tragic," the other engineer said. Shaking his head, he pressed the button for the elevator. It arrived seconds later, and he keyed in for the lowest level available that the elevator could go. Not expecting an answer, I ran a quick diagnostic check on my weapon while we continued our descent.

"New Berlin, as we know it, was founded on the ruins of the first German colony," the first engineer said without making eye contact. "The catacombs are the original foundation as well as housing for some of our redundant support systems. That's where the Volk, as they call themselves, buried their dead. There's a lot of dead Nazis down there."

"Okay, so why the escort if they're all dead?"

The two engineers shook their heads again. They apparently enjoyed making out that I was an idiot. Keeping my HK-17 pointed towards the floor, I turned my whole body to face them. I'm not a big fan of being condescended to at the best of times. Even less so when I'm wearing an Exo-suit and brandishing a semi-automatic weapon. They sized me up in silence as I glared at both of them. They took the hint.

"Most of the Germans here are descended from the original colonists. Although they grin and smile politely in public, there's a sizeable minority that hold the National Socialist viewpoint. They come down into the catacombs from time to time to perform certain rituals or celebrate Hitler's birthday, that type of thing. Security usually chases 'em off, but last year one of these Sons of the Fourth Reich attacked an engineering crew. One of our guys nearly died."

"Nah man, that's all BS," the second engineer said with a smile. "I hear the real reason they're down here is that they're looking for leftover technology or an artefact. Some type of weapon or somethin'. Same thing that has MARSCORP digging up half the planet."

I stopped listening at that point. After learning Neo-Nazis were on Big Red, I decided to stop asking questions. Questions only brought more confusing answers.

"Here we go," the first engineer said. He pulled out an ugly revolver from his toolkit and slid it into his waist band.

The lift lurched to a halt.

I raised my weapon as the lift doors slid open. We were too far down for me to access real-time information from the satellites, so I pulled up an image of the catacombs' layout and took a step forward. I checked both corridor directions. Seeing the area was clear, I gestured for the engineers to step out. They locked access to the lift. Then, using one of their handheld devices, they inputted the location of the system they needed to check directly into my helmet. With a steady and controlled pace, I took point, searching every nook and cranny of the winding, dim corridor until we arrived at our destination.

The two engineers dove into their work, eager to complete it and return to surface level. I stood guard and wondered how I would do if I had to deal with a Terran or Marsie. All our training simulations had been based around fighting aliens. Although the principals were the same, I wondered if it would be as easy for me to pull the trigger on a fellow human. I watched the engineers as they hunched over their work and wondered, if needed, could I point my HK-17 at them and squeeze the trigger. For a brief moment, a part of me was tempted. I experienced one second of strange, dizzying clarity when I knew it to be the right thing to do, but I shook it off and continued to stand guard.

The psychologists were right; the Rigs had done a number on us.

Within a half hour, the engineers completed their task and we beat a hasty retreat to the lifts.

"Thanks for that," the second one said as he punched in the code to bring us back to surface level. "Everyone gets the jitters down here. It's just creepy."

"Then why not move everything to a more secure level?" I asked, hoping this question wouldn't unleash another confusing answer.

"It would cost too much," the first engineer said, replacing his revolver back into his toolkit. "The systems down there are redundant. The primary and secondary back-ups are in secure locations. We use the redundant systems as a fallback plan. Realistically, the chances of the primary and secondary systems going down at the same time is incalculable. It couldn't happen, but we need to maintain everything down there just in case."

Satisfied with their answer, I faced the doorway and waited for the lift to bring us back home.

"I'm Charles, by the way," the first engineer said, extending a friendly hand to me. "And this here, is Benjamin."

"Darren," I replied, shaking their hands, "but people call me Dub."

"You had many dealings with the Marsies, Dub?" Charles asked.

"Not much. They only let us into the Rec on the weekend. I chatted with one or two but nothing much more than that."

"They're a weird, weird people," Benjamin said with a knowing smile. "They keep to themselves, which is fine, but remember…they may look like you, but they're not. Never turn your back on a Marsie, especially a German one."

"The war was seventy years ago. Are you telling me they still have a grudge?"

Charles and Benjamin looked at one another and started laughing.

"You really are brand new," Charles choked out between laughs. "The Volk don't believe they lost the war. Most of 'em landed before it broke out."

Benjamin slapped my shoulder and wiped a tear of laughter from his eye. "You hear about the Old Man?" he asked.

"No."

"He's a high-ranking Nazi who escaped before the end of the war. A confidant of Hitler's, or so they say. He lives in Command and Control under armed guard. The Germans worship him like a god. Ask around. It's pretty damn weird."

"I will," I replied, desperately urging the lift to ascend faster. The more people talked to me about Big Red, the stranger this place got.

"**H**is brain patterns seem to be returning to normal," Doctor Lucas said, breaking my train of thought.

Doctor Ling stood up from her seat and walked over to the monitors at the end of the room. She took her time studying several of them before checking other read-outs.

"Remarkable," she uttered to herself.

"I do feel much better," I called out to her. "Could you please loosen these straps? They're really tight."

Glancing at the monitors and back at me, the doctors conferred with each other in whispers.

"It's rude to whisper," I said, feigning indignity.

After a few moments, Doctor Ling approached my trolley and stood over me. "I apologise, Darren. That was rude to whisper. I can loosen your straps, but we still need to keep you confined until we can be sure you're not a danger to yourself."

"Or anyone else."

She smiled politely at that but didn't respond. She loosened the leather straps from the underside of the trolley, allowing me to move my hands more freely.

"Would you like a coffee or water?" she asked as I moved my hands around, happy that I could now scratch myself.

"Coffee, please."

Doctor Ling nodded. She opened the double doors and spoke to the armed guards outside. One of them departed as she turned to retake her place beside me. I managed a quick glimpse at my subdued colleagues and tried to search their faces for someone I recognised, but the doors slammed shut before I could.

The doctor sat down and picked up her files and tablet.

"How do you feel talking about Recruit Singh's death?"

"Sad. Really sad. It's not like we knew each other that long, but I felt close to her. She was a good person and didn't deserve to go out like that."

"Did you find yourself dwelling on her death for a long time afterwards?"

My memories were still hazy, but even without being able to recall, the sadness of Tazz's suicide pervaded the fog that choked my mind.

"Yes, but I got on with it. There was no point in dwelling on it or letting it bring me down. I was saddened by her loss, but I kept on going. Thinking about it wasn't going to bring her, Jacque, or Lionel back."

The psychologist scribbled something else on her notepad before continuing. "Did you ever think about her last words? What they meant?"

"Yeah, of course, I did. I spent ages trying to figure it out, but in the end, it meant nothing. As much as I don't like to admit it, she was clearly troubled. She hid it beneath a mask of strength, but she was in pain. Blaming herself for Jacque's and Lionel's death forced that mask off and pushed her over the edge."

"So, you don't think she meant anything at all by what she said?"

I shifted in my bed uncomfortably and felt the hidden cylinder poke into my thigh.

"At the time, I thought it was something about us being Hollows. Tazz thought we were clones, programmed with false memories. I know now we were more like drone pilots."

A rap sounded on the double doors, causing Doctor Ling to place her files and notes beside her again before answering the knock. One of the orderlies held two coffee cups and awkwardly gestured at another armed guard behind him.

"A message from General Barrymore," he said and slipped past her as she accepted the message from the guard.

The orderly placed her coffee carefully beside her chair before handing me mine. He paused for a second to make sure I could sip from it without scalding myself. Then he glanced at Doctor Lucas, who was still engrossed in her work.

"Everything's ready," he whispered. "Strike Team One, Two, and Three are in place. Our people are committed. As soon as Big Bird sends the signal, we move. You know what you have to do."

"Kill them all?" I asked, already knowing the answer.

"Kill them all," he replied and tapped me gently on the hand before retreating towards the double doors.

Doctor Ling returned. I sipped on my coffee as I watched her confer with Doctor Lucas.

I could see she was concerned about something. "Louise used to say that bad news tastes better with coffee," I said, nodding at her nearby cup.

She forced a grin, claimed her seat, and took a quick sip.

"I take it the general isn't happy with our progress?" I said.

She ran an exasperated hand through her finely brushed hair, causing strands to fall back lazily onto her face. She gently brushed the loose strands aside, while trying to maintain her composure.

"The general doesn't understand the consequences of pushing you too hard, and I won't risk your well-being by introducing...more advanced techniques.

I won't gamble with your sanity like that, Darren. You've served Earth for long enough."

"We do whatever it takes to protect Terra."

"Yes, we do," she said and sighed. "Is your coffee okay?"

"It's perfect." I smiled back and took a sip to demonstrate.

My hands wrapped around the cardboard grip on the outside of the cup. I maintained eye contact as my fingers slowly probed the cardboard for what I was looking for. The little finger on my right hand found the thin, metal strip. Taking another mouthful of coffee as a pretext, I moved that section of the cup from the doctor's view. Then I carefully shimmied the metal strip down until I could conceal it in my right palm. It wouldn't be long now and I had to be ready, although I still wasn't a hundred percent sure for what.

"Let's try something else," Doctor Ling said finally. "You've made great progress in the last two hours, but let's see if you can focus on specific events further into your tour of duty to see if we can fast-track this process a bit. I'll ask a specific question and see if you can recall it, okay?"

"Sure," I replied, placing the half-full coffee cup on one of the nearby monitors. I manoeuvred the metal strip between my fingers, as I'd been taught, and, using the rest of my hand as cover, began easing it into the lock on my right-hand strap.

"Great. Tell me if you can remember the first real combat situation you were in."

As the weeks passed, we began to adapt to our new lives and roles in New Berlin. We worked five days on and two days off, but work days could vary in length. If you were lucky, you worked twelve hours and had time to hit the Rec or the gym before grabbing eight hours of shut eye. If it was a bad day—due to manpower shortages, injuries, or sickness—you could easily work an eighteen-hour shift. On more than one occasion, I had time for only an hour or two of sleep before another long day began.

Our duties ranged from guarding a bulkhead or airlock to providing security at the hangar bays, Command and Control, or the civilian population centres. As we continued to prove ourselves, the higher-ups began unlocking the other mysterious areas of New Berlin; so, although we were still confined to our living quarters and the Rec when on our own time, they began trusting us with securing and protecting other sections of Mars' primary colony.

We saw no aliens during those first few months, not even live hostiles. In a lot of ways, what happened on Big Red was shielded from us because the powers-that-be entertained serious doubts about our loyalty and combat efficiency. As we continued to acclimate and prove ourselves, they slowly lifted the veil.

The first time I saw the effects of the hidden war, I was stationed at the underground hangar bay. Wave after wave of troop transports arrived one day crammed full of MOF soldiers clad in Exo-suits. They carried their wounded and fallen comrades towards the nearby bullet trains ready to take them to the medical treatment area or, in a lot of cases, the morgue. I remember standing in the same position, guarding the entrance to the transport area and watching endless columns of screaming and crying men and women (and sometimes boys and girls) walk or being carried with limbs missing and horrified looks plastered on their faces.

Some of them looked through me as they passed, as if willing me to be real enough that they could tell me their story but knowing that without having experienced their horror myself, I would never understand. I learned later that the Insectoids had launched an unprovoked attack on one of the Forward Bases by the border and massacred over a thousand full-time personnel.

Such was life on Big Red.

Due to sickness, injury, and the accidental deaths of several Second Battalion soldiers, our overall effective fighting force dropped to below a thousand active personnel. This didn't stop the powers-that-be from continuing to utilise us for the defence and protection of New Berlin while sending out the veterans to guard the outer colonies and Forward Bases. A constant influx of UEAF soldiers continued to be ferried down from the fleet and shipped off to where they were needed most, telling us that the conflict we found ourselves surrounded by was intensifying.

Rumours circulated that the various Insectoid hives had agreed to a truce amongst each other and decided to focus their collective energies on driving us from Big Red in a co-ordinated strike, but we paid those little heed. After witnessing the damage inflicted by the hostiles at the hangar bay, I was quite happy with guarding bulkheads or breaking up drunken fights between Marsies and Terrans.

Around this time, they began reorganising our platoons and filling in the gaps. With Richie still (allegedly) confined to the medical treatment area, we were due to get replacements, and these came in the form of Farmer and Noid.

Farmer was an old guy who was cool and laid back, very soft spoken and polite. He always had something interesting to say and he pulled his weight, so he fit in well. Noid was a different story altogether. I'd met her briefly during the original assessment. Although I hadn't interacted with her much since arriving on Big Red, I'd heard stories.

Basically, she was the anti-Tazz. She was a good soldier if she didn't have to interact with anyone, but she had a reputation for being headstrong, rude, and not working well in a team. During section training exercises in the Rig, she continually got us killed by ignoring orders or trying to complete the mission objective on her own. She was exceptionally paranoid, earning her nickname from her random outbursts that people were out to get her. Just by observing her for a few minutes, you could tell she wasn't quite right, but Corporal Owens and the powers-that-be didn't care.

Our first mission outside of New Berlin was relatively straightforward, in theory. Section One was ordered to escort a MARSCORP asset across Terran-controlled territory to Trump Colony, dump him with the Americans, and return home. Since we were cutting through the centre of the area under Terran control and hundreds of kilometres from anything resembling a war zone, the chances of enemy contact was highly unlikely, but the asset was deemed important enough to have a military escort; and it's not like we had the option to refuse.

Smack had become our unofficial Section Leader but remained officially unconfirmed by the corporal.

She was eager for this whole thing to go off without a hitch. She double and triple checked all our equipment, even going so far as to brush the grains of Martian sand from our boots to make us look as presentable as possible. It didn't work, but we were glad to have someone who tried to fill the void left by Tazz.

In our gear and led by Corporal Owens, we arrived at the hangar bay. Corporal Owens approached a group of waiting MARSCORP suits to meet the asset and receive any last-minute instructions. Personally, I wasn't a big fan of the suits. They walked around all day with their heads held high as if making eye contact with someone they deemed inferior would infect them with the terrible, crippling disease of poverty or low social status. I was surprised to see that we weren't going to be escorting any of them but a ten-year-old boy.

The boy wore the civilian version of an Exo-suit called a Bio-suit. It was the basic version of what we wore but with far thinner armour and without the military capabilities like homing in on a target or calling in a drone strike. The corporal returned with the boy following close behind and ordered us to climb aboard a nearby lander. We did as we were told. After strapping in and stashing our HKs, we chatted amongst each other.

The lander—a high-speed hover craft—was a civilian transport, so a bunch of Marsies and a few Terran scientists were already aboard. They fell quiet at the sight of us, probably concerned by the fact that we wore Exo or Bio-suits while their only protection was the hull's thick skin. One of the scientists turned pale and ran right off in terror, deeming our presence a premonition of the journey's doom. We laughed.

The lander inched forward after a few minutes, positioning itself on the landing pad to be brought to the surface. When the platform jolted upwards, I recalled the last time I rode a transport and found myself worried that Captain Lockhart piloted the ship. As if sensing my concern, Smack loaded up "Song 2" from her music library and patched it (at full volume) through our mutual communications network, causing me to flinch in my seat. Everyone laughed again.

By the time we reached the surface, I had finished my mock-tirade of abuse against Smack and promised future retaliation. The lander moved around the parameter of New Berlin's protective dome, giving us another view of the city that we still knew so little about. We gazed out of the lander windows and tried to soak up every detail, guessing what the various tall towers and buildings were for and even tried to spot where we resided in this extra-terrestrial maze. It didn't last long, though. Once clear of the parameter, the lander blasted off at full speed, hurtling us across the Martian wasteland toward the American sphere of influence on Big Red.

The thankfully coherent and sane-sounding pilot of the lander told us over the intercom to expect a journey of over four hours, depending on the possibility of high winds hitting us from the north-east, but it didn't sound like anything this little lander couldn't handle. To pass the time, we talked amongst each other, listened to music, or read from our arm consoles.

I thought about Kat and Louise. It had been months since I'd last seen them. Although it would only be a few days from their perspective, it was hard not to imagine them a year older when we did meet again. As my thoughts focused on them, I found myself looking at the asset who sat next to the corporal, with his eyes fixed straight ahead, unblinking. He was disciplined for a ten-year-old, I had to give him that. I wondered what MARSCORP was doing with someone that young but figured he was the child of high-level execs returning home from a sightseeing trip or something.

After two hours, my eyes grew heavy and I began to drift off, soothed by the reassuring whispers of the Voice of God. I leaned back in my seat, rested my helmet against the bulkhead, and allowed my brain to slowly switch off and drift...

BAM!

The loudest noise I ever heard exploded around me. I gripped my seat in panic as the transport shuddered in a series of violent lurches. I found myself being jerked forward. The seat straps held me in place, but my helmet thudded viciously against the bulkhead. This happened several times, and I couldn't seem to focus my vision enough to see why. Everything spun. Everyone screamed and shouted. The lander bounced and bucked wildly. I managed to turn my head enough to spot a giant hole a few seats to my left, opposite the corporal and the boy. I forced my head to the right and saw that we were no longer hovering but skidding at full speed over the Martian landscape, ploughing through ancient rock and sand.

The lander abruptly stopped with another violent jolt. My helmet bashed into the reinforced hull again.

Bewildered, I could hear alarmed yet muffled shouts around me. My head spun. I felt disorientated and sick. Remembering my training, I tapped the emergency diagnostic button on my console. I couldn't quite read the information that pulled up on my helmet screen, but I made out the symbols that indicated my Exo-suit hadn't been breached; I was in one piece.

"Dub, you all right?" Smack called out on a private channel.

I felt as though I was ready to throw up, but that

was the last thing I wanted to do in my Exo-suit.

"Yeah. Yeah, I'm all right," I groaned back as I unstrapped my seat belt.

I tumbled forward on wobbly legs and grabbed my HK-17. The inside of the lander was a mess. The civilians sitting ahead of us were stretched out and twisted, like weird pieces of living art, but they weren't alive. None of them wore Bio-suits, so even if the force of the impact hadn't killed them, they would have fallen victim to the gaping hole in the lander hull sucking out the atmosphere, heat, and air.

"What happened?" Nordie groaned as he too unstrapped himself and turned to check on Big Mo.

"Corporal? You okay?" I said as soon as I saw the unmoving body of Corporal Owens slumped forward in his seat.

The ten-year-old beside him was fidgeting wildly with his straps, so I took a few uncertain paces forward and unclipped him. Taking the boy by his left arm, I clicked on his console to run a diagnostic before pushing the corporal back onto his seat to check him, too. There was no need to run a diagnostic on him, though. Even with the reinforced smart fibres of an Exo-suit, they can't protect you from everything. Jagged shards of metal from whatever had caused the explosion had punctured his chest and lungs. He was dead.

"Was it an accident?" Intense Dan shouted as he stumbled forward over the mattress of dead civilians. "Did the engines blow?"

"Smack, the corporal's dead. You're running the show now," I reported and returned my attention back to the boy. He looked a bit shaken, but he was uninjured.

Smack appeared beside me and looked down at our fallen corporal before taking a deep breath. "Okay, listen up," she began, in the most authoritative voice she could muster, "I'm running the show until we get back to New Berlin. Nordie, Mo, get into the cockpit and check on the pilots. See if you can access the lander's logs to find out what happened. Intense Dan, double check those civilians. They're probably all dead, but I don't want to find out that we missed someone we could have saved. Dub, Farmer, Noid, outside. See what you can see and get me our location. Check the engines, too. Let's hustle, people."

Without any delay, we broke up and dived into our tasks without question. Smack remained behind with the boy as Farmer, Noid and I climbed over the shattered wreckage of the lander towards the massive hole in the hull. I paused as I studied the burned, curved edges of the blast outline, and then I turned to look at Noid. Wordlessly, she nodded at me in agreement.

"Smack," I called out urgently, "I'm not an expert, but this looks a hell of a lot like the burn marks from a particle weapon. Recommend we go hot."

Although no one said anything for a few seconds, I heard everyone collectively gasp in fear over the channel.

"Understood. Go hot."

We cocked our HK-17s simultaneously, released the trigger safety, and clicked on the particle battery charger. Interestingly, you can fire live bullets on Big Red. Something to do with the atmosphere and gravity, which means you get even better range than back on Terra.

What makes the HK-17 a favourite of the MOF is the 'HK' part of it—short for Hybrid Killer. If needed, you can switch to a particle-based weapon. Since the technology was still relatively new to us, the scientists back home hadn't developed a power source strong enough to create a fully particle-based weapon, so it was more like a shot-gun add-on built into your assault rifle. You could fire about five high-energy blasts per minute in between recharges.

Keeping my weapon high, I jumped out of the lander and trained my sights on the surrounding clumps of rock. We were hundreds of kilometres from the nearest reported Insectoid nest, but we had to assume we had been ambushed. I paced forward. My hand trembled as it did at the start of every Rig exercise. Behind me, Farmer studied the burn marks from the blast while Noid, with her own weapon readied, worked her way back to the lander engines. Even without looking directly at her, I tracked her progress via the satellite real-time feed and a minimised screen on my helmet followed her from my Exo-suit's rear helmet camera.

"Looks like we're about two hundred klicks southeast of Trump Colony," I reported to Smack as I studied the satellite feed. "We haven't gone off course, though, so if the pilots sent off a distress signal, drones from New Berlin should be able to home in on us."

"Good," Smack replied. "Any sign of hostiles?"

I approached the nearest pile of rocks and carefully checked every position someone could conceal themselves in. Confident that it was secure, I risked a glance over the rocks to study the plain that enveloped us. It was silent and unmoving.

"Nothing on visual and no movement detected by the satellites. Running a heat search now. This will take a minute or two."

"Copy."

"The engines are totalled," Noid roared. "There's no way this pile of crap is moving again. Must have been shot twice."

"Understood."

"The flight crew's dead," Nordie chimed in. "The computer reported a distress signal had been sent. But if this is an ambush, they could have jammed it."

Dan started to speak, but Smack cut right across

him.

"Okay, people, we have to assume we're under attack. Everyone outside, all-around cover. Dub, where are those heat readings?"

"Coming," I replied, tapping my arm console and willing it to work faster. There was serious lag time from the satellites, which was unusual and unnerving. I continued scanning the horizon but saw no sign of movement.

"I'm not getting anything from New Berlin," Noid shouted again. The anger in her voice rose. "We could be getting jammed."

"Same here," Intense Dan said. A sliver of fear cut through his normally calm voice.

"C'mon people," Smack said firmly. "Defensive parameter. Now! Everyone watch your arcs. Dub, we need that body-heat read. Where is it?"

Feeling the rising sense of urgency, I considered bashing my arm console onto jagged rocks to see if that would speed up the process when the results finally came through on my screen. I blinked once in case I was reading it wrong. Then, with a controlled eye-blink, I sent the feed to the entire Section without saying a word. I slowly raised my HK-17 and pointed at the rocky, dust-covered ground two metres in front of me.

We were surrounded.

"FIRE!" Smack roared.

Without any conscious thought, my warrior instinct kicked in. I squeezed the trigger and watched as a ferocious Insectoid erupted from the soil. I dropped it quickly enough before jumping forward and using its body as a shield, firing rapidly at the dozen other monsters that exploded from their hiding places. The heat-seeking satellite feed imposed itself on the 3D map of the area, showing our positions relative to those of the enemy. Because we opened fire, the

Insectoid warriors scurried from their positions and tried to swarm us. The battle cries of my comrades and the roar of gunfire came from every direction. My heart pounded like a drum as the hostiles drove right at me, like giant spiders from your worst nightmares on steroids.

I moved my HK-17 from position to position, cutting down the enemy as they scuttled up the bug holes they had carefully prepared. In the distance, a sole particle weapon fired on our position. Although accurate enough to pin-point something as big as a lander, the shooter wasn't skilled enough to land a direct hit on us.

After halting the advance of the Insectoids in my arc of fire, I whipped out a plasma grenade and hurled it down the nearest bug hole before hitting the ground. The explosion turned the entire area I landed on into a bowl of jelly. By the time I kneeled up with my weapon ready to fire, enemy movement ahead and on my helmet screen had ceased.

I turned to Farmer, who was on my right flank, and saw him surrounded by the bodies of dead or dying Insectoids, all screaming in terrifying roars of pain and anger. Raising my weapon, I fired another stream of bullets at the hostiles trying to overrun his position, carving them to pieces in the crossfire. I paused for a moment, carefully scanning the ground around me but couldn't detect any movement.

I accessed my rear-view helmet camera with an eyeblink. Panning around, I surveyed the ongoing battle behind me. We had held the parameter so far, but despite the dozens of dead aliens that lay at our feet, they were still coming. They seemed to be probing our lines of defence with diversionary attacks before withdrawing or hiding behind the carcasses of their dead comrades. My heart continued to pound viciously, but I controlled my breathing to keep my nerve and held my ground, ready for the next assault.

"Hold the line," Smack shouted over the comm and then paused long enough to fire a few sporadic bursts. "They know what we're made of now. The second wave will be coming. Watch your arcs and shoot anything that has more than two legs."

"DEFEND THEM. PROTECT TERRA."

The Voice grew repetitive. It had whispered to me all through the first attack, just below the surface, guiding my hands and eyes to every prospective target, urging me to do what was necessary. Now it spoke as loudly as if it were standing beside me, with its lips pressed against my ear.

"KILL THEM ALL. TERRA NEEDS YOU. FEAR IS THE ENEMY. KILL FEAR. PROTECT TERRA."

"Shut the hell up," Nordie growled in between deep gasps of breath.

"What's wrong, Nordie? Did the Voice threaten you with a united Ireland if you don't fight hard enough?" I goaded, hoping to break the tension.

"Don't you start," Nordie hissed, but I hoped he at least thought it was a little funny.

"Here they come!" Smack roared, and the sound of weapons fire erupted again.

I threw myself up against a nearby pile of rocks and moved my HK-17 from bug hole to bug hole, firing controlled bursts, trying to hit them head-on as they emerged from the ground. While changing magazines, I blasted the particle weapon one-handed and watched the silent but deadly energy discharge slice through the approaching attackers, but it didn't slow their overall momentum. They didn't wail in despair for a wounded comrade or show momentary reluctance at shying away from the terror of the battlefield. The enemy teemed relentlessly from their bug holes, shrieking wildly and clambering over their fallen without hesitation, eager to hack us to pieces.

"Aarrggghhh!"

I turned in time to see two Insectoids flank Farmer's position and drive their razor tipped limbs through his Exo-suit. His face contorted in pain and horror as they savagely ripped his body apart, tearing his flesh to pieces until he was nothing more than strips of muscle, blood, and pulverised bone.

I lobbed a plasma grenade at them and ducked for cover, feeling a grim satisfaction that I had at least destroyed his killers and sent them to whatever the Insectoid's version of hell was.

Shocked by what I had witnessed them doing to Farmer, I raised my weapon a split second too slow as three more of the creatures scurried within striking distance. I managed to take out one with a spray of bullets and wounded the second one across its left legs, but the third one weaved and bobbed between my line of fire and got close enough to lash out at me.

For a heartbeat, I thought I was dead. It occurred too quickly for me to fully realise what had happened, but I found myself knocked roughly to the ground, with my HK-17 landing out of reach. I looked up to see my entire field of vision occupied by a giant, hellish spider-like creature and opened my mouth to scream, but nothing came out. It raised its front two legs to deliver the death blow and I thought that was it. My time had come. Whether stunned from the fall or in shock at seeing something so unnaturally inhuman so close, my body froze. I couldn't move. Death's icy embrace pulled me ever closer.

"DRAW YOUR KNIFE. STRIKE HARD. DO IT NOW."

Unlike Nordie, I didn't believe in fighting against my Voice. Without conscious thought, my body reacted. Like a spectator watching a fight from a safe distance, I saw my hand draw my knife and lunge desperately upwards at the creature's exposed underbelly. The

117

blade pierced its thick, black, rubbery skin, causing it to jump back while squealing. Knowing I had a second or two to react, I rolled out of the creature's path and grabbed my HK. Still lying down, I turned. When it approached again, I squeezed the trigger and blew a hole in its head before wiping out its four allies that scarpered close behind, eager to dismember me and punch a hole through our lines.

"I'm hit!" Intense Dan cried out from his position. The pain in his voice was unmistakeably brutal.

"Gotcha," Big Mo hollered back as he ran to rescue our wounded comrade.

"Pull back to the lander! Hold the damned line!" Smack ordered.

Panting from exhaustion, I continued the cycle of firing my weapon and rapidly reloading. The Martian landscape around me was littered with a carpet of eight-legged arachnids, and its red soil was stained with the green tar-like blood of the enemy, but they kept up their advance. As if in warning, the Insectoid particle weapon struck the side of the lander again, blowing another hole in it. From a tactical situation, it didn't look as though we had long left. At that moment, I would have given anything to hold Louise and Kat, even for a second.

"YOU WILL NOT DIE. YOU HAVE ALWAYS BEEN HERE. PROTECT TERRA."

I'd heard the Voice say a lot of strange things, but I pushed its words from my mind and basked in the reassuring sense of warmth it filled me with.

"We need an evac!" Noid shouted, carving through another wave of the ever-encroaching hostiles with a shotgun-like blast of her particle beam.

"Still nothing on the comm channels. We need to knock out that jamming device," Big Mo replied as he simultaneously fought off the advancing enemy and tried to tend to Intense Dan.

"Switch to local channels. There may be someone nearby," Smack ordered, trying to hide the tinge of fear in her voice.

We managed to keep our defensive parameter intact but had fallen back to within a few metres of the lander. The enemy occupied the high ground around us and pockets of them blended in among the carcasses, waiting for the last push. Like lines of worker ants, they methodically tightened the noose ever-so-slowly, inching closer, drawing us into expending what little ammunition we had left as they prepared for one last decisive strike that would wipe us out.

"I'm nearly out of ammo," Nordie said. "Smack, what do we do?"

Tense seconds of silence followed. For all intents and purposes, it was over. We had nowhere to hide, barely any cover, and were running low on bullets. Five shots a minute from our particle discharges would buy us a minute or two at best, but with so much time needed to recharge in between, it was ultimately hopeless. All we had left was taking out as many of them with us as possible. Noid pulled out a plasma grenade and gripped it tightly in her left hand. I silently did the same and tried to make my peace with a cruel, uncaring universe that would have me die on some barren wasteland, so far from home.

"Maybe I can help?" the ten-year-old said abruptly.

In the heat of battle, I had completely forgotten he was there, cowering behind Smack. He stood now, gazing in awe at the carnage that surrounded us.

"No offense, kid," Smack said, without taking her eyes off the enemy that encircled us, "but unless you can grow bullets or order a tactical nuclear strike..."

The boy raised his hand and pointed at something in the sky. "Inbound," he muttered. His finger traced the path of an invisible object.

I risked a glance at Nordie, who shrugged in response.

"You won't have long," the boy continued, "I can only keep them at bay for so long. When it happens, they'll wake up again."

We were all baffled by the boy's words, but it was Nordie who first twigged something was off. "Why aren't they attacking?"

I scanned the horizon and could clearly make out the enemy running from position to position, circling us. But Nordie was right; they should have begun their assault. For stupid hive-minded insects, they were adept at probing for weakness. Although most of their tactics involved using overwhelming strength of numbers to win, it was strange that at this stage of the battle they chose to hold off. They just kept running about in circles.

"The transport's nearby, but it'll be gone soon," the boy said. "They won't hear you with the jammer on. I can't keep holding them back. You need to act now."

I lowered my weapon and turned to face the boy. Dropping to one knee, I looked directly at his face behind his helmet visor and saw his brow furrowed in concentration as his hand continued to trace something in the sky, something that was steadily moving away from us.

"Kid," I said in the softest voice I could muster given the situation we were in, "are you telling me you're stopping them from attacking us? And there's transport nearby? You know this isn't a game, right?"

The boy continued looking straight up at the Martian sky. "Kat called you 'faddy' when she first learned to speak. Your happiest childhood memory is on a beach on a sunny day. You ran from the waves and laughed when they splashed you. So young. You were attracted to Tazz but never would have done anything about it because..."

"Wow, wow, wow!" I shouted at the boy. Standing up, I took a few paces back in shock.

I didn't speak much about Kat since arriving and had never told anyone about her first words. I knew the memory of the beach, but that could have been a generalisation. As for Tazz, he was plain wrong. We were mates, that was it. I was in a committed relationship.

"Who told you to say that stuff?" Smack asked the boy, keeping her gun trained on the enemy.

"Connect the dots," the boy groaned. The irritation in his voice grew. "I can read minds, and right now I'm holding back the enemy. It's getting harder by the second, and our one hope of escape is moving rapidly out of range. Knock the jammer out while I can still hold them. I'm losing strength."

This was all too much to take, but the Voice whispered for me to act, so I acted. I pulled up a map of the area on my left arm console and held it in front of the boy. "Where's the jammer? Can you find it?"

The boy said nothing for a moment. Then he lowered his arm and held his hand over the console. Without looking, his index finger circled the map slowly before landing on a nearby bug hole and steadily traced a line to a spot a few hundred metres away from our current position. I marked the spot and turned to Smack.

"Give me what ammo you can spare. I'll knock it out. Stand by to call that transport. Don't wait for me."

They didn't sound like my words, but that was my voice speaking and my lips moving. I suppose, it felt like the right thing to do, so I went with it.

Smack looked right at me but hesitated. I could tell she wanted to volunteer to join me—she was our de facto leader after all—but I saw the fear in her eyes. And I didn't blame her. I was terrified to the core, too.

She handed me the last of her ammo. I shoved it into my Exo-suit belt, lifted my weapon, and charged headfirst into the morass of alien bodies.

All I remember thinking was I had to make it to the ridgeline. From there, it was a straight run to the bug hole and a few hundred metres to the jamming device. I ignored the charred and splattered carcasses of the enemy, as well as the odd glimmer of movement from my periphery vision. I was too scared to turn my head and see those creatures lying in wait and expected to feel the sharp thrust of their legs boring through my body at any time. Thankfully, I made it to the ridgeline intact, only pausing for a few seconds to get my bearings and regain my nerve.

All around me, Insectoid warriors rushed back and forth, jostling with one another or nervously twitching up on the ridge, ready to surge down and kill us. I gripped my weapon tight, feeling a hundred alien eyes on me, but nothing moved towards me. I took a few steps, moving my HK-17 from creature to creature, ready to take out anything that got too close for comfort, but they continued ignoring me. It sent a chill up my spine to be standing so close that I could reach out and touch one.

As certain as I could be that they weren't going to attack me, I picked up the pace. Keeping a close eye on the map on my helmet visor, I dodged and weaved between the hulking bodies of the enemy until I found the bug hole. I checked to make sure none had followed me before hunching down. Then, with night vision mode activated on my helmet's settings, I continued down into the tunnel.

Darkness closed in and an overwhelming wave of claustrophobia gripped me. These tunnels were wide enough for a single bug to move in on all eight legs, meaning it was too small in height for a human, but I kept my head down and continued moving. My trembling hands gripped my HK as if it was life or death, and my sight was constantly aligned to it, ready to kill the first thing that looked at me wrong. Constantly checking the map, I continued farther down the winding corridor until I came across a cavern connected to several other corridors.

I ventured a quick look into the chamber and noted three enemy warriors scurrying around and a large, black rectangular device in their midst. I was unsure if the boy was restraining these three, due to the range, so I decided to complete my mission as quickly as possible before running like hell out of there.

I pulled out my last three cylindrical plasma grenades. Careful not to be spotted, I planted them into the soft, sandy soil of the cavern floor. The Voice whispered for me to move closer to ensure the destruction of the jamming device, but I took a calculated risk that in this confined space, three grenades would be more than enough to at least bring the ceiling down on this place. I flicked open one of the grenade caps and paired the trigger to my arm console. Confident that I could detonate it with the push of a button, I turned and retraced my steps up through the corridor.

My legs ached. Adrenaline coursing through my tired body was all that kept me moving. The night vision filter in my helmet kept the shadows from turning and twisting into nightmarish creatures. On more than one occasion I fought the urge to believe that the walls were closing in on me, but I kept moving. I had to. I couldn't die here, not so far from Terra. So far from Kat and Louise.

I reached the mouth of the bug hole, exhausted but grateful to remove the night vision filter and see light again. Several of the creatures turned to study me but none reacted. Bracing myself, I pressed the button to detonate the grenades and, less than a second later, felt the whole terrain reverberate, knocking me onto the ground.

"Smack, I'm out. Send the signal," I coughed into the comm.

A cloud of smoke and dust belched out of the bug hole as I pulled myself to my feet and raised my weapon. It took less than a second for me to realise I was in trouble. Every single Insectoid in proximity had turned to face me, their alien eyes fixed as if noticing me for the first time. I tightened my grip on the trigger, wondering if I should make the first move or if they were still under a trance. Then they charged.

I blasted my HK like a madman, taking out every hostile close enough to lash out, but they kept pouring over one another to get at me. It was too late for me. I knew it was over when I clipped in my last magazine. But when I squeezed the trigger again, they all exploded. It happened in slow motion; their bodies raced towards me and then the seams of their flesh burst open to send sprays of green blood in every direction, staining my Exo-suit from head to toe. For a second, I thought I had done it. Maybe on Big Red I had mind control powers to make things explode or something, but a crackling noise cut through my comm, answering my question. I heard a pop-punk beat and a voice singing over familiar words, and I laughed the laugh of a man who had narrowly survived a bloody death.

"Hey baby, baby, you look so fine. Something, something, something up all night. Hey gorgeous, something, something, something, call me princess. Something, something else, after recess..."

Captain Lockhart's transport rained down deadly bullets and missile fire, carving through a swath of the enemy. Alien body parts flew in every direction, leaving nothing intact. They scarpered towards nearby bug holes for cover, but the transport's guns fired continuously, determined to unleash death upon them.

"...Something, something, until the crack of dawn. Something, something, early morning. Yeow!" the Captain sang without a note in his head.

The transport hovered overhead, spinning wildly, exterminating as many of the fleeing enemy as possible. The enemy particle weapon narrowly missed the transport, causing it to tilt before it homed in on the nearby emplacement. There was a flash as the transport machine guns opened up, followed by another as two missiles erupted and smashed into the weapon and its users, giving them a nice, fiery death.

"...Yeah, yeah, I'm your queen of Ares. Yeah, yeah, but I'm still your princess..."

By the time what was left of my section made it to the ridgeline, the remaining Insectoids had scarpered back into their tunnels, leaving me standing there exposed and covered in alien entrails while Captain Lockhart serenaded us with his new favourite pop-punk song. The entire section patted me for a job well done, but I was too dazed to hear their words. I wiped as much slime off me as possible as the captain landed his transport and opened the transport doors.

Intense Dan had suffered a leg wound, so we hauled him in first. Thankfully, the smart fibres of the suit sealed around the wound to stop the bleeding, but it was obvious he needed surgery as soon as possible. The ten-year-old looked at me as I helped him up and patted him on the back in thanks. I was weirded out by what he had said and even more so by his telepathic claim, but I stopped trying to make sense of Big Red a long time ago. I was just grateful to be alive.

Exhausted, we strapped ourselves in before Captain Lockhart sealed the door and banged on the cockpit for us to take off. He checked a nearby console before clicking his helmet visor up and gave us the thumbs up. We each did the same and took a minute to look at each other with a combination of pride that we had survived and horror at what we had witnessed.

"What in the hell were you crazies doing down there?" the captain shouted, despite the fact there was still no noise to shout over. "Don't you know we have a war on?"

"We were supposed to escort the kid to Trump Colony..."

"You mean Nixon Colony?" the captain shouted back inquisitively.

"Sure," Smack said, side-tracked, "but we were ambushed. Can you take us back to New Berlin?"

The captain laughed and fell back into the nearest unoccupied seat. He reached into his Exo-suit compartments and pulled out a pre-rolled joint. Grinning like a madman, he placed it in his lips, lit it, took a few long drags before responding.

"You kids really don't know what's going on?" he asked, and exhaled a large cloud of smoke into the confined space we occupied. Everyone else appeared stunned by his actions, but I breathed deep, hoping to get a hit off the second-hand fumes.

"Our little cold war escalated into a hot one over the last few hours," he continued, taking another series of long puffs before holding it aloft. "Any takers?"

I didn't hesitate a second. Unstrapping myself, I stepped forward to accept it. He bared his yellowed teeth as I took a long, hard drag.

"Dub??" Smack said, sounding more like a disgusted mother than a twenty-something-year-old soldier.

I shrugged and nodded at Nordie, who quickly joined me. After handing it over, I returned to my seat and buckled in, feeling much better about the day's events.

Captain Lockhart gestured at Nordie to finish the joint before sparking another one. "It's all-out war," he said with glazed-over eyes. "Simultaneous ground attacks across most of our Forward Bases. Nixon Colony is standing by to be overrun. The crafty bastards even tunnelled into the interior and attacked the mining and research posts right in the middle of our turf. They must have planned it for years."

"What about New Berlin?" Big Mo asked.

"It got its guts ripped out, but it's still standing," the captain replied after taking another long drag. "That's where we're going now, although we probably won't be there for long."

"My parents are at Trump Colony," the boy said abruptly, and we all turned to look at him. His face remained sombre, but fear tinged his voice.

"Don't worry, kid," the captain coughed out, trying to sound as reassuring as possible. "A lot of the civilians and execs were evacuated as soon as the fighting got inside the parameter. I flew a lot of them out myself."

Smack instinctively placed an arm around the boy to reassure him.

"Yep, Big Red's going straight to hell," Captain Lockhart said, trying to make himself more comfortable in his seat. "It's like the Tet Offensive all over again. Never thought I'd see anything as bad twice in a lifetime."

We fell silent at the captain's words, too stunned that the major colonies were under attack. We now found ourselves embroiled right in the middle of a life or death struggle to keep Mars in the Terran fold. It could've been the drugs in my system that sharpened me to Lockhart's words, but I replayed them slowly in my head. Something niggled at me, not just from what he said, but from the moment we awoke on Phobos.

"What do you mean 'again'?" I asked, trying to not sound too stoned.

The Captain looked at me with heavy eyes. "Again?"

"You said 'again,'" I said, hoping I made sense. "You said you never thought you'd see anything like the Tet Offensive again. Do you mean you saw it on a documentary?"

"You're stoned, Dub," Nordie said with a laugh.

Big Mo and Noid looked up at me and then at the captain. Evidently, they caught what I was trying to say.

"A documentary? Nope. I was there. It wasn't pretty. This isn't, either," the captain replied with a yawn. He closed his eyes and nestled himself into his seat for a snooze.

"Captain," I said, louder this time for everyone to hear. "The Tet Offensive was nearly fifty years ago in the Vietnam war. You don't even look forty."

"Thank you," he said with a smile. "I'm thirty-five. And it wasn't that long ago."

He let that linger in the air along with the weed smoke before his eyes opened fully and sat bolt upright in his chair and looked at all of us.

"I completely forgot," he said with a wry smile. "You're the Hollows, aren't you? The newbies?"

"Captain, what year is it?" Smack asked, catching on.

"The year? Well, you all know what year it is." He stood up from his seat and made to head for the cockpit.

"Tell them," the boy mumbled, stopping the captain in his tracks.

He paused and turned to face us again, looking unusually serious. "It's not my place..."

"What year is it?" Noid yelled at him.

"It's 1975."

He gave us a final nod and locked himself into the cockpit.

We questioned the boy, but he didn't say anything else for the duration of the flight back to New Berlin. Big Mo and Noid were insistent about squeezing him for more information, but considering the fact he was ten years old and probably terrified his parents might be dead, Smack ordered them to stand down. They reluctantly did so, although Noid grumbled loudly enough for all of us to hear that the boy better not be reading our minds.

Captain Lockhart remained secured in the cockpit and didn't join us at any stage or blast music at us, which was at least a minor relief. As we pulled in towards New Berlin, we could see from the side windows of the transport that he wasn't joking. Even in the thin, Martian atmosphere, the billowing black columns of smoke were visible from half a dozen klicks away. As we got closer, we gazed in stony silence at the sheer extent of the carnage.

All along the parameter of the dome lay the charred bodies of dead Insectoids with pieces of Exo-suit armour scattered around them. The colony itself was in bad shape with entire towers and buildings completely missing, reduced to smouldering rubble and ash. Several different vessels hovered above the ruins of the colony, either in damage control effort or to hunt down enemy stragglers. We descended in silence towards the landing pad, which remained intact, and then dropped mechanically into the hangar bay. We lowered our visors in preparation for the drop in atmosphere before Noid unlatched the door, and myself and Big Mo carried Intense Dan out into the hangar bay. He lost consciousness about halfway back, but his Exo-suit had stopped the bleeding successfully and hopefully kept him from losing his leg permanently.

The hangar bay was packed with a variety of different vehicles and transports, many of them labelled as MARSCORP property. Bustling with activity, rows of wounded and dying MOF soldiers flowed towards the hangar bay doors or moved towards the make-shift triage areas the medical teams had set up.

I gave the boy one last pat on the shoulder. "You gonna be okay, kid?"

He nodded his response to me. I should have left it there, but the question burned inside me.

"What are you?" I asked.

He looked up at me through his visor with the eyes of a ten-year-old, but something much deeper lingered behind them.

"I'm just like you," he whispered, "but MARSCORP made me better."

I pushed the boy's cryptic answer aside as Smack escorted him away to find someone to hand him over to while we raced to get Intense Dan checked. We eased him down into a row of injured personnel and flagged a doctor. The doctor checked the readout on Intense Dan's console and immediately called for a gurney to take him for emergency surgery. Helpless, we watched as they took our comrade away before Smack re-joined us.

"It's all gone to hell," she sighed.

"What's happening?" Big Mo asked.

"You mean aside from the fact it's 1975?" Noid interrupted angrily. "I can't believe you're all going to do this again. Every time something weird comes up, everyone pretends that it's fine or it doesn't exist. Am

I the only sane one here? We've just found out we're forty years in the past on Mars. And they have weird little kids that can read minds. Is no one else going to do anything or say anything about it?"

"Cool it, Noid," Nordie said.

"I will NOT cool it," she roared back. "Not only am I on a stinking red death trap, was nearly killed by giant space spiders, but it's now over a decade before I was born? I'm about to lose my shit!"

"Cool it!" Smack shouted back, pushing hard against Noid's Exo-suit.

Without warning, Noid lunged at Smack and struck her full force in the chest. The Exo-suit easily absorbed the blow, but the act alone caused Smack to flip and swing a full force kick at Noid. Big Mo, Nordie, and I threw ourselves into the scuffle, desperate to break it up before someone realised they still had a few rounds in the chamber of their HK. We had just torn them apart when a voice roared across our comm channel.

"What in the hell is going on here?" Mad Jack demanded.

We fell into a straight line as he marched over to us.

"What is the meaning of this?" he asked.

"Apologies, sir," Smack said, saluting. "We were ambushed and took losses. We're a bit wound up. It won't happen again, sir."

Mad Jack studied the dried blood and entrails that still caked our Exo-suits before looking at us one at a time through his own visor.

"Section One," he said vaguely, as if struggling to recall our names. "Yes. Yes, of course. You returned the asset. Well done for keeping him alive. I look forward to reading your report. My condolences for your loss. I'm afraid that won't be the only loss you'll be mourning before this day is through."

"Sir, Corporal Owens is dead, too. Permission to be dismissed and report to Sergeant Hopkins for orders?"

Mad Jack paused for a moment and checked something on his arm console.

"Sergeant Hopkins gave his life in defence of this installation. Report to Sergeant O'Malley for debriefing and reassignment. Dismissed."

We saluted and watched as the colonel turned to leave, but Noid evidently hadn't calmed down.

"Sir," she called after him, "is it 1975?"

Mad Jack stopped dead in his tracks. After a few moments, he slowly faced us. He studied each of us before focusing directly on Noid.

"There are far more important things at stake than the date, Private. I suggest you drop this matter until the current crisis has passed."

"Sir, with all due respect," she pressed, "we've just waded through Insectoid blood and barely made it back. We deserve the truth."

Nobody moved. Nobody flinched. The rest of us remained perfectly still with our gazes straight ahead, barely breathing.

"Yes. The year is 1975, but that's all I'm prepared to say at this time. Don't push your luck, Private. We've lost a lot of good people here today. What's one more?"

He let that linger in the air for a moment before turning and marching away. Several seconds later we deemed it safe enough to exhale. Following Smack's lead, we made for the exit to report to our new sergeant. Although Noid continued to simmer and we were all trying to process the colonel's confirmation of the year, we didn't speak about it, at least not then. The aftermath of the attack was too all-encompassing for us to dwell on something that felt surprisingly trivial. We were on Big Red, which was strange enough. Throw in time travel and it somehow paled in comparison.

We found our new sergeant co-ordinating the clean-up operation in the Rec. The normally pristine recreational area looked as if it had taken a direct missile hit. The shops and food areas were devastated. The metal furniture, seating, and rails were twisted and torn. You couldn't walk five paces without seeing the splattered remains of a lumbering hostile or the crimson pools of human blood. MOF soldiers probed the devastation, shooting the Insectoids where they lay to ensure they were dead or signalling for help when they found a trapped or wounded Marsie civilian or Terran soldier.

Sergeant O'Malley took one look at our alien blood-soaked Exo-suits and treated us like real soldiers, not just Hollows. Smack brought him up to speed on what had happened to us. In return, the sergeant gave us a brief account of what took place in our absence.

Just as Lockhart said, there had been a massive co-ordinated attack by the enemy across all Terran-dominated Mars with the fighting still fiercely raging to hold Trump (or Nixon) Colony. Having repelled the enemy attack on New Berlin, all excess soldiers were being sent to the front or for counter-attacks on the research stations the enemy had seized.

Dread and a sense of duty to serve and fight on the front lines overwhelmed me, but the sergeant advised us that we were needed here. The Second Battalion had taken a hit, but we had enough active soldiers to commit to the defence of New Berlin, freeing up the seasoned veterans to drive the invaders from our territory.

In the great war of 1975/76, we were assigned to guard duty.

16

"That sounds intense. Seeing a real life extra-terrestrial, meeting a kid from the Myers program, and learning you were sent back to 1975, all on the same day? How did that make you feel?" Doctor Ling asked.

A dozen smart answers I could have given the doctor flitted through my mind but feeling more in charge of my faculties and less bitter about the events that brought me here, I decided to be straight with her.

"Honestly, we were too confused to make sense of everything at the time. Noid was right about something, though. We were far too docile about the strange events unfolding around us. Sure, we discussed them in depth, but ultimately we accepted them and moved on."

"Why do you think that is?"

"Noid had us convinced it was all part of the programming. The Voice of God brainwashing on our Hollow bodies prior to being activated made us more accepting of the views of our superiors. Or maybe we were all chosen for the program because we were more susceptible to orders given from authority figures."

I studied the doctor, wondering if we had built enough rapport for her to tell me the truth.

"Do you know the answer?"

Doctor Ling shifted in her seat and brushed another loose strand of hair behind her ear.

"Darren, I wish I could..."

The double doors swung open. A stocky woman with hair cropped close to her head dressed in MOF colours and sporting the insignia of a Special Forces soldier entered the room, flanked by a half dozen other masked lackies. She ignored the two doctors and zoned in on me.

"Sergeant Major, I've already spoken with the general. Corporal Loughlin is making excellent progress and is showing an improved ability to recall..."

Doctor Ling trailed off as two of the masked soldiers gripped the end of the trolley and started pulling it towards the doors.

"Stop this. Stop this now," Doctor Lucas exclaimed, leaping up from her consoles. One of the soldiers grabbed her and shoved her back down on her seat before pointing his HK at her. She raised her trembling hands and froze.

"UEAF Command has ordered the general to take all measures necessary to determine what happened to the Second Battalion," the sergeant major said, still studying my chart. Then she dropped it onto my legs and tilted her head to study me in the same way the full-timers used to look at me when I was a Hollow.

"Salient," she mouthed almost inaudibly to me.

Baffled by what she meant, I continued looking up at her, trying to place those eyes that burned with such fearsome determination.

"Come with us, doctor," she said, finally breaking eye contact with me.

Something about her looked vaguely familiar. She had the look of the battle-hardened MOF veterans who served in the war of '75/'76, but her eyes were more intense. I wondered if we had crossed paths.

"You can't expose him to this," Doctor Ling said as she rose from her seat, ignoring the HK-17 pointed at her. "We've made real progress. If we add to his trauma there's no telling what effect it will have on his psyche. I need more time. He's already able to recall the start of the war of '75. Please, I'm begging you..."

The sergeant major gave the slightest of nods, and her soldiers wheeled me towards the double doors, carelessly slamming my trolley through them.

"Your presence is required, too, Doctor Ling. We'll get to the bottom of this."

As they pushed me back into the room I had awoken in hours before, I craned my neck to look up at the sergeant major and saw one of her subordinates grip Doctor Ling by the arm and drag her to her feet. He escorted her at gunpoint. I turned from side to side, scanning the faces of my subdued fellow soldiers. They lay in their bunks in various positions, almost comatose but conscious. Several gazes followed me as I passed by, but no one spoke or gestured at me. Another set of double doors banged open nearby. Struggling against my restraints, I twisted myself awkwardly around and spotted another group of soldiers pushing Big Mo's trolley behind us. He remained passive and unmoving, staring up at the ceiling.

"Is he okay?" I asked. "He's in my section. That's Big Mo. Can he talk?"

No one answered my question, adding to my rising frustration. I pulled at my restraints in a vain attempt to loosen them, but to no avail.

"Remain still," the sergeant major commanded as we reached the exit to the room.

I recognised the corridor in which I had lined up over a year previously, but instead of going back out the doors leading to where we completed the assessment, the trolley swung right, and they pushed me towards the doors of a lift. The six soldiers, the sergeant major, and Doctor Ling all formed a protective ring around me as one of the soldiers pushed the button for the lift and typed in a security code. After a few seconds, the doors eased open, and they shoved my trolley inside. They took their positions again, waiting for the second trolley with Big Mo to enter before the doors slammed shut. Two rows of soldiers blocked me from getting a good view of my comrade.

"Mo? Mo?" I called to him but got no response. "Mo? Where's the section? Mo? Report?"

"This will destabilise him further," Doctor Ling pleaded. "Listen to him. He's getting worked up. Give me more time. I promise I'll find out what happened."

"Orders," the sergeant major replied.

"I can remember. I can try to remember," I begged, unsure of what was happening. My mind went blurry. Everything was so bright. I didn't like what was happening. Why was I restrained? I had a section. Big Mo needed to report. We were under attack. A section under attack needs its corporal.

"Let me out!" I screamed as loud as I could. My voice echoed off the sterile metal walls of the lift. I rocked wildly against my restraints, pulling as hard as I could, willing them to buckle.

"Kill them all," Big Mo groaned in response, but he sounded far away.

"Darren? Darren, it's Doctor Ling. You need to calm down. Nothing is going to happen to you. Just breathe."

I heard her words, but they didn't soothe me. It felt as though a thousand fire ants were crawling over my skin and burrowing into my skull. I desperately wanted to scratch at them, to pull my skin off and never feel that sensation again.

"Darren. Focus. You need to focus. Breathe. You need to calm yourself. Do it for your section."

I closed my eyes and tried to centre myself. I thought of Kat and Louise and focused my thoughts.

I began to calm. I was in a lift in an EISEN complex in London. Something had happened to us on Big Red. I was surrounded by people who wanted to help me and my stranded comrades, who were in trouble.

"Darren," Doctor Ling said; her voice was like a calming oasis. "What happened after the ambush? Focus your thoughts. What happened next? We don't have much time."

The war escalated steadily after the initial assault. The hostiles changed the rules by not only attacking military targets, but also attacking our civilian population centres, which forced the MOF to respond in kind. Our forces launched violent reprisals against enemy nests inside their own territory, and the MOF's undisputed air superiority allowed the fleet to begin planetary bombardment against enemy outposts and positions. A long-standing rule of conflict on Big Red effectively meant that orbiting vessels weren't to be used in conflict with the hostiles. This unspoken agreement remained in place for over twenty years, mainly to prevent retribution against the civilian population, but also to prevent retaliation against MARSCORP's drilling operations. Likewise, the hostiles didn't target our civilian population centres, so when they broke the rules first, there wasn't a major outcry about using orbital bombardment, even if it did grate on MARSCORP. The local Marsie population supported our actions at first but began to resent the increasing presence of MOF personnel in their colonies. They blamed us for the massive loss of life that followed in retaliatory attacks.

Although the Second Battalion had suffered casualties in the first attack on New Berlin, our forces were largely intact, so we quickly assumed the security portfolio for the colony. For the first few weeks after the attack, our lives became routine. We patrolled, we guarded, we broke up fights between Marsies and off-duty **MOF** soldiers, we filled out reports, we arrested seditionists. Boring stuff.

Four months after the start of the war, it showed no signs of abating. Smack had been promoted to acting corporal of the section and I became the team commander. Moving up the ranks never interested me, though. I just wanted to do my time and go home, but no one else was that motivated to take on added responsibilities for no extra pay. Eventually Smack wore me down, so as a favour to her, I took on the role and did a pretty good job at it.

Intense Dan re-joined us after a few weeks, fully healed but with a massive scar on his right thigh. Following the ambush, he was less intense, but it was great to have him back. We also got a new influx of replacements to bolster our numbers. And under Sergeant O'Malley's leadership, we were given more platoon-based assignments, allowing us to work closely with the other sections of One Platoon. We all knew each other from bunking only metres apart, but it gave us a greater sense of family, which was something we needed following all our losses.

That day began like a dozen others. I roused the section, covering for Smack who had to get stitches after breaking up a bar-fight between some Fourth Reichers and visiting Americans. I hustled everyone into the showers, to breakfast, and then straight into their Exo-suits. After getting locked and loaded, we marched towards Command and Control. On the way we intercepted acting Corporal Smithy from Two Section and Team Commander Breezy from Three Section and all the soldiers under their command. Since this was the first time One Platoon was given the honour of guarding inside Command and Control, the centre of all **MOF** operations on Big Red, everyone looked their best with glistening HKs and polished suits.

Arriving early outside the entrance to Command and Control, we completed last minute checks on one another. Thankfully, Smack showed up just in the nick of time. Trying not to look self-conscious about the row of stitches across her right cheek, she whispered her thanks and then, after checking in with everybody else, led us through the entrance for the security checks.

While walking in single file through a narrow corridor, an invisible beam scanned us one at a time, searching for contraband or traces of non-Terran DNA, before a high-pitched bleep signalled us to proceed. Stepping through the heavily guarded entrance and into the hustle and bustle of Command and Control was breath-taking, in a sad type of way.

It's not as though we had a lot to look forward to on Big Red. Sure, the Rigs were good for killing a few hours and spending time in the Rec kept boredom at bay, but Command and Control—or C&C as it was more popularly known—had remained a mystery to us. It was where all the big dogs got to hang out. Finally, after months of repetitive tasks and guarding bulkheads, we were being rewarded with a glimpse into the nerve centre of Terran operations on this dusty wasteland.

C&C looked like something in a sci-fi movie. It stood over three levels high and was crammed full of computers, monitors, and other strange equipment. It held hundreds of analysts running back and forth, co-ordinating every facet of the war right down to keeping the bullet trains on time. The bottom level looked to be where all the action happened, at least from what I could see. Covering the far wall, a massive viewing screen was split into hundreds of different images, showing everything from soldiers in combat and MARSCORP's never-ending drilling operations to monitoring the movement of Marsies going about their daily lives.

Rows of busy bureaucrats bashed commands into their consoles, screamed into headsets, or ran back and forth with stacks of files to report to **MOF** officers. We filed up against one of the walls and silently watched as an **MOF** officer dismissed the night watch before we took our positions. They lined us up in groups of ones and twos, spreading us throughout all three levels to guard the various entrances as a precaution in the event of an attack. As amazing as it seemed initially, the novelty wore off fast enough.

After a few hours of standing and watching, I spied two familiar faces in the crowd of top brass **MARSCORP** execs and sour-faced pencil pushers. The ten-year-old we were supposed to escort to Trump Colony and Doctor Milton, who had tried to explain compression travel to us back on Phobos, separated from a meeting of execs and made for the exit. Knowing my place, I kept my gaze straight as they approached the entrance to the lift I guarded. I expected them to walk straight past, but the boy stopped a few paces ahead of me and smiled.

"Private Loughlin, it's good to see you."

"Thanks. And you, too," I responded, unsure if I was allowed to talk, and suddenly aware I didn't even know the boy's name.

"Of course, you can talk," the boy said with a wry smile, "and you can call me Dennis. I'm sure you remember Doctor Milton?"

The doctor fidgeted with his spectacles as he took a closer look at me.

"Ah, yes," the doctor smiled, recognising my face. "One of the first batch of..."

"They call us Hollows."

"Hollows," the doctor said in disgust, pursing his lips. "I can't say that's very apt. There's nothing hollow about you. And from what I hear, you've been preforming beyond expectations."

"Thank you, sir," I replied, not knowing what else to say.

"I wanted to thank you and your team for saving me," Dennis continued, "I could sense your overwhelming fear, but you still acted like professionals and got me out of there. I'd be dead if it weren't for you."

"We'd be dead if you hadn't stopped the Insectoids from attacking us in the end. I'd say that makes us even."

"That was nothing," Dennis replied sheepishly.

"That was something. I have to ask, though. You said you were like me. Are you a Hollow, too? How did you..."

"We can't discuss other programs," Doctor Milton prompted Dennis and placed a protective arm around his young ward.

Dennis looked up at the doctor and nodded his agreement before returning his attention to me. His childlike face appeared to blush from embarrassment, but those cool, dark eyes made him look far older than his ten years.

"Still, I am grateful, Private Loughlin. If there's ever anything..."

He trailed off as all the lights in C&C flickered. Everyone stopped and looked around in silent disbelief until they all switched fully off. After a few seconds, the monitors followed, throwing the room into complete darkness. Instinctively, I flicked on my helmet visor, activated night vision mode, and checked the satellite uplink. Everyone in the platoon radio-checked with one another, and we were relieved to know we could still communicate.

However, the room erupted into panicked shouts as they fumbled in the darkness for torches or tried to access the emergency backups. After adjusting my own visor filter, I switched on my HK-17s torch light and raised it high enough to allow Doctor Milton and a terrified Dennis to see around.

"Main power's down," someone called out.

"How is that even possible?" another voice cried out.

"Switch to backups!"

"No response from backup redundant systems."

Over the growing sense of fear that swept the pitch-black room, Smack called Sergeant O'Malley and reported the power loss. Static came through, followed by crackling and popping noises. The popping noises continued at random intervals across the common channel for a few seconds—eerily familiar. It took me a moment to register the noise before my blood froze. Gunfire.

"Possible shots fired," Smack shouted into her helmet mic. "Hold your positions."

I faced the nearby door and readied my weapon. From my Exo-suit rear camera, I tracked Smack as she left her position and found the nearest officer to report her concerns. A minute or two after that a nearby engineer rigged up a connection to one of our Exo-suits and connected that to a portable device, allowing one of the higher-ups to call around and get a situation report. It didn't take long to find out that New Berlin was under attack.

"Stupid. Stupid. Stupid," I told myself as I raced through the darkened corridors. Although we had been able to reach several different MOF units and positions, we had an incomplete picture of what was happening, preventing the powers-that-be from co-ordinating a defence of New Berlin. At a high-ranking general's behest, we had pried open one of the doors and Section One split up to get as much information about what was happening on the ground as possible, and the other sections remained to protect those of importance.

Big Mo and Nordie were sent back towards the Rec to search for Sergeant O'Malley or whoever was in command, Noid and Intense Dan were ordered to ensure no hostiles had breached the parameter of the C&C building, Smack was dispatched to find the nearest command posts, and our four newbies Fish, Rocker, Gizmo and Buckle were escorting engineers to get the main power back on. They ordered me to navigate the winding corridors of the C&C building with the sole mission of contacting the semi-mythical Old Man, who resided as a permanent guest of MARSCORP. I always got the fun assignments.

Following the map read-out on my helmet visor, I moved through the complex, occasionally coming across petrified civilians in the dark. I directed them to find shelter and continued with my mission. Thankfully, the intuitive filters in my visor blanked out the darkness that enveloped New Berlin, making everything look like a dull and hazy day, but it couldn't filter out the sporadic sound of gunfire echoing through the bulkheads or the pleas of help cutting through the comm channels.

Despite my visor read-outs and night vision, I got lost twice. Eventually I found the correct room at the top of the C&C tower. Exhausted from climbing so many stairs, I was fit to drop by the time I approached the room at the end of the corridor. I spotted the six armed guards well before they spotted me. Probably thinking I was an intruder, one of them fired his gun. I flinched as the bullet pinged harmlessly off my Exo-suit armour. Dropping to a knee, I raised my weapon and aimed at the perpetrator. I could see them clear enough to know that they had no night vision, giving me the advantage.

"MOF," I shouted, "lower your weapons or I'll open fire."

I flicked on my HK-17s laser sights for added effect and watched as they lowered their handguns. I crept forward, keeping my weapon pointed at them until I was an arm's length away. Then I flicked on my torch, giving them the opportunity to see me, and I studied them in turn. They each wore strange black uniforms without insignia and rank, and all of them sported blonde hair and blue eyes.

"You speak German?" one of them asked me in a heavy accent.

"No, English. **New Berlin** is under attack. We're working to get main power back online, but we believe the enemy has breached the parameter. Objectives and effective strength unknown."

The six soldiers looked at one another before their leader spoke again.

"Will we be evacuating?"

"Unknown. I was ordered to update you. I don't have any further information."

147

An awkward silence followed. They continued to look at me as if I had all the answers. I slowly inched away. Having fulfilled my orders, I wanted nothing more than to return to my comrades.

"Wait here," the leader said. Before I could protest, he opened the room's door and entered. I caught a glimpse of a carpeted but sparsely furnished apartment with a roaring, open fire and the silhouette of an old man seated in front of it, with his back to the doorway. The young German soldier stepped forward, said something in his native language, and the door slammed shut. His comrades continued looking at me with blank expressions. I studied them back, still gripping my HK-17.

"So, who is he?" I asked, doubtful I'd get a straight answer.

"Our father," one of them replied.

Even in the dim light from my torch, I could see clearly enough that they weren't related. I decided to stop talking, knowing how little it was worth asking questions on Big Red. You rarely got the answers you wanted. If you did, they just led to more questions.

I was about to force small talk when my visor signalled movement from the corridor behind me. Turning, I raised my weapon and studied the quick progression of the four dots on the map laid out on my helmet screen.

"C&C," I spoke into my mic, "this is Echo One-Niner. Mission accomplished but detecting four life forms moving towards target. Did you send back up?"

I watched as the blips moved closer and whispered to the guards to standby. Two of them dropped to a knee while the other three stood behind me, with their guns pointed in the general direction. I remained front and centre, hoping I would draw the brunt of the attack since I held the advantage of an Exo-suit.

"That's a negative, Echo One-Niner. No friendlies

sent. Internal sensors coming back online. Standby."

I looked at the four dots approaching and readied myself. My suit's uplink to the satellites was patchy at best in **New Berlin,** so I couldn't run any other hi-tech scans to determine if they were a stray patrol or the enemy. I'd have to wait until they got closer.

"Standby," I whispered to the Germans.

"Halt!" I shouted to the approaching group, "MOF. Identify yourself."

I zoomed in with my helmet's targeting sensors as close as I could. Even with the lights out and night vision on, the feed was grainy. I could make out four figures with two legs and two arms, but that didn't mean they weren't hostile.

"We are friends," another voice called out in the darkness. Relieved, I urged them to continue walking forward but kept my HK-17 aimed at them until I could verify it wasn't an elaborate trap. Once I finished scanning all four with my torch light, I lowered my weapon and turned to make my excuses to the original guards. And that's when it happened.

At first, I thought it was a joke. Nordie always tried to jump on my back when he had a few too many beers, so for a split second I thought he had snuck up behind the Germans. But when two sets of hands wrapped around my helmet, trying to pry it off while the original five guards rushed me to grab my weapon, I knew it wasn't a joke.

"Stop!" I roared as I swung my right elbow behind me, catching one of my attackers in the ribs. I slammed my bodyweight backwards and crushed the last one into the bulkhead; he slumped to the floor. One of the other guards tried to grab the barrel of my assault rifle from my hands, but I lunged it into his stomach, winding him.

"Stand down!" I shouted, showing incredible restraint as another attacker tried to kick my legs out from under me.

A series of gunshots rang out, harmlessly pinging off my Exo-suit. A scream of pain errupted as one of the bullets ricocheted off my armour and struck one of the Germans. The approaching party of four lay wounded or incapacitated. With no one at my back, I wheeled around and brought my weapon to bear on the remaining five.

"Last warning," I screamed at them as my blood boiled from the betrayal. They said something to each other in German, and a part of me expected them to lower their weapons. They must have known their bullets couldn't damage my Exo-suit. They had no other option. Or so I thought.

Maybe it was desperation or ingrained refusal to surrender, but all five of them opened fire on me at the same time. The sound of bullets bouncing off my Exo-suit reminded me of when I would listen to heavy rain pattering off the tin roof of a shed, a long-forgotten memory from my childhood. Anger and frustration washed over that pleasant thought, replacing it with the Voice of God, as angry and vehement as ever I had heard it.

"KILL THEM ALL. THEY HAVE BETRAYED TERRA. KILL TRAITORS. KILL THEM ALL."

Without hesitation, I squeezed my HKs trigger and blasted all five of them. They dropped like sacks of potatoes and crashed onto the floor—twisted and bullet riddled. I could hear my heavy breath as I unclipped the empty magazine and clicked in a new one, but I stayed rooted to the floor. Through the night vision filter, I could see their lifeless bodies, but I didn't want to step closer. Killing hostile aliens was one thing, but to kill flesh and blood humans, even if they were lousy Volk Marsies, struck me as a step too far. I felt as if I had stepped out of my body, as if I was watching someone else commit these actions, but that someone else looked a lot like me. Those same hands that held Kat as a new-born had just mowed down five living, breathing human beings. I had ended everything about them, all their hopes and dreams, in the time it had taken to exhale.

The Voice tried to whisper and soothe me, telling me I had no other option, when the lights in the corridor powered back on. The sight around me was even more horrifying than I imagined in the grim darkness. They lay there lifeless as their life's blood oozed from the bullet holes I had put in them. Their empty eyes gazed in every direction but mine. I took a step forward without thinking and found myself standing in a pool of blood. I wanted to vomit and scream at the same time. Dread at what I had done and the consequences of my actions struck me hard in the gut.

"C&C," I called into my mic, "it's Echo One-Niner. There's been a complication. I..."

"Understood, Echo One-Niner," Mad Jack's familiar voice replied. "We regained access to the helmet live-feeds several minutes ago."

I felt dizzy. They would never send me home now. The Germans never had a chance to kill or even wound me in my Exo-suit. I could have stridden up to them, beaten them senseless, and taken their weapons one-by-one, but I murdered them. I had given in to the darkness that lingered below the surface, using the Voice's prompts as rationalisation to take their lives.

"You're clear, Echo One-Niner, they were hostiles. You had justification and you used appropriate force. Well done, son."

"Sir?" I asked, bewildered by what I was hearing.

"Internal sensors are back online. This isn't an enemy incursion. This is an armed rebellion by the Fourth Reichers. The use of deadly force has been authorised. Take any measures to pacify the area and

151

return to C&C for new orders."

I turned and saw the original five attackers all lying on the corridor floor. One had a bullet wound to the stomach, three were unconscious, and the last one was nursing a severe wound to the head.

"Sir, where will I escort the prisoners to—"

I barely finished the last syllable before the colonel cut me off.

"Negative, Echo One-Niner. No prisoners. These are insurgents. There is no Geneva Convention here. Terminate them."

"Sir, can you confirm your last order?" I asked.

"Echo One-Niner. You will point your HK-17 at each of the five rebels and shoot them in the head. We are taking heavy casualties. Your section is missing and presumed dead. Kill them all. That is an order."

I thought about Smack, Big Mo, Noid, Dan, and Nordie missing. I imagined their lifeless bodies carpeting a lonely corridor and felt anger rise in me. I switched to autopilot mode as I stepped toward the first wounded German. I could see everything through my own eyes, but it was more like watching a movie or playing a videogame. I experienced the moment, but I remained detached. It was me, but it wasn't.

I raised my assault rifle and aimed it at the first wounded Marsie. Looking at me, he extended a bloodied hand and said something in his own language. I squeezed the trigger and watched as the bullet blew a hole in his head, splattering his brain matter across the walls. Mechanically, I faced the second, third and fourth unconscious soldiers and did the same. I hesitated for a moment as I raised my weapon again to finish the last one. He too looked at me with pleading eyes, but he could speak English.

"Please, don't," he begged, with genuine terror in his eyes. "We just want to be free. We don't want our children to have to—"

152

I pulled the trigger and silenced him.

"Orders completed, sir," I reported back to C&C.

"Good," the colonel said. "Now secure the room. I've sent override access to your arm console. Try not to kill the Old Man, unless he poses a direct threat. MARSCORP needs him alive. For now."

"Understood, sir."

I approached the doorway to the room and ran my left arm console over the scanner by the door. The door slid open, and I rushed in with my HK-17 moving from side to side, ready to identify targets. The first soldier who had entered earlier stood away from the silhouette by the fire, in the centre of the room, with his gun pointed at me. I considered asking him to stand down but fired first.

His body dropped from the fatal shot, so I swung around and aimed at the man in the chair. A frightened woman with short blonde hair sat on the floor beside him. One of her hands was on his shaking one, and her other hand trembled as it held an old-fashioned Luger. She screamed at the sight of what I had done, dropped the gun without prompting, and buried her face into the arm of the old man. From my vantage point, I still couldn't make out anything about him apart from his shaking hand and even that looked more like a medical condition than out of fear.

"It isn't here," the woman shrieked in between sobs, "you'll never find it if you kill him."

Ignoring her, I kicked the handgun away. I was tempted to take a few steps towards the old man to see his face, but I turned and searched the rest of the apartment. It was small enough with two bedrooms, a kitchen, a study, and a bathroom that I quickly confirmed no one else present. Keeping my eyes trained on the blonde woman and the Old Man, I called the colonel.

"C&C, room secured. One male and one female

present. Orders?"

There was a momentary pause. I pointed my HK at the woman in anticipation.

"Stand down, Echo One-Niner. A team has been dispatched to secure the room. Return to C&C when you're relieved."

"Understood, sir," I replied and felt an urge to ask, "Sir, who is he?"

I felt foolish asking when all it would have taken was a few steps to catch a glimpse, but something kept me rooted to the spot. A strange sense of dread had pervaded every part of me since stepping into the room. Something instinctual told me whoever sat in that chair represented something dangerous and evil. The Voice whispered a name, but I couldn't make it out.

"The ghost of Christmas past," Mad Jack said after a moment's deliberation. "Wait outside. There are some things on Big Red you're not quite ready for. Good job, Echo One-Niner."

I took a last lingering look at the woman and the back of the chair the Old Man sat on before following the colonel's orders and stepping outside. The urge to vomit hit me when I saw the bloodbath I had created, but I held it together when I heard reinforcements approaching.

"Dub. I never thought you had it in you," Herman the German from Second Platoon said as he approached and studied my handiwork. He kicked at one of the lifeless bodies and looked at me with his trademark stony face.

"I'm surprised you're not heartbroken," his comrade Benjy replied, gazing around at the massacre.

"They're not my people," Herman said and, taking aim with his own HK-17, fired another shot into one of the dead guards.

"Sit-rep," I said, sounding calmer than I had

expected. Herman kept looking at me. Benjy answered instead.

"A large group of Fourth Reichers stormed the living area. Took a bunch of us out while we were sleeping. It's a bloodbath. They still have the Rec, the landing bay, and MARSCORP HQ, but we beat them back from an attack on C&C and retook the power station. It'd be over a hell of a lot faster, but some of 'em have particle weapons and they're cutting our people to pieces."

"Any word on my section?"

"Nope, but we're coming from the far side of the colony. They could be fine."

It would have been easy to call them, but I couldn't bring myself to do it. Not only did I not want to run the risk of distracting them in a firefight, but I didn't know what I'd do if I called and got no answer. After patting Benjy goodbye, I started down the corridor and returned to C&C.

"It wasn't your fault, Darren. You did as you were ordered. It wasn't your fault."

From somewhere in the distance, I could hear Doctor Ling's concerned voice call out to me. I was still in the lift, but whether we had gotten on seconds ago or hours, I couldn't tell. It felt as though the fabric of my life was being ripped at the seams and rewoven at random intervals. I had no sense of bearing. Memories rose and crashed through my skull as realistically as though it were real life. One minute I was on Big Red, fighting for my life, and the next I was back on Terra. I couldn't make sense of the conflicting images.

"He's losing cohesion," a fading, echoing voice called out from somewhere. Far away, far from my location, a familiar-looking doctor shone a light into a set of eyes, but they were too far away to be mine. I was here, wherever here was.

"Just keep him conscious," another voice snapped.

It sounded like Smack, but that couldn't be. Smack was with me back on Big Red. Or was she? I saw an image of a lifeless Smack staring back at me with cold, unmoving eyes. I spotted someone's hands far away, reaching out to touch her tenderly. A voice that sounded eerily reminiscent of my own called out to her as a set of hands shook her, but she remained unmoving. That didn't make sense. Smack was still alive.

"I told you. He's in a fragile state. We have no way of knowing what he went through before he came back or the effects compression travel had on his mind because of that. He doesn't know where he is. Let me speak to the general."

I saw Nordie slumped over, too, a small chunk of his side missing from a particle blast. Even wounded, he had managed to kill his attacker. His hands were wrapped around the throat of a lifeless soldier dressed in black; the two of them locked in a cruel and macabre dance. I tried to call to him, to tell him to wake up, but no words came out. Wherever I was, I couldn't speak. I could only bear witness to these strange and disturbing images, a mere spectator to someone else's life.

"You'll see the general soon. Until then, the order stands."

What order? There was no order here in the void. No sense of right or wrong, up or down. No past, present, or future. Everything was everywhere and nowhere at the same time. Images danced and grew before shattering into a million shards and disappearing into me. I could feel them but not control them. Fear gripped me. Fear of losing control, of not knowing where I was. I was floating, but I didn't know where to.

"Damn you!" the faraway voice shouted.

Doctor Ling shouldn't be angry. She was a nice person. Was she my friend? Probably. It made sense that we would be friends. In the distance, she shone a light into that person's eyes again. Eyelids blinked, slowly at first and then more rapidly as the light continued to shine on them.

"He's starting to come around," she murmured. "Darren? Darren? Can you hear me? Blink if you can hear me."

I felt myself float upwards, closer to where those eyes were. I wondered what it would be like to see out of them. Like looking out of windows from the top of a high building, I imagined.

"Darren? You need to focus on the sound of my voice. I'm here with you."

I sensed a warmth coming from somewhere below me. It reminded me of the sensation of someone holding my hand and gently caressing it. Tenderness rushed through me for the first time in a long time, so I tried to float faster and higher. I moved closer to the voices on the outside, but something dragged and clawed at me. It couldn't stop me, yet it continued pulling. It was something cold and foreign. Something unnatural. It shouldn't be here. Not with me. Not with Darren. I moved faster, but it kept its icy grip. I ignored it.

"Darren? Darren? Are you okay?"

"No," I groaned and moved my head from side to side in case the words hadn't escape my throat. "I don't know what's real."

"Memory fragmentation, disorientation, and feelings of disassociation are common side effects of compression travel. These feelings are amplified because of your traumatic experiences, and because you returned too soon. You will be fine again soon. I promise."

I could hear the genuine concern in her voice, but I found it hard to believe her or hold my attention on what she was saying.

"You need to focus on my words. Let me be your anchor. Concentrate on me. We'll get through this together."

"Okay," I said weakly, "but you have to promise me something."

"Anything."

"Send me back to Big Red. I have to go back. Send me back."

I forced myself to look up at the doctor as I spoke. Instead of looking back at me, though, she shot the sergeant major a look. I couldn't decipher it; it wasn't a flash of anger or concern or fear. It was something else. What could I have said to have made the doctor flash that look? What was wrong about asking to be sent back to Big Red? The colony, the people, and the artefacts were all still up there. Just communications were down. Didn't they know that? I was positive I had told them.

New Berlin was in one piece. I knew that for a fact.

By the time I reached C&C, power had been fully restored and the reinforced doors opened. Outside, rows of unarmoured and wounded soldiers lay shouting, screaming, and cursing the German Volk insurgents. Many more lay silent, unmoving.

After passing the security scan, I found C&C in its natural state of chaos as the many operators and analysts bustled around and the various big screens on the main wall showed dozens of combat situations in real-time. As I searched for Mad Jack to report, I kept checking the different feeds from soldiers' body cameras, hoping to spot a glimpse of a familiar face.

"Private Loughlin," the colonel said after accepting my salute. "Well done. How do you feel, soldier?"

"I'm eager to re-join my section, sir."

The colonel pointed to a nearby computer and typed in a series of commands. It brought up a list with my section's names on it, as well as their health status. All of them were blank, except mine.

"The insurrectionists are using crude jamming devices that are wreaking havoc with our shortwave communication channels and satellite uplinks. We're working on overcoming that problem, but, for the moment, we have to consider your section as MIA."

"Yes, sir," I said, but my heart sank at the thought of them all dead.

Taking me by the arm, he led me over to another console and pulled up a map of the Rec. He pointed to several dots that remained static by the main terminal door. "I have a section of MOF personnel pinned down here," he said as he typed a few buttons to transfer the information to my Exo-suit's visor read-out. "They're unarmoured and they've taken casualties. I want you to take command and pacify the area. Our top priority is to clear MARSCORP and retake the hangar bays, but some of our troops may be trapped in the living area. I need you to get to them. I'll send reinforcements as soon as I have them to spare."

"Understood, sir," I said and saluted.

The colonel returned the salute but stopped me as I was about to walk away.

"Private, you handled yourself well back there. My order still stands. Terminate any rebel on sight."

I nodded and tried to force what I had done to the back of my mind. Everything had happened so fast, but I wasn't sure if I could do it again.

"If we locate any civilians, where will I direct them to, sir?"

The colonel smiled at me and patted me on the shoulder.

"All civilians have been advised to remain confined to their quarters. Anyone claiming to be a civilian in the combat zone is to be considered an enemy combatant and dealt with as such. Do I make myself clear?"

"Yes, sir."

"Good. The Volk have gotten the carrot for a long time now. It's time to give them the stick. After today, they will never again resist Terran rule. Dismissed, soldier."

I saluted again. Unnerved by what I had heard, I hastily made for the exit. Everything struck me at once. I found myself in the middle of a dizzying, swirling nightmare. Outside C&C, I raised my helmet visor and dry retched, convinced the contents of my stomach would spill onto the floor, but nothing came out. I paused for a moment, on my knees, spitting before I forced myself up. I pushed everything from my mind and focused on the soldiers pinned down by the Rec entrance. After checking my HK was fully loaded, I ran through the corridors towards the Rec.

The closer I got, the louder machine guns fire and plasma grenade explosions grew. The corridors outside C&C bore all the hallmarks of intense close combat fighting, with empty bullet casings, scorched pieces of wall panelling, debris of all kinds, and the occasional carcass of a friend or foe. I paused as soon as I came across fallen MOF comrades. Although I recognised many of those faces, I felt relieved and disgusted at myself when I noticed they weren't my friends.

I approached the Rec door cautiously and called the beleaguered, trapped section over the comm before opening the entrance doors. A spray of machine gun fire from the second floor greeted me, so I raised my HK and returned fire, blasting until I eliminated the enemy soldier.

"You took your sweet time, Hollow," a soldier in MOF Red'n'Blacks hissed at me.

A number of smart or insulting responses came to mind that I could have made in response, but I didn't feel like talking. I had a job to do. I turned and studied the walls and entrances along the enemy line of fire and saw no evidence of particle beam blasts. That didn't mean there wasn't one up there somewhere, just that the Fourth Reichers hadn't used it yet.

"I count three enemy positions," I said to the section, replaying my helmet camera footage from the first few seconds I entered. "A two-person group a few metres away trying to sneak along the wall to throw plasma grenades at you, a light machine gun emplacement on level two approximately one hundred metres to my left, and a four-person team making their way down the stairs to flank you."

Before the section could respond, I stepped into the line of fire again and, aiming to my right, fired a controlled burst at the two would-be grenadiers sneaking up on our position, mowing them down. As a barrage of bullets rained down on me from the second level, I brought my weapon around to bear and fired another series of shots at the light machine gun emplacement, landing headshots to the gunner and his assistant before dropping to a knee and aiming towards where the last group would emerge from.

I switched my HK-17 to particle beam mode, cocked the top of it like you would a shot gun, and waited for all four to emerge from the stairwell. Upon seeing me, they dived for cover. I squeezed the trigger and couldn't resist a smile as the green energy blast annihilated everything in its path, vaporising two of the enemy and cutting the remaining two in half, killing them instantly. Content that all the rebels were dead, I returned my attention to the section still hunched down behind me.

"There may be snipers, so stay low. We'll clear the first level and then work our way up."

I didn't wait for their response but took a cautious step forward, moving my weapon back and forth, covering as many angles as possible. The section fell in behind me, and we quickly moved through the wreckage of the first level, clearing every shop, store, and stall as we went. The devastation looked much worse than after the attack by the Insectoids, but this time the bodies of Terrans and Marsies littered the terrain. We checked them as we passed but found no survivors. It looked as if it had been a brutal fight, with the off-duty MOF personnel having sprung straight into action as soon as the first shots rang out. We found clusters of them surrounding enemy positions or around the bodies of lone gunmen, evidently having thrown themselves into the line of fire rather than flee with the civilians. After confirming the first level clear, we stormed up the stairwell to the second level. That's where I found Nordie.

A chunk of his side—not just his side armour—was missing, no doubt as a result from the fringes of a particle beam blast. He lay in a pool of his own blood. His hands were gripped around the throat of a black-uniformed Fourth Reicher who wore a contorted look of agony on his face. Undoubtedly, they had died terrible deaths, but as grief stricken as I was, a part of me felt proud that my friend had taken his murderer with him. I dropped to a knee and opened my visor to look down at the hollow, empty eyes of my friend. I'm not ashamed to admit that hot, stinging tears ran down my face at the thought of never talking to him, hearing his quips, provoking him for fun, or sharing the aftermath of a joint again. I patted his shoulder and silently promised to come back for him and give him a proper burial.

"We should move," someone said as the section continued scanning any possible position an enemy could hide themselves in. We were out in the open, so I understood the danger, but I needed a moment to say goodbye.

Clicking my helmet visor back down, I took point again. As we continued our search of the second level, I found at least a dozen people I knew to varying degrees, all wearing their jumpsuits or civilian clothing and lying around tables of food or drink. The enemy had mowed them down perfidiously as they relaxed after a fourteen or sixteen-hour day defending New Berlin from enemy attack.

Each of them had come to Big Red against their will and had spent that time training or fighting the alien hostiles who wished to drive us from this planet. They had sacrificed so much for the native Marsies, descendants of a murderous regime back on Terra, and all so they could live peacefully. As thanks, the Fourth Reichers had stabbed them in the back when they were at their most vulnerable. My heart hardened. Rage filled me as we passed every fallen comrade.

We cleared the second and third levels without incident. Before moving towards the Second Battalion living areas, I notified C&C. I sent a coded broadcast over the open comm channels in the hopes that someone would pick it up due to my proximity, but I received no response. I was concerned about the confined space in the corridors connecting the individual rooms; without adequate cover, a single particle blast would take me down. The moment we overrode the door, we surged forward, moving into the first series of rooms. We found no survivors, only the bodies of our brethren in various stages of undress, murdered as they changed or prepared for bed. Once inside the living area, I got a garbled communication from someone requesting backup in the armoury, so we stealthily made our way towards it, creeping closer to the sounds of sporadic gunfire.

Once we were close enough to cut through the jamming device, the soldier identified himself as Elvis from Third Platoon and advised us that he barricaded himself into the armoury to prevent the insurgents from gaining access to our HKs and Exo-suits. After transferring data concerning the enemy's location and confirming they had particle weapons, I split the section into two and laid out our plan of attack. Elvis would draw their fire, and one group would hit them on their left flank while I spearheaded an attack on their right. When everyone knew what they were doing, we divided up and moved into position.

Elvis let out a series of gunshots to signal the commencement of the plan, and I rushed down the corridor with my HK-17 at the ready. Two insurgents revealed their position to return fire. I dropped them as Elvis flared up again. A particle blast rang out in response, so I hit the ground instinctively, but one of the soldiers behind me wasn't quick enough, and it blew a hole through his chest. Angry, I let out a roar and answered with my own particle blast, taking the rebel's head clean off. After I pulled myself to my feet, I moved forward again and stormed their position as the other part of the section struck. In seconds, we cut them to pieces.

Two wounded Fourth Reichers survived the encounter. In the aftermath, I watched with bemusement as the MOF soldiers tended to their wounds, as if they were fellow Terrans.

"What are you doing?" I asked, as Elvis showed up.

"Rendering medical aid," one of the soldiers snapped back at me.

I studied the two fallen rebels and noted the bullet wounds in their chests and arms.

"Why?"

"Is your Hollow brain malfunctioning?" another of the MOF soldiers shouted back. "So we can take 'em alive for interrogation."

"Oh, I see."

I lowered my weapon and took careful aim at the first wounded prisoner. One of the soldiers pushed his colleague out of the way as I squeezed the trigger, killing the rebel instantly. Without prompting, Elvis did the same and shot the second Fourth Reicher to the shouts and roars of the MOF soldiers. Several of them instinctively pointed their weapons at us. None of them had cocked their HKs to activate particle beam mode, though, so it was a futile gesture.

"Standing orders say no prisoners, no survivors," I said to the barrel of a gun pointed harmlessly at my visor. Elvis aimed his own weapon at the ringleader. Following a few tense moments, the section lowered their weapons but couldn't conceal the horror of what we had done.

"C&C, this is Echo One-Niner. Rec, Second Battalion armoury, and habitable areas have been pacified. Orders?"

When reinforcements were sent to help us establish a security parameter around the Rec and living areas, I claimed Nordie's body and carried him to the nearest medical area to be tagged and bagged. It didn't feel right to leave him there on his own, so while I waited for a doctor to register him, I stood vigil and wondered what the higher-ups in EISEN would tell his family. I reached into his Exo-suit's external compartments and found a pre-rolled joint and lighter. Unafraid of the consequences, I proceeded to spark it up, inhaled deep puffs of the joint, and exhaled a large cloud onto his face, wishing it could deliver him some final measure of peace.

Captain Lockhart's drunken, off-key singing echoed down the corridors long before I saw him. I expected him to keep walking, but he paused as soon as he saw me hunched over Nordie. For a few moments, he fell uncharacteristically silent.

"It doesn't get easier, does it?" he said in a far quieter voice than usual. He hunched down beside me and studied Nordie before silently accepting the joint I passed him.

"It seems like such a waste," I said, still trying to make sense of everything.

The captain placed the joint between his lips and patted me on the shoulder. He then reached into a grimy satchel and pulled out a bottle of bourbon. After taking the cap off, he took a large swig, and then he offered it to me. I graciously accepted and whispered a silent goodbye as I drank to Nordie's memory.

"I've buried a lot of friends, back home and here," the captain said in between long swigs. "The pain does get easier in time, but it always stays with you. The trick is to use it. Use it to not end up like them. Cling to it so it keeps you alive and gets you home."

I took the joint back and tapped it, careful not to stain Nordie with ash.

"We only have a few months left. That's all. Just a few more months and we all could've made it back. Why did this have to happen now?"

Captain Lockhart shot me a strange look, one where I thought he wanted to flash that deranged grin, but, as drunk as he was, he managed to retain a look of seriousness.

"You have to know deep down that they're not going to send you back, right? At least not now."

I looked him right in the eye. "We signed a year contract. They have to send us back," I said defiantly. My anger rose at the thought of having to stay here longer than planned.

"Sure. And I'm sure they will send you back as they promised. When they have compression fully worked out. From what I hear, it's a one-way journey. Anyone who takes the return journey ends up with their brains scrambled. They're working on it, but I don't think they'll have it figured in the next few months."

Stunned, I stood and stared at the captain. He rose in response and offered me the bottle again, like a gesture of peace. I took another long and hard swig.

"You know what?" I said. "I'm not even surprised by that anymore. That sounds exactly like something the MOF would do to us. Send us on a one-way mission and dangle false hope about sending us back on time."

"Welcome to Big Red," Captain Lockhart said. Accepting his bourbon bottle back, he threw it into his satchel. "We have always been here."

He slapped me hard on the shoulder, mumbled something about having to pilot a flight, and then stumbled down the corridor, singing.

It took a full day and night for order to be restored to New Berlin. We continued operations against the rebel forces with little food or rest, determined to stamp Terran supremacy on New Berlin once and for all. The bloodiest battles took place in MARSCORP HQ, where the insurgents fought to the last soldier, often blowing themselves up with plasma grenades in a vain attempt to take as many of us with them as possible.

Once a semblance of order had been restored, an unofficial reign of terror was unleashed against the civilian populace, with reprisal attacks and summary executions meted out against suspected Fourth Reicher sympathisers. MARSCORP employees and their families or anyone who collaborated with the MOF were exempt, but that still gave us free reign to punish thousands of civilians.

We became blood mad at the unnecessary loss of so many of our colleagues. We were infuriated at the sense of entitlement the Marsies possessed and how they could so underhandedly stage an insurrection while we were fighting and dying for their very freedom. The powers-that-be utilised this terrible fury and unofficially sanctioned any actions that we deemed necessary to break the spirit of the inhabitants of New Berlin.

The rank-and-file MOF soldiers often took part in these atrocities, but they were spearheaded by Second Battalion for the most part. We had taken the brunt of the casualties in the fighting and showed no qualms about exacting revenge. The zeal we applied to the task disgusted even the most hardened full-timer veterans, but no one opposed us. After the horrors of collective punishment we unleashed, they referred to us as 'Hollows' less and less. 'Vampires' or 'Wolves' became the new terms of choice, although rarely said to our faces.

We treated the Volk Marsies with more savagery than we had ever shown the enemy. Stories abounded of civilians being stomped to death for their suspected loyalties. The Star of David was carved into the foreheads of the families of rebel soldiers as a sign of their betrayal. We led gangs of petrified civilians down into the crypts where the bones of their Nazi ancestors lay and made them watch us as we destroyed their tombs with sledgehammers. At gunpoint, we made them desecrate their own family graves before we flooded the whole crypt with poisonous gas, hoping to kill any die-hard hold-outs and ensuring the civilians couldn't sneak down and repair the damage later.

We forced whole families to clean the battle damage caused by their petty rebellion and showed no emotion as they cried, mopping up the blood of their fallen soldiers and ours. Any act of defiance, either real or perceived was quickly rectified with a severe beating from the butt of a HK. Male or female, young or old, few emerged from the conflict without visible scars. We ransacked houses, burned down schools, destroyed their monuments and places of worship, and forbade them from receiving medical treatment. In the end, it was estimated that hundreds died in retaliation, although official figures were never released.

After our vengeance ran its course and simmered down, all **MOF** and **MARSCORP** facilities were in a pristine state, every inch glimmering from the hard labour of the civilian workforce, while their own houses and living areas lay smouldering. Security increased three-fold as martial law was declared and internment without trial was introduced for even the smallest of offences. The Old Man, his followers, and everyone who resided in **New Berlin** had the message beaten into them. They were here for as long as they were tolerated. Non-Terran born humans could never flee to Terra, so if anything like this were to happen again, we were ready to cleanse them in their entirety from Big Red. After that, the Second Battalion became synonymous with brutality.

With a semblance of normality returned, I found myself not only in a reduced strength section but a reduced strength battalion. Half of the battalion had been killed in the rebellion, most in the opening stages but a large portion in the operations to retake the colony. Nordie and the newbies had all been killed, and Smack, Noid, and Intense Dan were in critical condition, leaving Big Mo and me. Thankfully, a new batch of Hollows had been activated to bolster our numbers, so we were promoted to acting corporals and given control of a platoon each. The higher-ups had learned a lot from their experiences with us. Having proved ourselves, it made sense to let experienced Hollows train, orientate, and integrate the new Hollows.

I met my new platoon on the exact same platform that I had stepped off over six months ago and found myself amazed at their fresh and bewildered faces. I looked around at my fellow **MOF** soldiers and saw the same sombre look etched onto their faces. Without noticing it, we had become veterans. We had waded through alien and Marsie blood and come out the other side—stronger, tougher, and more resilient.

I led my newbies to Mad Jack's briefing and smiled with amusement as they learned, for the first time, the ways of Big Red and their duties. The colonel didn't mention the recent clash with the Fourth Reichers but did mention the escalating conflict along our borders with the hostiles and strongly hinted that they, too, would see combat. That didn't surprise me. They had chosen us, and after extensive Rig training and real-world combat, we excelled. Whatever the selection process was in 2018, we were proving ourselves as equals to veterans who had been shipped in from various armed branches in 1975.

Knowing how difficult the first month could be for any recruit, I took on a father figure mantle. I made myself available to anyone who wanted to talk or reconcile the fact that their consciousness had been separated from their bodies and implanted into a cloned version of themselves. I actively took part in the Rig training exercises, giving individual coaching to those who needed it, as Tazz once did for us. I found myself thinking about her more and more in those days and became determined that no one under my command would experience her fate. I wanted all of them to come through their tour of service in one piece and be shipped home to their real lives afterwards.

Unfortunately, that wasn't meant to be. Big Red had a way of sensing your hopes and desires, twisting and gnawing at them, and spitting them back out. Destiny had another outcome in mind for us and despite my best efforts, few of them would set foot on Terra again.

The sound of the lift doors opening snapped me out of my trance. I was calmer, but a barb of fear lodged deep in my chest. Doctor Ling kept talking to me, determined for me to cling to the present as much as possible. I could see in her eyes that she feared for me, that whatever was coming next would make or break me.

I focused my energy on not drifting away. I looked around at the black-clad soldiers and tried to concentrate on every single detail to anchor me to the here and now. My trolley lurched forward with the sergeant major at the front, leading me to wherever we were going.

The sounds hit me first. The noise of dozens, possibly hundreds of people, all talking at the same time, busily trying to say their piece. It sounded like a packed office block with people all in close proximity, urgently trying to get their individual tasks done.

The lights came next. The glare of countless monitors and screens and the powerful ceiling lights cast illumination on all three levels. As they wheeled me out of the lift, I blinked two or three times to ensure I wasn't trapped in another memory. I shifted on my trolley to look back at Doctor Ling, who stared at me. With my jaw aghast, I turned from side to side, soaking up everything in sight, willing it not to be true. I blinked again, hoping to disrupt the false memory and make the real location reveal itself, but nothing changed.

I was back in C&C.

"What the...?" I managed to fumble out, too shocked and confused to string a whole sentence together. It didn't make sense. They told me I was back on Terra. I was wearing Terran greens. Before I got shot, I had reached the Compression Matrix and been transported back to Terra. It couldn't be.

How was this possible?

Lieutenant-General Barrymore stood monitoring a nearby console. He turned at the sound of our approach. The sergeant major saluted and said something quietly to him before he stepped forward. A wry smile curled up on his face.

"Well, well, Corporal. Welcome home. I'm told you weren't feeling well on the way up here. I trust you have improved?"

I was too busy moving my head from side to side, searching for signs of treachery, to respond straight away.

"This can't be..." I stammered. "You told me I was home. You said you couldn't reach the colonies."

"This has only ever been about the Second Battalion, Corporal. I want to know what happened to you out there and where the rest of your team is."

"But compression," I replied, feeling my mind begin to fracture under the confusion. "We woke up back in London. You said we were confused by the compression. That's how I escaped..."

I trailed off and looked accusingly at Doctor Ling. I wanted to feel betrayed by her, but I experienced such loss and confusion that I couldn't bring myself to scream at the one person who I thought had been trying to protect me. She looked as though she wanted to say something, but her lips remained locked.

"Where is the rest of the Second Battalion, Corporal? I know you know more than you're letting on. No more games. I want an update."

The general glared hard at me as if a single look could break me, but I didn't have an answer for him. As hard as I tried and as much as I wanted to answer his questions, I couldn't recall even the slightest. I could see a firefight but had no idea of where it was or against whom. I didn't have the answers he wanted.

"I don't know, sir. I can't remember."

"General, I believe him. This won't do him any good," the doctor pleaded. "Return him to my care and I'll provide you with the answers as soon as possible."

"Negative, Doctor. We have too much depending on this. You had your chance."

The general returned his attention to me. In a slow, mechanical movement, he reached for the holster on his hip, removed his sidearm, cocked it, and pointed it right at me. The guards blocked Doctor Ling from moving to stand in front of me while I stared down the barrel of a gun.

"I have been authorised to take any steps deemed necessary to find out what happened to the rest of the Second Battalion. I will not hesitate to shoot you and every one of your colleagues to get to the bottom of this matter."

As if to illustrate his point, the general flipped the safety off and continued to aim it at my head.

"I will ask you one last time, Corporal. What happened to the Second Battalion?"

My heart pounded as I searched for answers. Deep down, a voice whispered the fate of the Second Battalion, but I couldn't make out the words. Their location lay buried deep below my consciousness, screaming to be found, but no matter how hard I tried, I couldn't say it aloud.

I looked into the general's eyes and saw no fear. I believed in what he said. He would kill me to get to the truth.

"It's his son," Doctor Ling blurted out, earning a

glare from Lieutenant-General Barrymore. I heard the sound of weapons being raised and pointed at the doctor, but it didn't silence her. "Tell him what happened to Private Barrymore. You have to remember. Is he still alive?"

I looked from the doctor to the general and tried to place that name. It sounded so familiar; it was definitely someone I knew, but I couldn't recollect his face.

"Daniel Barrymore," Doctor Ling prompted from behind me.

"Daniel?" I asked, confused for a moment before the answer struck me. "Intense Dan? You're his father, sir?"

His hand trembled ever so slightly as I spoke, but he said nothing in response and continued aiming at me.

"Intense Dan is fine, sir. I know that for a fact. He was with me right up until the end. He was right behind me when we tried to evacuate..."

"You left him there," the lieutenant-general shouted at me, pushing his sidearm closer to me for emphasis. His face glowed red with anger. The slightest misspoken word and I had no doubt he would squeeze that trigger and kill me.

"No, sir. He still has a part to play in all of this. He—"

"Sir," a young officer called to the general, interrupting me. "We're picking up something. A signal of some sort. It's garbled, but it looks like the point of origin is New Berlin."

General Barrymore hesitated as if deciding whether it would be better to shoot me now or later. After a few moments, he lowered his sidearm, flipped the safety back on, holstered it, and turned to face the young officer.

"Are you sure?" he said, with a noticeable hint of

desperation in his voice. When he stepped away from me, I took a deep breath to steady myself and tried not to think how close I had come to being murdered.

Up on the main screen a series of jumping and broken images played, interspersed with interference and indecipherable sounds. Several of the soldiers surrounding Big Mo and I inched forward to get a better look, giving Doctor Ling the opportunity to reach her hand over and gently caress my head.

"We are on Terra, aren't we?" I asked, realising what was happening and why they had brought me here.

"Yes," the doctor replied. "You're in C&C in the London installation. They wanted to see if they could jog your memory by making you believe you were still on **New Berlin**. I told them it wouldn't work."

I looked up at the broken images on the viewer and wondered what they were, but heavy interference marred any details.

"Darren, what happens next is out of my control. The general will stop at nothing to find out what happened to his son and the rest of your battalion. He already has his mind made up that you know what happened up there, and he will kill you if you don't tell him what he wants to know."

"Why not check the records?" I asked. "We were set to return in 1976. Surely there would be a historical record of what happened to us on Mars."

Doctor Ling shook her head sadly. "Everything about the program is black-ops. Apart from psyche, medical, and personnel records, we have limited information on your operations, certainly nothing towards the end of the war. We know you were sent to do a lot of...questionable things, but we don't know the specifics. That's why you need to remember. Please, you have to try your hardest."

Okay," I said, looking up at the main viewer again.

"But one way or another, I think we're about to reach our end-game on this one."

Doctor Ling squeezed my hand but said nothing.

As 1975 ended and 1976 began, the war had reached a new level of intensity. We managed to secure our borders and continued to launch strategic raids into enemy territory, but at considerable cost. Even with air superiority, the death toll continued to mount. And to everyone involved, there was no end in sight. Every time our forces gained an advantage, poised to deliver a knockout blow, another hostile faction from somewhere else on our borders launched a series of attacks in solidarity, forcing us to withdraw and counterattack. Rumours spread that our continued use of the fleet to bombard enemy positions was beginning to draw the ire of certain factions within the UEAF, who feared further retaliation against MARSCORP personnel, property, and excavation operations.

In response, the powers-that-be began decreasing the levels of aerial bombardment as a prelude to opening peace talks with the Insectoids to find a peaceful resolution to the war. As the weeks dragged on, whispers spread that we were on the verge of signing an agreement granting MARSCORP mining concessions in certain contested areas and confirming the status quo of our current borders. The MOF leadership, although technically subservient to the whims of MARSCORP, still wanted to end the war on a high note and so, as the talks dragged on, Operation Blood Moon was born.

The logic behind Blood Moon was simple. The

MOF leadership feared that the hostiles would perceive the MARSCORP initiated peace talks as a sign of weakness, so they wanted to plan one massive offensive operation to show that the Mars Occupation Force had the will and ability to escalate the war even further if the need arose. The plan was to launch a series of all-out offensives across our borders while simultaneously striking at something of value to the enemy.

Every Forward Base guarding the border would launch a simultaneous incursion into enemy territory and attempt to cause maximum damage. At the same time, an advance force would land behind enemy lines and assault, what we were told, was one of their holy sites. Due to our reputation for ferocity and our desire to take revenge, they named Second Battalion as the advance force. That surprised a lot of us, since most of the time we were considered glorified security guards, but it made sense to me; it was a risky manoeuvre with a high probability of casualties. No point risking a Battalion of battle-hardened veterans when you had expendable Hollows to do the job.

Following the Reicher Rebellion, I ran my own platoon as an acting corporal, mainly due to the lack of experienced or uninjured NCO's. After successfully helping my platoon pass recruit training, I was given a battlefield promotion to full corporal along with Smack and Noid, who both had their own platoons. Intense Dan and Big Mo became team commanders for sections under my command, so I felt confident that I had the people around me to get the job done.

Prior to the Operation, most of the battalion was shipped out to Forward Base Lima, leaving behind some of the greener units and newly arrived reinforcements to safe-guard New Berlin in our absence. It took us several hours to reach our destination in Utopia Planitia. Despite fears that the enemy might learn of our movements and ambush us, the journey was uneventful. It also marked the farthest I had ever travelled from **New Berlin** since my arrival, but the novelty of seeing new Martian terrain had long since worn off. I wanted to get in, get the job done, and go home.

We landed outside the Forward Base amid their own preparations for the up-and-coming offensive. We had all our equipment and ammo with us already, so to pass the time we drilled our platoons while the Second Battalion officers set up their command post. Mad Jack had already gone through the plan with us in detail. In turn, we dished it out to the soldiers under our command. It was simple and straightforward: The in-orbit fleet would bombard the surrounding enemy area. Then the Forward Base Lima Strike Team would assault enemy nests and positions, and we would get airlifted to the mouth of the underground target, about forty klicks away. The Second Battalions orders involved seizing control of the area, fighting our way down into the subterranean caverns, setting explosive charges, and evacuating. Once safely in the air, we'd detonate the charges, blowing the entire area to smithereens and showing the Insectoids that we meant business.

The following morning, we completed our last series of checks and took off in our transports for the initial bombardment. We were under a thousand strong, half being the original batch of Hollows and the other half comprising of newbies. I was proud of how hard they trained and how they adapted to life on Big Red so much more quickly than we had. They hadn't seen any real action, but I had a feeling they'd do well enough.

When we were a few minutes out from the target, the bombardment began. Those who could rushed to the nearest window to watch the action. In the dark, we could barely see the terrain below us, but the particle blasts from the orbiting cruisers lit up the night sky in brief, fiery flashes, casting an unusual green hue across the blood-red sand and rock. In the distance, we watched as the destructive force of our ships pummelled the Martian landscape with feverish intensity, so that every single Insectoid on this godforsaken rock would forever know the wrath of the Terrans. We cheered as the fleet smashed fiery death into Big Red, but whether they were doing any serious damage to the enemy was the real question.

With perfect timing, we landed seconds after the bombardment ended and, like columns of worker ants, streamed out of the transports. A defensive parameter was established. Everyone else formed into their companies and approached the entrance to the holy site at a series of caves in the mountain's base. With weapons high, we broke into our order of march and surged down the winding corridors, ready to inflict death and devastation on anything that opposed us.

To aid the success of the mission, a few telepaths were assigned to us, but they were officially dubbed as observers from MARSCORP since not many people officially knew about the Myers program. Nobody believed they were observers, but it was easier than explaining they could read your thoughts at a whim without you realising it. I was surprised and glad to see Dennis with us. It felt strange having such a young boy on a military operation, but I knew he could be a massive help if we got stuck.

It took under ten minutes of navigating through the bleak, haunting corridors before we reached our destination—a massive cavern located beneath the base of the mountain. The size of the cavern was breathtaking. Even using the torchlight from my HK I could barely make out the roof. I gazed in awe at the monstrous alien statues and depictions carved into the rock walls and marvelled at the smooth polished ground. In the distance, I could make out chambers dotted along the cavern walls, which I guessed to be crypts or tombs.

I tried not to get distracted by the sheer effort of building something like this so far underground, but it was hard. Words will never describe the awe-inspiring degree of effort or alien beauty of that place and here we were, ready to obliterate it. That was the first time that I thought what we had been told about the Insectoids wasn't true. We believed they were mindless drones, incapable of thinking by themselves, in thrall to a hive mind that ruled them, but here they showed themselves capable of creating stunning works of art. It didn't make sense to me that unthinking beasts possessed the capability or the inclination to create something so beautiful, as strange and foreign as it looked to me.

Nevertheless, we set to work placing and arming the explosives in strategic points all around the cavern. So far, we hadn't come across a single hostile. Several of the MARSCORP execs explored the chambers while we worked, but we paid them no heed and stayed out of their way. We had finished placing the last of the charges and were about to begin evacuating when the word I had prayed I wouldn't hear echoed throughout the comm channel.

"CONTACT!"

At least a dozen HK-17s opened up in response. In the time I turned with my weapon at the ready, an entire platoon had already been wiped out. Every single chamber on the northern side of the cavern opened and hundreds of furious Insectoids streamed out. They smashed into our lines like a tidal wave, obliterating everything in their path. Even the telepaths were unable to stem their wrath. By the

184

time we knew we were under attack, other chamber doors around us opened, surrounding us completely. It was a massacre.

Fighting against the terror that threatened to freeze me, I screamed for my platoon to form into all-around cover and engage the enemy. The screams and shouts of the dying filled the comm channel, so I switched it off and listened only to my team while waiting for orders from the command post. Within seconds, any semblance of order collapsed. Those who were able to grouped together, but the enemy attacked from every position, climbing over the piles of their own dead to smash into our fractured formations. It didn't take a military strategist to work out that we were on the verge of annihilation.

Continuing to fire my weapon and unsure of what to do, I ordered my platoon to move back towards the exit. Insectoids came at us from every direction, slashing, stabbing, and howling for our blood. Every time I dropped one, two more took its place. No matter where I looked an eight-legged creature was mowing down an Exo-suited ally. I called into my helmet mic, desperate to link up with someone, anyone, but horrible, blood curdling screams came in response.

They say the battle—or rather, the massacre— lasted around eleven minutes. To me, it felt like seconds. One moment, a thousand of us fought in a life-or-death struggle. The next moment, barely a fifth of us remained. My platoon and a few others banded together and fought our way towards the exit and back up the corridor. All I remember was the relentless sound of gunfire and the horrible, nightmarish screams.

At one point in the run towards the surface, the scalpel-pointed limb of an Insectoid warrior struck me in the leg. I remembered the excruciating pain and hitting the dusty floor. I can still see the twisted face of the demon creature that planned to hack me into a thousand pieces, but Smack saved me. She grabbed me by the shoulders, hauled me up onto her back and, blasting her own HK-17 relentlessly, managed to drag me topside.

I didn't know how many made it out. After being thrown on the nearest transport, it lifted off immediately to escape. Back on the ground, the moment the last soldier fled from the mouth of the cave, the explosives were triggered. It took a few seconds, but the massive explosion fried every living thing in those bloody corridors and caused a portion of the mountain's base to collapse. Whether from blood loss or shock, I lost consciousness soon after.

I woke up in the New Berlin medical bay two days later. Dressed in a medical gown, I found my right leg heavily bandaged but was thankful that, despite the pain, I could still move it. The screams and cries of those we left behind echoed in my skull, but the medical area was surprisingly calm and peaceful. It didn't take long for a doctor to notice I had regained consciousness. He informed me that I had undergone successful emergency surgery and should anticipate a full recovery. No long-term issues or side effects were expected. At least not physical ones.

I had expected Smack, Big Mo, Intense Dan, even Noid to visit me first but to my surprise, it was Mad Jack. I saluted him as soon as he entered the room and replied politely as he asked about my injury. I didn't know him well enough to read him accurately, but the extent of awkward small talk gave me the impression he was tip-toeing around something.

I decided to jump straight into it. "How many of us survived the operation, sir?"

"Operation Blood Moon was a success, fulfilling every one of our goals," he said. "Unfortunately, casualties were higher than projected. We can account for one-hundred-and-sixty-four members of the advance force. The rest either died in combat, from their injuries, or were killed in the explosion. Their loss will be mourned by all members of the MOF, but their heroism and sacrifice will expedite the end of this war."

"I understand, sir." I trailed off, unsure of what else to say. With so many dead, what else was there to say?

"The doctors tell me you'll make a full recovery and are expected to return to duty within the next few days," he continued. "Your platoon has been reformed. For your continued dedication and hard work, I'd like to make you acting sergeant. This war isn't over yet, son. I need people like you who I can trust to get the job done."

Technically speaking, I was already an acting sergeant. It wasn't exactly a promotion, but I tried to see it as the good-natured gesture I hoped it was.

"Thank you, sir. I'd be happy to serve in whatever capacity you see fit. At least until I rotate home in a few weeks."

That statement weighed heavily in the air for a few moments. Then the colonel sighed, removed his beret, and took a seat at the foot of my bed.

"You're a good soldier. Can I convince you to stay on until we've brought the war to its natural conclusion?"

As tough and exhausting as it was on Big Red, I enjoyed the work and believed I was making a difference. But I also knew that a large portion of the people I had arrived with were dead. The longer I remained, the lower my chances of leaving became.

"Thank you for the opportunity, sir. I greatly appreciate the faith you have in me," I said, trying to pick and choose my words carefully. "As much as I'd like to stay and get the job done, I want to get home to my family. I'd be lying if I said I wasn't tempted to do another tour at a later date, but I need to see them."

The colonel looked away for a moment before returning his full attention to me. "I have to be straight with you, son. That's not going to happen. We've had an issue with compression travel that seems to affect the psychological well-being of subjects. Something to do with the patterns breaking down on the return trip. I've been advised that our people are working on it. They should have it fixed in the near future. Until then, all trips are one-way."

My entire world collapsed in on itself at hearing those words. I had fought, bled, been shot at and killed without question for over ten months. And now, when I should be gearing up to return home, back to my life, it was snatched away from me. Despite the fact that Lockhart had mentioned this was a one-way trip, hearing it first-hand from Mad Jack, anger and frustration grew in me. I maintained my composure, but inside I neared boiling point.

"Sir, respectfully, I signed a contract for a year-long tour of duty. I have given you and the program everything, every part of me without question. I understand there may be issues which cause delays with sending us back, and I accept that, but I respectfully request to be discharged when my time is up, so I can wait out of harm's way until the problem is solved."

Mad Jack stood abruptly and, putting his beret back on, gave me a hard stare. Any traces of empathy or rapport vanished, replaced by the harsh words of a veteran superior officer.

"I'm afraid that's not possible, soldier. You signed a contract stating that the MOF could extend your term of service in extenuating circumstances, and this is as extenuating as it gets. You will continue to serve as you have done or you can linger in solitary confinement. Either way, you will not be dismissed. Do I make myself clear?"

"Sir, that was never explained..."

"You should have read your contract clearly before signing," Mad Jack cut across me and walked towards the door, where he paused. "Take the next few days to recuperate and report directly to me as soon as you've been cleared for duty."

I opened my mouth to beg, plead, or just plain shout, but the colonel was already gone and with him any chance of my leaving Big Red. I stared up at the ceiling and wondered if he told the truth. Was it an excuse or were they planning on keeping us here indefinitely? Maybe that had always been the plan.

Then it hit me. One of the possible reasons why they had chosen us was because we were nobodies back on Terra, faces in a crowd. We could die on Big Red and they'd cover it up. They would tell our families we died in a traffic accident, a mugging, or that we never showed up for the assessment. Most of us didn't know each other prior to joining, so it was doubtful that our families could connect with each other. In that unlikeliest of events, EISEN would use their considerable resources to silence them.

They could hold on to us for as long as they wanted, and we had no one to turn to. Even if we managed to board a ship, we'd find ourselves in 1976, in a completely different world before many of us had even been born.

25

"That must have been distressing," Doctor Ling said. I noted a slight sound of suspicion in her voice as she connected the dots. Or at least what she thought the dots were. "But something must have changed if you were discharged less than three months later?"

I opened my mouth to respond, but the high-pitched sound of interference from the main viewer stopped me. All eyes in the room focused on the grainy images up on screen as they came into focus. The images remained black and white, but I could make out people running back and forth. It took a second to recognise several of them were in Exo-suits and, from the looks of it, were engaged in a firefight. From the camera angles it appeared to be security footage.

"Is that **New Berlin**?" General Barrymore said, with a hint of relief in his voice. "Is this real-time? Is that happening now?"

One of the analysts nearby punched a few commands into his console before studying the footage on his own screen more closely.

"Negative, sir. It's got a time stamp showing it to be from...1975."

"The Reicher Rebellion," I said, studying the footage more closely. "Look, that's the Rec!"

The camera angle seemed to be from the ceiling but gave a bird's eye view of the entire room and panned around to follow the action. Although it wasn't crystal clear, I noted a small gang of Fourth Reichers emerge from our living area and begin to fire into the crowd.

191

My blood boiled as I watched bodies drop to the floor and the Reichers mercilessly mowing down everyone in sight.

"How can that be?" demanded the general.

"It's not being sent from 1975, sir," the analyst replied. "It's footage of an event from 1975 being transmitted now."

"Transmitted by whom?"

"Unsure, sir. It's definitely coming from **New Berlin** through one of the emergency channels, but nothing else is included in the transmission."

Everyone in the room remained glued to the footage. Even Doctor Ling took a few paces forward and studied it with morbid fascination as the battle for the Rec intensified. Even though I couldn't be sure, I thought I spotted Nordie rushing towards the attackers, close to the spot where he had died. I closed my eyes and tried not to remember.

What happened next was so sudden that it gave me a fright. A deep voice cut over the footage and uttered a single word.

"Salient."

The chatter in the room melted into nothing. My head dropped against my pillow as the walls came crashing down. In an instant, I lived an entire life. Who I was became clear. The broken fractures of a shattered life pieced together forming a whole, complete picture. Memories floated up from the treasure chest hidden in the deepest recesses of my mind—gleaming, shiny, and pure. An intense, almost orgasmic energy flowed through my body connecting me, rebuilding me, revitalising me in every possible way.

I wanted to laugh, to scream out to the whole world, to tell them all it was me. I was here. I had finally returned. I wanted to, but I didn't. I remained as still as possible as I reached for the piece of metal smuggled to me on my coffee cup. As I had practiced a hundred times, I effortlessly slid the strip of metal into my fingers and began to work the lock on the straps that confined me. When I heard the click and knew I had freed my right-hand constraint, I darted a careful look around the room. Confident that everyone still focused on the images on the screen, I freed myself from my left-hand restraint and undid the one around my waist.

"Salient."

The voice rang out again, but that was only for show. We were all awake, every one of us, every Hollow solider. I could feel it in my bones. Reaching under me, I pulled out the plasma grenade and flicked the cap on it. I adjusted one of the settings before pressing my thumb down on the top, activating it as a Deadman's Switch. I held it aloft and smiled.

"Grenade!" one of the guards roared, and a dozen HKs pointed directly at me. Doctor Ling's jaw dropped in horror, and the general wheeled around to see what was happening. The sergeant major positioned herself near the general and placed a hand on her sidearm, ready to whip it out.

"I wouldn't," I shouted at the nearby guards. "Not one of you is close enough to shoot me and grab this bad boy before I let go. If anyone so much as sneezes in my direction, I let go."

"D-Darren, w-what are you—" a baffled Doctor Ling stammered, but the general cut her off.

"Lower it, Corporal. That's an order," he growled, as his face burned red again.

"Darren, you have to stop this. You're not thinking—"

"I said lower it, Corporal. I know you want to go home, so you won't do this. Give me the grenade."

"Order your soldiers to stand down," I responded, trying to make sure they all kept their eyes on me.

The general took a step forward and raised his hands to placate me.

"Corporal, give me the grenade, and then we can talk."

"I don't think so, sir."

"Salient," the voice called out again.

The general opened his mouth to say something, but it was too late. Everyone was in position. He froze at the sound of a sidearm cocking at the back of his head. The guards looked at one another and back to me, trying to make sense of why the sergeant major pointed her gun at the general. Big Mo extended his own hand. While gripping a plasma grenade and holding it to the side of one of the guard's heads, he removed the sidearm from his holster.

"Order them to stand down," the sergeant major said to the general as confused shouts erupted around the room. Groups of black-uniformed soldiers began disarming each other as those loyal to me took control of C&C. General Barrymore looked from side to side, realising he had lost control of the situation.

"Stand down," he ordered through gritted teeth.

I continued to hold the plasma grenade until the guards were disarmed and subdued. Big Mo stripped them of their weapons and tied their hands with cable ties. Then the guards loyal to us ushered their former comrades into the centre of the room and ordered them and all the analysts to lie face-down on the floor with their restrained hands behind their heads.

"I'll have you all shot for this," the general hissed as the sergeant major removed his own sidearm from his holster.

Big Mo handed me one of the HKs. After disarming the plasma grenade, I threw my arms around him and let out an ecstatic roar.

"We did it," Big Mo laughed into my ear. "After all these years, we finally made it back."

"Are you ready?" I asked, releasing myself from his grip and patting his smiling face.

"Let's do it."

I turned and glared at the general and Doctor Ling, both of who remained standing.

"On their knees," I ordered.

The sergeant major and Big Mo shoved them to the ground. The doctor continued gaping at me in disbelief, trying to make sense of what was happening, but I had more pressing concerns. I turned to face the sergeant major and extended a hand. She handed me the general's sidearm but remained silent. Those cool eyes studied me. I couldn't withhold the urge to smile any longer.

"Good to see you again, Smack."

"You too, Dub," she grinned proudly and enveloped me in her own bear hug. I held my friend a moment before reluctantly letting go, knowing we still had a mission to complete.

"Get me a sit-rep," I said to her, seeing past the wrinkles and age lines etched over her face.

Still holding her handgun, she removed the sergeant major insignia from the front of her uniform and carelessly threw it at the general. Turning to type commands into a nearby console, she took a few seconds to study the various readouts before returning her attention to me.

"Strike Team One, Two, and Three all report objectives fulfilled. We have full control of this installation, the Lunar Colony, and New Berlin."

"Any update on the fleet yet?"

"Not yet, but that will take a bit longer."

"Okay. Have our people switch to back-up channels. Cut internal and external communications but continue to monitor all incoming. Lock down this base."

"On it," she replied. She picked up a headset and

barked orders to our units.

"Darren, what the hell is going on?" Doctor Ling shrieked at me. "Why are you doing this? Have you been brainwashed by the hostiles?"

I wanted to laugh out loud at that.

"No, good doctor," I said, squatting down in front of her so we were more or less at the same height. "You can't blame what's happening today on someone else. Today is the day of reckoning, the day when you and your kind have to own what you did to us. You have no one to blame but yourselves."

"I don't understand," she replied, on the verge of tears.

"No," I conceded, "you probably don't. But he does." I nodded at the general.

The general glared back at me with violent hatred, but he said nothing.

"Tell her," I goaded him. "Tell her what's going on. Tell her the reason why you're all going to die today."

General Barrymore remained defiantly tight-lipped, even as I pointed my gun at him. Realising he wasn't going to play fair, I stood, took aim at one of the guards on the floor, and pulled the trigger. A shot rang out, sending blood and brain matter all over the floor.

The doctor screamed.

I aimed my gun at the next soldier and turned to the general.

"Tell her. Tell her what this is really about. Tell her why we're here."

For a moment, I thought the general was going to play hardball. That didn't faze me, though. I had plenty of creative ways to make him talk. Before I could pull the trigger again, he spoke.

"We left them there," he said, barely speaking louder than a whisper. "We never brought them home. We left them there for over forty years."

In the days that followed the massacre, I found myself unable to focus on anything else. I had escaped certain death back in the cavern, but my mind seemed intent on forcing me to relive those horrible moments. Every time I closed my eyes all I could see was a horde of those foul creatures, trampling over one another to hack me to pieces. I saw the faces of my fallen comrades. Their terrible, pain-filled screams rattled around my brain non-stop. I found no respite in sleep; for the few minutes that I was lucky enough to lose consciousness, those images followed me. I tried my best to block it all out, to focus on something, anything else, but I was as trapped in those bleak tunnels as the shattered bones and torn flesh of my platoon.

The doctors did their best with me. They sent me to councillors and prescribed me drugs, but I didn't take them. After all the lies the powers-that-be had told me since arriving on Big Red, I didn't trust anyone in authority to look after my well-being. I stashed the pills under my pillow and considered what my next move would be.

I tried to think about Louise and Kat, but every time I did, I felt nothing but shame wash over me. It was nearly a year since I had last seen them, and I wondered, if I ever escaped Big Red, what type of person I would be. I thought of how easy it had been for me to execute the Reichers in cold blood and if that was a result of my training or something that had always been in me, buried under layers of civility. I could never imagine hurting Louise or Kat in any way, but I never thought myself as being capable of taking another life. I desperately wanted to see them, but I wasn't sure if there was anything left of me for them to recognise.

After my release from the medical bay, I reported to Mad Jack as ordered. He gave me a pat on the shoulder, handed me acting sergeant stripes, and sent me back to the remnants of the Second Battalion to carry on with my duties. Those who had survived the massacre were placed on light duties while we recuperated, so I hoped that the extra free time would allow me to burn off some steam and get over what I had experienced.

I was wrong.

Every haunted and shocked face I saw reflected my own pain and horror. I threw myself into my duties and tried to find solace in the company of Smack, Big Mo, Intense Dan, and even Noid, but we were all burnt out. We spent time together, went for drinks, worked out in the gym, played cards, and sometimes laughed, but something had changed in us. We had looked point-blank into the face of evil and survived, but in so doing we lost a small piece of our souls.

As tough as those days were, I didn't expect things to get any harder for us, but once again they did. Following our attack on the Insectoids holy site, a massive retaliatory raid against Forward Base Lima resulted in the deaths of a thousand full-time MOF soldiers and support staff. Many of the full-time MOF soldiers stationed in or passing through New Berlin had either served there or knew someone who had, and they blamed us in their anger.

The word "Hollow" became more prevalent and visceral, following us wherever we went. Drunken soldiers would curse us and call us cowards, traitors, and blood-thirsty robots. Rumours spread that no massacre took place on our mission. They said we betrayed the MOF to the hostiles to save ourselves and surrendered the real soldiers at Forward Base Lima by giving the enemy access to the facility. One evening, a group of drunken enlisted soldiers threw an empty whiskey bottle in my direction and cursed me as a vampire. I had them brought up on charges, but they only got a slap on the wrist.

Every passing day became more and more unbearable. I silently held out hope that Doctor Milton or one of the MARSCORP scientists would resolve the issue with the Compression Matrix and send us home, but as my birthday came and went my hopes diminished. A year after we arrived on Big Red, those of us who had been a part of the first batch gathered for drinks in the Rec and commiserated over the hardships we had endured.

No one spoke about it openly, but I could see it in their eyes, that twinkle of hope fading away. That night, I found Big Mo tightening a noose around his neck in the shower area, ready to take his own life. He looked at me with those big brown eyes. Without him saying a word, he told me he couldn't take it anymore. I talked him down, got him to his bunk, and stayed awake for the rest of the night to stop him from trying it again, but that was the final straw. Something needed to be done.

The next day, once we were on our own time again, I gathered Big Mo, Smack, Intense Dan, and Noid and went to the Rec, taking a spot close to where I had discovered Nordie's lifeless body. We discussed everything we had been through and agreed that we needed to take action. To remain on Big Red any longer was a death sentence. We had served our time; now we wanted to go home.

"They can't keep us here indefinitely," Intense

Dan said, staring into the bottom of his beer. "They'll have to send us back soon. As frustrated as we are, I think we should give them the benefit of the doubt."

"You heard what Dub said the colonel told him," Smack responded, and took a long swing from her bottle of wine. "They can keep us here indefinitely. It was in that stupid contract we signed, the one they never let us read."

"The longer we stay here, the more likely we are to die," Big Mo mumbled, unable to make eye contact with anyone.

"Finally, you guys are starting to wake up," Noid said victoriously, with a weaselly grin plastered across her face.

"So, what can we do about it?" Smack continued. "How exactly do we take action?"

We each took a swig of our drinks while we thought about it. There was a limit to how much we could pester the powers-that-be about before we crossed the line. They were the gatekeepers. If they decided they didn't want to let us go, how could we persuade them?

"We use force," Noid said, leaning in close to us, whispering. "We take the number one lesson they taught us and use it against them. We go in at gunpoint and make them send us back."

She sat back in her chair and let that sink in for a few moments before waving a hand at a waiter to order another round of drinks.

"You're forgetting the Compression Matrix is on Phobos," Big Mo said, slowly stroking his stubbly chin. "Even if it could be done, we'd need enough transports to bring the rest of the Second Battalion up there. That's at least ten troop carriers."

We fell silent again as the waiter returned with our drinks. I paid for the round using my wristband and waited for him to move out of earshot. "Big Mo's right," I said to the table. "I'm not ruling it out, but I think we should focus on something less drastic first. Let me talk to Dennis and Doctor Milton. Dennis feels as if he owes us something. He could shed light on the situation. It's at least worth approaching Doctor Milton about, too. We're his creations, after all."

I could tell Noid wasn't happy with that; she wanted to go in guns blazing, but I had no intention of letting us get killed trying to break out of Big Red. We talked about it for the rest of the night. In the end, everyone conceded to my plan. I would approach Dennis and the doctor to figure this out, or at least gain some information that could be helpful.

What could go wrong with that?

The next day, I got Smack to take over training of my new platoon. Dressed in my Exo-suit, I made for the C&C building. Security was tight but thankfully mostly managed by the Second Battalion, so I blended right in. I waited by the main doors and chatted with colleagues or paced back and forth, as if on patrol, all the while closely watching the comings and goings of the top brass, the MARSCORP execs, and the hundreds of drone-like analysts. It took a few hours, but I spotted Dennis walking towards C&C flanked by two armed minders. Working out exactly want I wanted to say without sounding too desperate, I moved into his field of vision, trying to not make it look too obvious that I was trying to catch his attention.

"Corporal Loughlin," he said, sounding pleasantly surprised to see me, "or should I say acting sergeant? It's good to see you again." He waved off his minders and waited for them to step out of earshot before turning to face me. "Of course, I'd be happy to help you. I'll seek out Doctor Milton later today and see what I can find out."

Damn mind readers.

We chatted for a few more minutes, with Dennis politely not pre-empting what I was thinking before we arranged to meet later. A part of me grew nervous for having taken this step. Although I wasn't technically breaking any rules, it felt as though I was betraying the MOF, but the fact that they were keeping me here for an indefinite amount of time washed away any sense of guilt. No matter what way they twisted it, that went against everything they told us at the start.

True to his word, Dennis spoke with Doctor Milton and persuaded him to meet with me. The Rec was far too public, so after sending his minders away, we met up in an empty corridor in one of the lower levels of New Berlin. As soon as they arrived, Doctor Milton began fidgeting with his glasses and lab coat, continuously adjusting them. These actions made him appear more nervous than normal, but he still greeted me warmly. After making small talk, I told him of our plight.

"We've done everything the MOF has asked us to do and have always been ready to serve and fight, but half our numbers are dead and they won't tell us when they'll let us go home. Can you tell us how long it will take to fix, Doctor?"

Doctor Milton took off his spectacles and wiped the lenses awkwardly on his stained coat before slipping them back on. "I'm afraid it's not as simple as that," he said, looking anywhere but at me. "There are so many factors to consider when it comes to a timeline. Obviously, the safety of your consciousness must be paramount during the transfer procedure, but there are other factors at play, too."

It was a lazy attempt at dodging the question, but if the doctor didn't want to meet me, he didn't have to come, so I chalked it up to typical nervous disposition and tried again.

"I understand it's far more complex when you factor in other considerations, but if you had everything you needed, how long until you could fix the problem and make compression safe enough for us to go home?"

The doctor rubbed his chin and looked off into space. "If they gave me the time to properly research the issue, carry out tests, and gave me access to you and your...kind...then, roughly...I don't know...five or six days?"

I blinked a few times and replayed the words in my head, scanning them, processing them, trying to be certain I hadn't misheard.

"Five or six d-days?" I said, stunned by the answer.

"Yes. Yes, about that. The hardest part would be focusing on what causes the temporary psychosis after consciousness has been downloaded back to the original host body. I'd need to carry out controlled tests on volunteers and in collaboration with the team in 2018. But I'm confident, with enough subjects, we could solve this problem."

The answer shocked me. From the way the colonel had made it out, I had expected it to take weeks or months to resolve but hearing it would take a couple of days caught me off guard.

"Can you start working on this now?" I nearly screamed but lowered my voice at the last minute. "Doctor, I will place the entire Second Battalion at your disposal. Including the first and second batch of Hollows. That's over seven hundred people. I can have a list of volunteers for you within the hour."

"It's not as simple as that," the doctor said, looking down at the ground as he shuffled his feet.

"Other factors," Dennis mouthed quietly and nodded towards the doctor.

"What other factors?" I demanded. "What's stopping this from happening?"

"Orders," the doctor mumbled. "After we activated the second batch on Phobos, the higher-ups thought they'd cracked it. We'd discovered and mastered a new form of interstellar travel, so I was ordered to move my lab here to New Berlin in preparation for the roll-out. Things changed when some of the volunteers we sent back began suffering severe mental breakdowns. This, coupled with the actions of your kind, spooked those further up the food chain. There is a major debate going on that if you get sent back, you could pose a security risk on Terra."

"What actions? I've only ever done what I was ordered to do."

"Therein lies the problem," the doctor said glumly, patting me on my armoured shoulder. "Code was added to your host body. That was the reason you knew how to march and follow basic commands after you were first activated, despite never having drilled in the MOF style before."

I remembered following orders and instinctively marching in time off the train platform with everyone else and wondering the same thing, but I never dwelled on it.

"Code was added to make you all more compliant, to make you not question your surroundings too much or have any hostile feelings towards your superiors. In short, it made you effective killing machines, but the problem is that this code has become integrated into your personalities. We can't remove it safely without causing damage to your core consciousness."

"I still don't understand..." I groaned, feeling my stomach churn.

"Yes, you do," Dennis whispered. "Many of you have adapted. You're questioning your environment. Even the fact that you're standing here, in flagrant disregard of your superior officer's orders, shows that you're starting to adapt. In time, you may even become uncontrollable, and that's the last thing they want back on Terra. The one thing that scares them more than ruthless killing machines that can be controlled via programming are ruthless killing machines that can make up their own minds. Think of the damage the Second Battalion could do back on Terra if the wrong hands gained control of your programming. Even worse, think of what you could do if you decided to take action yourselves."

"I'm not a machine," I mumbled. Dropping to my knees, I gripped my stomach. From the pain, a sea of acid worked its way through my body, slowly eating and gnawing at every inch of my insides.

"No. You're not a machine," Dennis said, lowering to a knee and studying my pained face. "That was a poor choice of words. You're more like a tool. A multifaceted one but a tool none the less. A tool can be used to build a house or, as you have so effectively proven, to take a life. Or in your case, *lives*."

The pain in my stomach increased with each breath. I could feel the burning, acidic sensation leak into my limbs, slowly gnawing away at everything that held me together. I fell onto the ground and writhed in agony. Doctor Milton's hands reached under my arms and sat me up against the corridor wall.

"The higher-ups were impressed by how you and your kind handled…what do you call them?" Dennis continued. He paused before turning to Doctor Milton to prompt him for the answer.

"Insectoids," the doctor said. His sad eyes looked down at me.

"Yes," Dennis laughed. "Insectoids. What really scared them was how brutally you treated the Marsie Volk after their little rebellion. You've all been programmed not to kill what you perceive to be human. That's what drove the one you called Tazz to kill herself, and even that surprised them. But you adapted, and when ordered, you complied. It's fascinating stuff, really."

"I'm sick," I groaned again, completely overwhelmed by the agony that pulsed throughout my body.

"Help is on the way," Doctor Milton said and gestured at something down the corridor. I was too weak to lift my head but could hear the sound of boots rapidly approach.

Dennis stripped me of my weapons and gently

patted me on the head. "Don't worry," he said soothingly. "It's a temporary telepathic imprint. It will pass in a few minutes."

"Why?" I choked out, unable to make eye contact.

"Because you're their leader. And because we wanted to catch you all off guard, and this seemed like the easiest way. Don't worry, Darren. MARSCORP and the Myers Program initiates are here to help. We'll fix you up as good as new, and then you can get right back to fighting these...Insectoids, is it?"

I wanted to speak, but I couldn't move my lips. I wanted to ask him about everything he was saying. I wanted to tell him he had seen them at the ambush. He froze them long enough for me to destroy the jamming device.

In response to my thoughts, Dennis laughed. "I didn't see any Insectoids, Darren. You did."

Gazing up at the massive viewing screen, I paced the C&C floor, willing the transmission to come through. Doctor Ling visibly shook at the sight of the dead soldier in front of her while the general continued to gaze off into space.

"Anything?" I called out to Smack.

"Nothing yet," she replied, checking the screen readouts.

I had anticipated this delay, but the entire plan hinged on taking the fleet. We could hold the colonies but never keep them with a fleet of ships ready to rain death upon us at any moment. I checked the watch I had taken off one of the captured soldiers and looked towards Smack again. Another update was due to arrive.

"Sir, quarantine measures are in full effect. The base has been locked down."

"Good. Make sure the security teams are fully locked in. Have we received any communications from any other EISEN facilities?"

Smack moved to another console and punched in a series of commands. "Negative, sir. Everyone's too focused on the blackout in the colonies to notice us."

"Good," I replied and continued pacing.

I looked down at the doctor again. Seeing the terror plastered all over her face, I felt a momentary tinge of empathy. I signalled to a couple of nearby co-conspirators to move the body to the corner. They did so without hesitation, leaving the doctor and general where they were.

"I never abandoned him," the general said quietly, still looking away into nothingness. "He must know that. I would never abandon him."

"You keep telling yourself that," I smirked.

"This can't be happening," Doctor Ling mumbled. "Darren, you have to come to your senses. There has to be a part of you in there that knows what you're doing is wrong."

I couldn't help but smile at that statement. It was so black and white and sugar-coated with plums on top. Deep down, the doctor was trying to rationalise a situation she had never been in before. Her trained mind worked to break down exactly what was happening, to discover the root cause, the fundamental emotional reaction that drove me to this. But this wasn't driven by anger, although that certainly was a motivator.

I was here to right a wrong.

I awakened, still in my Exo-suit, to the sound of gunfire. I instinctively flinched and tried to roll onto my feet, but straps held me tight. Tilting my head, I found myself restrained to a medical trolley in a laboratory I had never seen before. Windows to my left had their shades drawn, blocking any chance of me getting my bearings. I craned my neck, trying to study the room as much as possible. There was no one in here with me and nothing nearby that I could use to free myself. I fidgeted, trying to see if I could manoeuvre my left arm and activate my arm console, but the restraints held.

Outside, the sound of machinegun fire echoed closer and closer throughout the corridors. Fearing another assault by the Insectoids, I doubled my efforts to loosen my restraints, but to no avail. I couldn't even wriggle my arm out of the Exo-suit to free myself that way.

I heard a roar and a thump as something slammed into the lab door. I turned and trained my eyes on it. The sound of people running grew louder but faded quickly as people escaped the weapon's fire. Another series of blasts came from beyond the door, and I braced myself.

The door flew open. HK in hand, an Exo-suited-soldier scanned the room before training the weapon on me. For a second, I expected a bullet to my brain, but then I noticed the face behind the helmet visor. Smack lowered her weapon, marched over to me, and began undoing my straps.

"What the hell is going on?" I asked as she freed me. "Are we under attack?"

I swung my legs from the trolley and stretched my limbs while keeping an eye on the door. Without answering, Smack reached beneath the trolley and pulled out my HK and handed it to me. She then placed her hand on my back and, pushing me forward, began fumbling with one of the Exo-suit's compartments.

"What the hell are you doing?" I shouted at her.

I felt her wrench something out. Holding her hand aloft, she showed me the Exo-suit's transponder. She dropped it to the ground and smashed an armoured boot onto it, crushing it to pieces. After slinging her HK, she placed her hands on my shoulders.

"They came for us after they had come for you," Smack said firmly. "There isn't time for details, but they started rounding up the Second Battalion. Noid shot that little mindreading freak and we bolted. We came here for you. Now we're going to seize the Compression Matrix and go home. You in?"

It was too much to process, but I trusted Smack with my life and knew if she said there wasn't time for details, she meant it. I clicked my helmet visor down and raised my weapon, ready to move.

"Stay off the standard MOF comm channels," she said as we approached the door. "Stick to channel Sierra Seven-Niner. It's encrypted, and it'll link you to everyone else."

I did as I was told and, with a series of eyeblinks, opened the comm channel. Dozens of voices spoke calmly over the sounds of a raging battle, co-ordinating their actions with one another.

"Where are we?" I asked, noticing my satellite uplink was dead.

Smack peered around the corner of the door, checking to make sure it remained clear, and gestured for me to follow. With my HK at the ready, I covered our rear and moved quickly through the unfamiliar corridors.

"We're in the Research and Development area of MARSCORP HQ. Some of our guys retook this building during the Reicher Rebellion and figured this is where they'd take you. We have it mostly locked down, but there are still a few **MOF** personnel inside the parameter."

We moved through the maze of corridors without incident before stopping at a pair of double doors guarded by two of my platoon members. They greeted me as I walked through the doors into a large room filled with medical and scientific equipment. The room was packed with beds filled with our wounded. Everyone else hovered around a set of monitors at the side of a large, white-coloured machine at the far end of the room.

"What do you need me to do?" I asked, noticing Big Mo stationed at the monitors. They showed security camera footage from inside and outside the MARSCORP building. Even at a glance, I could see there was still heavy fighting going on.

"Motivate him to work faster," Smack said, nodding at Doctor Milton.

In a panic, he ran back and forth between consoles near the large machine, a dozen HKs egging him on. I felt a rush of anger and betrayal surge through me as I stepped towards him. He twitched nervously at the sight of me.

"Sit-rep," I demanded.

The doctor flashed me a terrified look but continued his task. The Compression Matrix looked to be the size of a house but, apart from some consoles and six compartments on the front of it, nothing indicated its function.

"I keep telling you all," the doctor cried back, "this

isn't going to work. I need time to calibrate it and run diagnostic tests. The slightest slip up and your brain patterns will degrade long before they reach Terra."

"No excuses," one of the Exo-suited soldiers shouted and prodded the doctor roughly with his HK. The doctor flinched and paused momentarily to rub his bruised ribs before shooting me a fearful expression.

"Lower your weapons," I ordered. Although they hesitated, everyone obeyed.

The doctor nodded his thanks to me as he adjusted a few settings on one of the consoles and studied one of the read-outs.

"You've got five minutes to do what you need to do before I start cutting off pieces of you," I growled, still stinging from the doctor's betrayal.

"I need more time," he pleaded. "I already told you it would take five or six days of testing. You can't expect me to resolve it all within five minutes."

"You'd better, doctor," I replied coolly. "If the MOF storms this room and there're any of us still here, you'll be the first to get a bullet in the brain."

I patted my HK for effect and turned to seek out Smack. She was hunched over one of the monitors, shouting orders into her helmet mic. I strode up beside her and studied the ongoing battle. From the looks of it, Second Battalion units had seized control of all the entrances, exits, and key areas within the facility. But outside, Exo-suited MOF soldiers were amassing for an assault. It would be a bloodbath.

"Doctor Milton says he needs days to get the Compression Matrix online correctly," I reported. "He reckons we could end up with our brains fried if it's not done right."

"He had better be wrong," Smack said, tapping one of the monitors. "They're moving tanks into position. We don't have much time."

I watched as four lumbering hover tanks moved around one of the street corners and inched towards the MARSCORP building. They were small and ugly, with long particle cannons pointed in our direction. In response, one of our units on the roof opened fire with a series of particle blasts, which barely scratched the red and black paint on the hovering monstrosity.

"I'll buy you as much time as I can," I said and turned to leave.

I felt Smack's hand grip my arm tightly to stop me.

"I need you," she whispered. "Think of Kat and Louise. Don't be a hero."

I had no desire to die on this hell-hole so far from home, but I felt a bond of loyalty to my people. We had done everything that was asked of us and all we wanted was to go home. I would have given anything, including my own life, if it meant they could escape this place and the horror that awaited us if they captured us alive.

"Send an advance team to secure the London facility," I advised. "Once they have control, send everyone back as fast as you can, but keep the doors open for us. We'll be hot on your heels."

Smack reluctantly nodded and let go of my arm. I patted Big Mo on the shoulder and trotted out of the room. Grabbing a nearby soldier to guide me down to the main lobby, I called Noid over the secure comm channel.

"Noid, where you at?"

"Main entrance, about to get overrun. You?"

"On my way."

I picked up the pace as I followed my fellow soldier down the winding steps to the bottom floor, while making mental notes of the directions we had taken. We passed the stunned but still breathing bodies of MARSCORP scientists before reaching a side entrance that led us out into the main lobby. A dozen Second Battalion soldiers were in positions around the lobby with their weapons aimed at the main entrance, ready for the brutal assault that was to come. Noid signalled to me from her position. Keeping my head down, I crouched over to her.

"They're going to hit us from multiple entry points," Noid reported, "but the main thrust will be here using those damn tanks to steamroll over us. Once they have the lobby, they'll clear the building room by room, floor by floor. We don't have the people to do anything other than slow them down. It's over."

"No way," I replied. "There's no way we came this far just to die in this stink hole." I pointed to the ceiling above us. "What's in those rooms? Anything of use?"

"Just offices, the whole way up."

She continued looking at me as if expecting a follow-up question, but I said nothing. Even with someone who irritated me as much as Noid did, I hoped that after a year of sleeping, eating, training, and fighting together, we were on the same wavelength. Even if we weren't, I gambled her own Voice of God would lead her to think outside-the-box in the name of self-preservation. I couldn't say it, for fear that a mind reader would be included in the actual assault and would pick it up, but I hoped she took my meaning.

"Pull your units back," I ordered.

She studied me closely for a few seconds before relaying the order. Giving me the slightest of nods, she disappeared back up the stairwell with the soldiers under her command and my guide at her heels, leaving me alone in the lobby.

"PROTECT TERRA. KILL THEM ALL. PROTECT TERRA."

My Voice of God sounded somewhat confused but still enthusiastic about the prospect of eliminating what it perceived to be the enemies of our planet. I waited a few minutes for Noid to move into position before toggling the frequencies on my helmet visor screen to find a channel that I knew the **MOF** soldiers outside would be monitoring.

"This is Echo One-Niner, respond."

There was a moment of silence, but I knew they were listening. An unknown voice responded before routing me to someone higher up the food chain. "Standby."

I waited for a few moments, wondering if they would patch me through to Mad Jack or even C&C, but the voice belonged to Dennis.

"Former acting Sergeant Loughlin, what a pleasant surprise," the cocky ten-year-old said.

"A surprise for me, too. I was told you were shot."

There was a pause before Dennis responded, which I hoped meant I had provoked him.

"A mere flesh wound. Are you calling to surrender? Have your people lay down their arms and walk single file out of the building. You have my assurances that no one will be executed for treason. No one needs to die here today, Darren, but rest assured, MARSCORP and the **Mars Occupation Force** do not negotiate with terrorists and mutineers. Stand down."

"That's a negative. I would recommend that you pull your forces back. There are a lot of innocent people in here that could get caught in the crossfire if you send in the tanks."

Another pause followed as Dennis considered my veiled threat against the MARSCORP personnel still inside the building. I had no idea how many there were and had no intention of harming a non-combatant, but I hoped to stall for as much time as possible. Assuming Smack could motivate Doctor Milton to get the Compression Matrix online in time, I figured there would still be a delay of a few minutes between when the first volunteers were sent back, took control of the London installation's Compression Matrix, and signalled back.

"MARSCORP doesn't want to see its innocent employees suffer," Dennis said in an unbelievably smarmy tone, "but, as an individual not representing the interests of anyone else in any official capacity, I'm prepared to speak with you, Darren, if you'll guarantee me safe passage. Let's talk this out before more innocent people lose their lives."

"You think I'm going to let you get close enough to drop me again, Dennis?"

"There are limits to what even I can do within a twenty-four-hour period, even without getting shot. Grant me safe passage. As a goodwill gesture, I'll bring one of your captured soldiers. At the very least, it will buy you a few minutes to calibrate the Compression Matrix. Before you ask, it doesn't take a mind reader to figure out why you're holed up in there."

I didn't trust Dennis in the slightest, but I also knew that if they sent in the tanks and seized the first floor, it would be a massacre. Our units stationed throughout the building would fight for every inch of ground, but a lot of people on both sides would lose their lives. I felt betrayed by the MOF for putting me in this situation. As much as I resented the hostility of the MOF soldiers, though, I didn't want to be responsible for their deaths for doing exactly what I had done for the last year, which was following orders.

"Okay," I replied. "Just you and the prisoner, but if you try anything or if any of those soldiers out there even sneeze in the direction of one of our positions, the deal is off and you get a bullet to the head. You don't need to be a mind reader to know I'm not bluffing."

"Agreed. Coming in."

I relayed orders to hold fire unless provoked and updated Smack. She advised that Doctor Milton had the Compression Matrix online but was still imputing data to send us back to our timeline. On a private channel, she conceded that even if we bought extra time with negotiations, we wouldn't get everyone back. Smack was one of the toughest people I had ever known, but she was sensitive and took things to heart. She hid it well behind her smiling and social exterior, but I knew the thought of abandoning anyone would eat away at her. We had come this far together. It didn't feel right to leave anyone behind.

"He's coming in," Noid reported from her position. "I have everything in place, but I sure hope we were thinking the same thing."

"Me, too."

Creeping from my position, I moved to the main desk directly in front of the reinforced glass doors in the lobby. They were thick enough to resist bullets, but a single particle beam blast would shatter them, so I made sure to keep as low as possible and clicked on the desk panel to release the door locks. Cocking my HKs particle beam on, I flicked off the safety and activated my helmet visor's targeting settings before moving to a more secure position behind a massive marble pillar to the left of the desk. I kept my eyes and weapon trained on the main entrance and watched Dennis and his prisoner ascend the dozen steps outside the main doors. With his hands up to show he was unarmed, he stepped through the doors into the lobby.

Like him, his prisoner wore a commercial Bio-suit but remained a few paces behind, making it difficult to identify him. I had no idea how many of our soldiers they had captured in the initial crackdown, so it could be anyone. I kept my weapon pointed at Dennis as he slowly paced forward.

"Darren," he said, gesturing towards his prisoner who was more intent on studying the artwork on the walls instead of identifying themselves to me, "my gift to you. My hope is that this will shed light on what you've been through, and it's my wish that it may even help you reconsider this rash course of action you and your people have taken. I can sense the hostility from you but know that we want to help. Mistakes have been made on both sides."

In a careful and controlled motion, Dennis clicked down his visor and then removed his helmet. He placed it on the ground and smiled at me before gesturing at the prisoner to do the same. The prisoner nodded in response, but his movements were slower, whether from injury or drugs, I couldn't tell. A tinge of nervousness cut through me.

"I mentioned to you before about some of the code that was included in your Hollow body which made the powers-that-be wary. If you remember, it's your ability to circumvent that code that really scares them. This should explain why."

The prisoner, still facing away from me, clicked down his visor and inched off his helmet. I saw long, slightly matted, jet black hair and soft, caramel-coloured skin. Then the prisoner faced me.

My heart stopped. I gasped.

For a few seconds, confusion rushed through me with the force of a sledgehammer. As my instincts kicked in, I feared it was an attack from Dennis. I tightened my grip on the trigger but didn't squeeze. I looked from him to the prisoner, unable to process what was happening, but Dennis remained frozen. He looked right at me with his hands held high, barely breathing. I tried to keep my gaze on him but couldn't help moving it to her. I blinked, half expecting her to vanish, but she remained.

"Tazz?"

It couldn't be. I had watched Tazz die—the image of her blowing herself up in the airlock forever engrained itself on my memory. Yet here she was. The Tazz I knew had shone like a star, but standing in front of me, she was a mere shadow of herself. Her once-smiling, bubbly face remained gaunt. Bags hung under her eyes, and even her soft brown skin appeared to have a tinge of grey to it. Her sad eyes looked exhausted and confused and blinked back at me without a hint of recognition.

"What is this?" I roared at Dennis. "I swear to God I will burn every inch of this building to the ground if you don't stop messing with my mind, Dennis. I watched Tazz die. Make this stop or I'll kill you right here and now."

At that moment, I forgot he was ten years old. I wanted to tear him limb from limb with my bare hands. I wanted to pull the flesh from his bones with my fingers while he screamed. To use my memories of Tazz like this was a step too far. I contemplated killing him right there and then.

"She's real, Darren. Go ahead, touch her. She won't disappear."

"Tazz is dead. I watched her die. Make this thing go away."

"No, you *remember* watching her die. It's a false memory designed to motivate you and your section to not get yourselves killed and to hide the fact that Jasmine here was taken for testing after her... malfunction."

I switched to the private channel with Smack and activated my helmet camera to transmit the footage directly to her. "Smack, do you see a second person here?" I forced out, trying not to stammer my words.

"Yeah, sure I do. Who is that? It looks like..."

She broke off. A long moment of silence stretched between us.

"Dub, I'm seeing Tazz. Is that who you're seeing?"

"Yes," I replied, too confused to make sense of

everything. "Check in with the other units just in case," I said and terminated our link.

"Jasmine," I called out, still expecting a trap, "is that you? Can you talk?"

She looked bewildered and unsure of herself. Whatever she had been through couldn't have been pleasant. She looked back at Dennis, who nodded at her to proceed. She took a few controlled steps towards me. Her gaze moved from my face to my HK-17.

"Yes," she replied meekly. Her brow furrowed as she struggled to recognise me, but she continued to walk towards me all the same.

"I remember her dying," I said to Dennis. "How did you do that to us? Why? Why would you put us through that?"

Dennis lowered his hand slowly but remained rooted in place, clearly sensing how volatile this situation was. I was confused and angry and a lethal shot.

"The first and the second batch of Hollows—to use the colloquial term—wasn't about experimenting with a new form of travel. It was about testing a new type of soldier. One that could do their duty without losing their humanity in the horrors of war. The **MOF** doesn't want mindless, drone-like killing machines. They want real soldiers with real-world experiences and feelings to motivate them to get the job done and come back alive. Altered memories and perceptions, it was believed, could help us build a new breed of soldier. One that encompassed all the joys and sorrows of the Terran experience but make the overall job easier on the human psyche."

"I don't understand."

"Of course, you don't," Dennis said, taking a single step towards me before freezing again. "That's the last of your programming trying to stop the walls in your mind from collapsing. That's why I'm here, Darren. It's my job—and those like me—to serve MARSCORP by maintaining company assets and property. Assets and property like you and your Hollow friends. I'm here to help you."

"So, what? You fill us with these false memories to make the overall experience more bearable? I've got a news flash for you, Dennis. I don't count being abducted and killing giant spiders on another planet as a lot of fun. Let me guess, that's fake, too?"

A smile broke across Dennis' face at that. I switched my attention back to Tazz for a second, who stood a few metres away. Her blank gaze studied every inch of me.

"No, most of that is true. You are on Big Red, and this is 1976. The only major things we've kept from you are Tazz's death and *who* you've been fighting. For the most part, everything else is true."

Something about what he said struck me. I could feel it in the recesses of my mind and in the pit of my stomach. Something about the way he laughed whenever I mentioned the Insectoids. Something that I felt or knew deep down but couldn't bring myself to admit.

"No," I said as the walls began to crumble.

I remembered the ambush, being surrounded by the hostiles, cutting them down relentlessly. I saw the aftermath of the attack on **New Berlin**—their dead littering the outskirts of the colony and intermingling with ours in the Rec. I heard the terrible noise of the screams and roars of pain as they hacked us to pieces in the cavern.

"Try harder," Dennis whispered, taking another step closer. "You're almost there. Let the walls fall down. When they do, we'll help you make sense of it all."

I saw Farmer get cut down and ripped to pieces by

those foul creatures, but the memory shimmered and grew hazy. I watched him die as if it had happened yesterday, but something changed. For a split second, I stood at the ambush site, seeing again the wreckage of the lander and those beasts rushing up from their bug holes. The same fear gripped me as I relayed the live feed back to the section and brought my weapon to bare, firing continuously as they emerged. For one gut-wrenching second, they stopped being Insectoids and turned into Bio-suited humans.

A particle blast hit Farmer in the chest a second before a grenade landed beside his corpse and exploded. As clear as daylight, two human soldiers surged over a pile of rocks and landed on his position, ready to charge our lines under a hail of weapons fire. I remembered tossing a grenade at them and the satisfaction of killing his murderers.

The scene changed, and I struck the ground hard from an explosion; my weapon flew from my hands. Instead of an Insectoid, I felt the weight of another human on me, desperately trying to pull the helmet from my Exo-suit. He pinned me down, but I managed to draw my knife and bury it deep into his unarmoured Bio-suit. He stumbled back, screaming in pain before I finished him off.

"There are no aliens on Big Red, Darren. Just humans killing humans, the way it's always been. We created this narrative to make it easier for you. To help you adapt. We dehumanised the enemy so you wouldn't feel guilt or pain and could return to Kat and Louise without all the baggage from the things you've done. We wanted to spare you that, Darren."

"Humans?" I said, desperately trying to process what I had done. The things I had done. My grip on the HKs trigger waivered as the flood of dark images rushed through my mind.

"We have always been here," Tazz said sadly.

I thought about the assault on the cavern. I could still see the strange carvings on the wall, but they didn't look so alien. I made out ancient and old images, depictions of humans as clear as day. The cavern no longer appeared dark and bleak; it seemed like something reminiscent of an ancient temple, like a relic found in Greece or Egypt. The enemy that flooded the cavern no longer had eight scalpel-pointed legs; they were humans, every one of them. They rushed to get their children out of the way as their soldiers counterattacked. They leapt over their dead, firing their own particle weapons and mowing us down. I winced at the pain of one of their home-made particle weapons cutting through my leg and recalled how Smack dragged me out, right before we destroyed their millennia-old temple.

"What have I done?" I said, sickened to the core as the faces of my victims floated to the surface of my mind. I lowered my weapon, too dazed, disgusted, and overwhelmed to think straight. I dropped to my knee to steady myself.

"You did what was necessary," Dennis said, close enough to place his hand on my armoured shoulder. "You did what we programmed you to do. You protected the interests of Terra against the Native Martians. They're human in the most basic sense, but they pose a threat to our security. Thanks to your actions, the war is all but over. We didn't want you to know any of this. If you stand down, we can make it all go away, just as we did with Tazz."

I forced myself to look at Tazz, and she stared back at me. A part of me hoped it was true, that she couldn't remember me or the rest of us. I didn't want her to know what monsters we had become.

"Stand down, Darren. Let us correct our mistake. We owe you that much."

Dennis continued looking at me but held his right

DAMIEN LARKIN

hand up and waved it towards the door. A dozen Exo-suited **MOF** soldiers made their way up the steps outside the main door, with their weapons trained at me and at our positions above.

"Dub," Noid called, "they're moving towards the main entrance. You ready?"

For the longest moment, I didn't know how to respond. I was a killer, a murderer. I had butchered people in cold-blood without even the courtesy of knowing why or remembering them. Every part of me felt sick and numb. I thought about staying there, letting them capture me. I wanted the memories to go away and never resurface, but that felt too easy. The anger locked deep down in me bubbled to the surface.

I hated everything about the **MOF** and every single person affiliated with it. I wanted to burn and destroy everything, to erase its name from history, to avenge the unnamed victims of Terran aggression. I looked at Dennis and then back to Tazz.

"Bring it down."

Uttering the last syllable, I rushed straight for Tazz. Dennis flinched at my sudden actions and dove out of the way. I scooped up a shocked Tazz in my arms and, like an Olympic athlete, bounded for the nearby stairwell as the explosion reverberated through the building. Large chunks of reinforced concrete crashed down from the ceiling, followed by tables, shattered consoles, and fractured debris from the charges Noid had set above us. The room directly above the lobby smashed onto the lobby floor in its entirety, crushing Dennis and sending the approaching **MOF** soldiers hurtling to the ground. From her position above us, Noid and her soldiers opened fire, mowing down approaching soldiers who survived the shock of the blast.

Gripping Tazz, I raced up the stairs, retracing the path I had taken earlier. By the time I reached the fifth floor, I was heaving and my limbs felt like lead, but I was determined to get Tazz to safety.

"They've breached the parameter," one of our units called out as the sound of particle fire and explosions intensified throughout the building.

"They have the roof," another voice shouted over the sound of gunfire. "Pulling back. We'll hold them at the stairwell."

The building rocked from the sheer force of one of the tank cannons blasting. I tried not to think of who had died in that devasting explosion as I navigated the corridors towards the Compression Matrix. Ceiling tiles and lights crashed to the ground as another volley struck the building.

"We can't hold them, there's too many," Noid screamed into her mic as another series of grenade blasts echoed through the corridors.

"All units, all units, retreat to the compression room. All units, pull back," Smack's voice screamed over the comm channel.

I rounded the last corridor as a stream of Second Battalion soldiers rushed through the double doors. Some of them stopped and took aim, but as soon as they noticed who I was, lowered their weapons. Several defenders had erected make-shift barriers along the corridor outside the room. They gestured for me to hurry as another violent blast shook the MARSCORP building. The whole office complex lurched at an impossible angle. For a terrifying moment, I thought the building would collapse in on us, but it held.

I climbed over the barricade as the sound of particle fire closed in on us from every direction. After pushing my way through the double doors, I placed Tazz back on her feet and escorted her to the monitors where Smack and Big Mo monitored the situation. Even with the battle raging, they tore themselves from the monitor long enough to see a beleaguered Tazz, who still didn't seem to know where she was or what was happening. Smack threw her arms around her and gave her a tight hug before returning her attention to the monitors. The sound of particle fire erupted from the corridor outside as our soldiers battled to keep the approaching MOF at bay.

"Doctor, you better be ready to go or there's a bullet with your name on it," Smack roared, tearing herself from the worsening scenes on the security monitors.

I followed Smack as she marched over to the doctor's console, cocked her weapon, and aimed it right at his head. Trembling, he pulled back on a lever, and the machine hummed to life. With a shaking hand, he pointed to a series of plastic boxes stacked neatly beside the Compression Matrix.

"Put the headgear on and take a bed. I have the coordinates locked in. Just tell me when," he said.

Smack nodded, and the first group of volunteers raced to pull on the headbands. An explosion rocked the room, causing one of our soldiers to smash through the double doors and crash into a nearby trolley, knocking it and its wounded occupant over. The few remaining uninjured Second Battalion soldiers kicked the doors open and let out a barrage of particle fire.

"Go now," I said to Smack, realising we had seconds to act.

I threw my arms around Tazz and embraced her as tightly as I could before rushing towards the double doors. A grenade detonation blew the doors off their hinges and knocked the defenders to the ground, and a wave of attackers charged forward. I dropped to a knee and fired my weapon before diving for cover, willing it to recharge faster. A particle blast sliced through the top of the trolley I hid behind, forcing me to roll over and position myself behind a fallen ceiling beam. I raised my weapon and fired again, striking one of the **MOF** soldiers square in the chest. Ducking, I hurled myself behind another trolley as the next wave of enemy fire opened up on me. Keeping as low as possible, I retreated towards the Compression Matrix where those of us still defending rapidly snatched headbands and screamed at Doctor Milton to start the transfer process.

I raised my weapon to shoot again, but my vision was filled with a shimmering green light. A tsunami of pain cut through my body as I fell backwards. I struck the ground hard and roared from the agonising pain that engulfed me. Looking down at my chest, I saw a large chunk of armour missing and a cauterised wound covered in burnt flesh. I let out a scream at seeing so much of me missing and my lungs grew tight. Intense Dan grabbed me by the shoulder and pulled me away from the vicious assault. I felt myself crammed into a confined spot and watched as the lights flickered off from another blast of the tank cannon.

Still screaming, I closed my eyes and faded into the darkness.

"**D**ub, we have the signal," Smack called out and received a rapturous cheer in response.

I breathed a sigh of relief and couldn't help but let out an ecstatic laugh. We had done it. After everything they put us through, all the years of suffering and misery had finally paid off. I turned and flashed the general a victorious smile.

"Details, Smack. I need details."

She paused and studied the incoming report. A smile curled onto her face the more she read.

"Two thirds of the fleet are under our direct control. The other third has been crippled by the package and pose no threat. Operations to mop up have begun, and the fleet has been moved to a defensive parameter around Big Red. The assault group is on course for Terra as we speak. Minimum casualties reported from the bombardment of the colonies. They've all agreed to unconditional surrender. We did it, Dub. We actually did it."

I took a deep breath and raised my hands in triumph, allowing myself to enjoy this moment. In one single operation, we had crippled the MOF and would soon hold all of Terra to ransom.

"You have your son to thank for this gift," I taunted the general. "He volunteered to smuggle the virus aboard the fleet and seized control of the flag ship. That was his personal 'thank you' to you."

The general shook his head vigorously, refusing to believe me. It didn't matter whether he believed me or not; it wouldn't change the fact that Terran supremacy on Big Red was over. MARSCORP would be dismantled, the MOF would be ousted, and after decades of brutal occupation, the planet would be given back to the natives, minus, of course, a small slice for the Hollow Legion. The Native Martians had thought me crazy when I proposed this plan to them well over fifteen years ago, but they would be rejoicing in the streets of New Berlin, Trump Colony, Putinsgrad, New Beijing, and Bolivar City. They would once again walk over their ancestral lands and embrace their newfound freedom.

A sense of relief washed over me. For the first time in a long time, something akin to satisfaction filled me, but I grounded myself; there was still work to be done.

"It's time to move to the next phase," I gloated over the general before walking to one of the consoles and picking up a headset. I signalled to Smack, who tuned me into our force's comm channel.

"All units, all units. This is Echo One-Niner. Switch to back-up channel four. Confirmation code Sierra Tango zero-seven-three-three-four-two. Commence."

Without prompting, Smack switched me over to the back-up channel. I waited a few seconds to confirm everyone had time to make the change before continuing.

"All units, phase two has been a success. All Terran units begin evacuation procedure. You all know the drill. Stay under the radar until we can have you picked up. Second Battalion, hold your positions and maintain radio silence. Echo One-Niner, out."

I took off the headset and watched as the Terran-based guards who sided with us began evacuating C&C and were replaced by the green uniforms of Second Battalion soldiers. Smack took her time to thank them as she left, and I couldn't blame her; she had spent years on Terra with them, grooming them and moving those she could trust into positions that would be of use to us when the day finally came. I didn't envy them, either; when the dust settled, the MOF would realise that this was an inside job. If even one of them was caught before we could negotiate their release in exchange for MOF personnel on Big Red, it could put each individual's freedom in jeopardy.

"You'll never get away with this," Doctor Ling said quietly, shaking her head in disbelief.

"I already have, Doctor. Even if I'm captured or stopped, everything is in motion. We have the fleet. Without it, Terra is powerless."

Grinning like a child, I turned away from the doctor and signalled again to Smack. "Open a channel to New Berlin. Send my compliments to Big Bird. It's time to start wrapping this up. I never thought I'd say this, but I'm looking forward to going home."

I regained consciousness on a hospital trolley, screaming in agony. At first, I thought it had worked, that we had made it back to Terra and escaped Big Red once and for all, but it wasn't meant to be. The **MOF** managed to knock the Compression Matrix offline before our consciousnesses could be transferred home. We were trapped and at the mercy of the very people we had been shooting at.

Thankfully, the death toll for our little insurrection was low. Although both sides suffered casualties, whether out of respect or a fraternal bond buried underneath the surface, both sides had tuned their particle weapons to the lowest frequency. It was strong enough to cut through the reinforced armour of the Exo-suit and cause damage to the flesh beneath it, but not necessarily strong enough to kill someone. Still, the Second Battalion and the **MOF** assault force experienced fatalities, and since we lost, they were going to make us suffer.

They patched us up before turfing us straight into solitary confinement. There was no court martial, no list of charges or a term of incarceration given; we were dragged from our beds, flung into a tiny cell, and left there.

After the first few days, I assumed it was a way to break us. I could hear the screams and shouts of my colleagues from the cells around me, so I figured they would process us one at a time, weeding out the leaders from the followers. I tried to ignore the overwhelming guilt I felt at letting everyone down. I convinced myself that it was the horrors of what I had experienced in the cavern that pushed me over the edge and that I needed psychological help to get back on track, but our jailors ignored me. Not even a week into my stay in that tiny box and I convinced myself my mind was descending into insanity. The cruelties I had visited upon the innocent haunted me until I could think of nothing else. My mood shifted rapidly from overwhelming anger at my captors to deep depression in the blink of an eye.

As the first week merged into the second, I spent my time screaming and shouting until hoarse, demanding to see a superior officer to plead my case. I banged the sides of my hands on the door until they were red-raw. Then I used my fists until the skin around my knuckles split. I didn't care if I risked a beating, I needed to interact with someone, to vent the bile that was building up in me, but our captors exacted their own form of torture on us: They ignored us.

No matter how much we screamed, shouted, roared, or shrieked, we received no admonishments. A gap in the door opened three times a day with our meals. Even then, the guards didn't engage us. If we didn't take our food tray fast enough, they tipped it onto the floor and sealed the door back up.

Eventually, we discovered that if we sat at the bottom of the door and spoke at a certain angle, we could communicate with one another—something to do with the acoustics of the corridor outside, so we co-ordinated a "Day of Noise," where everyone on the cellblock banged the door and shouted in the same rhythm in an attempt to force someone to interact with us, but it was in vain. Wherever they had incarcerated us was far from anyone who cared about our well-being.

I kept track of the days by scratching lines onto the wall with a small piece of stone I found in my cell. Two weeks...three weeks...four weeks passed. We talked with one another to pass the time or sent messages to other cellblocks via a massive game of Chinese Whispers.

"They can't keep us in here forever," I called out to anyone who would listen.

No response came back.

"They'll let us out," I continued. "They have to. Dennis the mind-freak said we're broken. They'll fix us. They'll find away. If they don't, then we'll find a way out of here."

Still, I was met with silence. When I opened my mouth to speak again, a series of echoes bounced back down the corridor in reply. I couldn't identify the sender through the reinforced doors, but the last voice came from a nearby cell.

"Message from Smack: Dub, stand down. Repeat, stand down."

"Message from Dub," I roared back, with anger permeating my voice. "Negative. Will not stand down. Plan needed."

I pressed my ear against the doors and listened as my answer moved from cell to cell back to wherever Smack lay incarcerated. A minute or two longer than normal passed before I got response.

"Message from Smack: Would rather end everything on own terms than lead Second Batt to death. Not a joke. Stand down."

Smack's response cut deep into me; she blamed herself for our predicament. I couldn't say anything more in response, as I held no intentions of pushing her while she dangled at the end of her tether. Instead, I worked out, paced my cell, and then worked out again.

By the end of the second month, someone higher

up the food chain must have felt sympathy for us because they started letting us out for exercise for an hour each week, but it came with a price. We were gagged, bound, and hooded. Chained to one another, they made us walk in a continuous circle before dumping us back into our dungeons. Although it was a welcome respite from that tiny cell, I viewed it as another form of torture, knowing I was so close to my comrades but unable to see them or speak to them in person.

I kept myself going by reaffirming that they would have to let us out one day. We signed a contract. We were soldiers. It was they who had betrayed us. I never asked for this. If they had told me what the program was at the start, I wouldn't have opted to join. They programmed me to be a killing machine and stuck me in a cloned body. What did they expect would happen? They needed to fix us and let us go home.

Desperate for company, I begged, threatened, and cajoled the Voice of God to whisper something to me, to give me words to endure another harsh day locked in a prison of my own thoughts, but for the first time since I heard it speak, it remained silent. I felt more and more alone with every passing minute and struggled daily with the dark thoughts that marched closer to the forefront of my mind.

"Talk to me," I pleaded with the Voice. "Please, you've always been here for me. Always. Just talk to me."

Silence answered.

"Please," I begged, "you've always told me what to do. I listened. I did it. You kept me safe, now keep me sane. Tell me what to do and I'll do it."

Again, the Voice refused to respond.

"Don't ignore me," I shrieked at the top of my lungs. "You're the reason I'm here. You're the reason

I did what I did. I killed those people—men, women, and children. I did it all because you made me."

This time I sensed something stir in the recesses of my mind. It was a whisper, but it sounded as clear as day.

"PROTECT TERRA."

The urge to scream until my lungs exploded overtook me. I balled my hands into fists and imagined tearing a physical version of the Voice limb from limb. I wanted to wrap my hands around its neck and watch it suffocate in its own blood.

"No," I roared, "I protected Terra. I did everything, gave everything for Terra. You owe me. Terra owes me."

A long moment passed before the Voice spoke again, sending me into a spiral of violent fury.

"PROTECT. TERRA."

I bashed my head against the wall, praying the pain would override the guilt, anger, sadness, and frustration. Sometimes, I struck myself so hard that I lost consciousness and would wake up with dried, crusty blood on my forehead and a meal or two dumped on the floor in front of my cell door. I understood then that the guards didn't care if we lived or died. If anything, we would make their lives easier if we killed ourselves. I don't know why, but that thought alone sustained me. None of this was my fault. I was a victim of circumstance. I never asked to be abducted, and I wouldn't end my life to convenience my abductors. They owed me, not the other way around.

As the months turned to years, I let that anger fester. It drove me to train harder, to keep my body fit, active, and lethal. I focused my mind solely on revenge. I wanted to punish those responsible for the plight of my brethren, to avenge the innocent humans hunted and exterminated on Big Red all for the sake

DAMIEN LARKIN

of corporate profits.

Two years of incarceration in and they eased up on the restrictions. They allowed us to have our hour's exercise without the use of shackles and a gag and even turned a blind eye to us talking to one another. When I first saw what was left of the Second Battalion, I was beyond shocked. Everyone gazed blankly at one another; the sparkle of freedom had long since vanished from our eyes. Our skin appeared faded, worn, and loose. Even though I could tell from the bulging biceps and toned figures that most had kept fit to kill time, everyone looked years older, a product of the environment we found ourselves in. For that fleeting hour, we talked, embraced, reminisced, and plotted.

I was the most eager to plan a breakout, but no one else had the stomach for another futile encounter. It saddened me to see my friends so broken that they believed the **MOF** would pardon us one day, set us free, and send us back to Terra. No one listened when I told them they would never let us return home, and I didn't press the matter as hard as I could have. Who was I to tear out the last, lingering thread of hope that sustained them through the day?

After three years we were taken to doctors for medical testing every month, to check our health and to figure out what went wrong with us. No one wanted to believe what I considered to be the most obvious reason; we were abductees here against our will.

Of course, blowback was inevitable. Caged animals always lashed out.

Five years in and they lifted the solitary aspect of our confinement. Under strict supervision, we were escorted to our own prison canteen and given permission to interact. They allowed us out of our cells more often and even gave us access to a limited supply of books. The guards still refused to interact with us apart from ordering us in and out of our cells, but I sensed no hostility from them and didn't recognise their faces. Newcomers, most likely. I filed that away as something I could possibly use to my advantage. They had no doubt been briefed on how dangerous we were, but they hadn't experienced our capabilities first hand. I saw that as an opportunity.

Around this time, I reconnected with Tazz, who was in a cell beside Smack on one of the other blocks. She appeared far more coherent than when I saw her at the MARSCORP building, but she still wasn't— what I'd consider—herself. We talked about home and shared stories about our children before falling into long and uncomfortable silences.

"I'm sorry you got caught up in all of this," I finally said.

She shifted her weight awkwardly and glanced down at her feet. "You've nothing to be sorry for. If I hadn't lost it, we wouldn't be in this mess. We could be home by now."

That comment caught me off guard. I had spent so long blaming the MOF, MARSCORP, even Dennis, that I hadn't considered all the variables. I wondered if Tazz would have been a stabilising force. She could have been that special ingredient that kept us all sane and stable, the voice of reason to talk us down from the brink of mutiny.

"I guess we'll never know," I said with a shrug, unsure of what else to say.

For the first time in a long time, Tazz made eye contact with me, and I saw a twinkle in her eye that reminded me of when we first arrived on Big Red.

"Thanks for trying, Dub," she said, forcing a half-smile. "I wish I'd gotten to know you better. All of you. I wish I'd been there to understand what you're all going through. But I can't imagine what it must have been like for you all. I don't recognise any of you anymore. You're all strangers to me now."

She patted me on the arm and returned to her cell. Reflecting on her words, I figured her response and outlook to be normal, given the circumstances. We had known each other a month before her 'death,' while the rest of us had spent a year bonding and sharing experiences. We had blood on our hands—she didn't.

Smack, Big Mo, Intense Dan, Noid, and I eventually emerged as the leaders of what remained of the Second Battalion. We did our best to keep morale up, organise games, and encourage people to get involved. We even petitioned our jailors for more freedoms or sit-down time with the warden. Nevertheless, suicides were inevitable. Like after the deaths of Lionel and Jacque, a domino effect happened as people decided to give up.

When five comrades passed in a single week, we staged a sit-in in the canteen, demanding access to mental health professionals and more freedoms. Our sit-in could've boiled over into a full-blown prison riot, but the powers-that-be caved in. We were given twenty-four-hour access to doctors and additional liberties such as gym time and recreation. That, at least, confirmed that as much as we were a thorn in the side of the higher-ups, they answered to someone higher up the food chain who didn't want us dead.

A decade in prison came and went. I wish I could say it flew past, but even with our privileges and minor freedoms, it was still prison. We spent countless hours locked away in our tiny cells with nothing to do but think. The memories of Kat and Louise faded over time; I could remember the emotions of the experiences I had with them, but not their faces. That was probably the cruellest thing about my incarceration and the one that hurt the most. I had no photos of them. I had no way of calling them, and even if I did, it was only 1986.

After two decades, they let us out. Without warning, a week after my forty-eighth birthday, the guards herded us after breakfast to the processing centre of our prison. We were locked into large group cells and one-by-one taken out for a medical examination, given a shower and a fresh set of clothes, a wristband with some credits, and assigned a case officer.

The case officers arranged for transport to take us to accommodations, but they refused to answer any questions regarding our abrupt release. After spending so long locked up, I was shocked by the sheer size of the massive dome that covered New Berlin. It stretched far and wide, covering the sky in every direction and reducing me to the size of an ant in comparison. All around, large buildings and towers seemed to have sprung up overnight, and the streets were far more packed with people than I remembered.

Military landers took the remaining few hundred of us in a convoy to a series of buildings at the outskirts of the colony, near the dome parameter. The buildings looked new and freshly painted on the outside, but the area around it appeared strewn in rubbish and litter. Despite the amount of apartment blocks in close proximity, all the doors and windows remained bolted. I couldn't detect any sign of movement or hear the sounds of people going about their daily lives.

They took us in groups to our new home and assigned us apartments, but it became evident that there wasn't enough room for everyone. In the end, five or six of us crammed into apartments designed for two people, setting up beds on the floor or wherever we found space. It wasn't ideal, but I certainly preferred it over my tiny cell, and I knew pretty much everyone well enough that it wasn't a shock.

We enjoyed the novelty of freedom at first. We took turns taking long showers or baths and explored the building and surrounding area, always expecting soldiers to leap out and drag us back into custody. But apart from irregular visits from our case officers, no one cared what we did.

We visited cheap restaurants, drank alcohol, and ventured farther and farther into the colony to see how much it had changed. A lot of the old buildings remained intact, but many were dwarfed by the newer skyscrapers and apartment blocks. Apart from the outskirts where we resided, we heard the German accent less and less, and practically all the signs and advertisements were in English the more we went into the centre of New Berlin.

After a few days of acclimating to this newer, updated-version of New Berlin, our money started to run out. Along with Smack, I paid a visit to the case officers' station at the prison to find out if someone in the MOF could send us home or at least give us the back-pay we were promised for our tour of duty. Within five minutes, we were escorted off the premises at gunpoint. They didn't even let us past the first checkpoint at the MOF Installation, so we had no choice but to fend for ourselves.

Despite the colony's explosive growth during the two decades of our imprisonment, jobs were scarce. We weren't allowed to leave New Berlin for one of the other colonies, forcing us to scour the city in droves looking for work, but everywhere we went, we were denied. Newbie MOF recruiters who had no idea who we were enticed us to enlist in the newly reorganised

MOF. Some of us were tempted, if only to see how far we'd get through the security checks, but that wasn't a realistic option. Even if they did want us back, we had been deeply scarred by the deceptions they programmed into us and had no desires to go back and shoot poorly-armed natives for a pay check.

As our credits dried up and our bellies began to rumble, it became clear that we needed to find work soon, so we looked closer to home. The fringe areas along the **New Berlin** dome had become the area where the original German settler population relocated to make way for the post-war arrivals. The Volk were seen as an underclass, a relic of a long-over war and marginalised, like us. Following their failed rebellion, their positions of power eroded over time and their culture actively suppressed in the name of assimilation. That didn't bother me; the fact that they had been allowed any position following the Allied invasion in 1954 had always been weird to me, but it presented an opportunity.

The German settlers despised us. Many remembered the atrocities we had committed against their population during the rebellion, but they also feared us, which prevented retaliation. To eke out a living, many of them had turned to organised crime, ranging from boot-legging and counterfeiting to drugs and weapons smuggling. With such profitable yet dangerous business, it made sense to have efficient and capable soldiers on the payroll. So, we became muscle for hire.

From the start, we made it clear we weren't contract killers and wouldn't engage in violence against any civilians, which brought ridicule, but we managed to get low-level jobs as bouncers and security for dive-bars. In a short amount of time, our reputations began to precede us. Even after two decades of imprisonment, the countless hours of Rig

243

training were still engrained in us, so no situation caught us off guard. Even when outnumbered, we were like crazed berserkers, using all that pent-up frustration and anger to dispatch anyone who got in our way.

It took time, but we eventually earned the grudging respect of the local Marsies. However, the jobs we worked were still low-key and barely enough to provide for everyone. We pooled our resources and avoided starvation, but it was clear we needed to earn more if we were to survive long-term on Big Red.

Around this time, fierce debates raged throughout the remnants of Second Battalion about what our future should be and if we should find a way of returning home. Although the majority wanted to make our future efforts based on returning to Terra, no one could agree on how. Even if we smuggled ourselves aboard a ship, we'd return to a timeline when our actual selves would be children and we'd do so as middle-aged adults, with no possibility of rebuilding our original lives.

Others argued for securing access to the Compression Matrix again to have us sent back to 2018, but we were nowhere near ready to undergo such a risky operation. The remainder opted to remain on Big Red and build new lives for themselves. Already dozens of couples paired off after our release from prison and managed to find steady work. In the end, it was outside-the-box thinking from Smack and a plan by me, Big Mo, and, to some degree, Noid that set everything in motion.

Smack, although worn down from our incarceration, still remained bitter over the MOF's betrayal. She wanted to hit back more than anything but was practical enough to know that we were in no position to seriously threaten them. Instead, she proposed we take all our innate knowledge and use it to build ourselves a future on Big Red and position ourselves to strike back at the MOF once we had the resources.

"It's simple," she started, gesturing with open palms as she spoke, "we cover all our bases. Provide for those who want to stay, those who want to return to Terra, and those who want to hit back at the MOF."

"I don't care what we do," Noid said, barely paying attention. "I just want to earn some cold, hard cash. Tons of it."

"Agreed," Smack said, "but we're never going to get rich breaking up bar fights. Think. What's the one thing we're all good at, even after all these years?"

"Drinking?" I asked half-jokingly, raising the whiskey bottle in my hand in mock salute.

"There's that," Smack replied before returning attention to the entire group. "Think about it. Virtual months spent in the Rigs, proper combat experience, and, our skills are still honed. What could we do with our skills to earn a decent living?"

She had the group's attention now. We stopped joking and glanced at one another while we thought about her words.

"What void in the market can we fill?" Smack pressed.

Big Mo's face lit up as a realisation dawned on him. "I was doing door work down at Kaiser Wilhelm's yesterday. You all know Fritz the bartender? He gets into this group chat with a bunch of half-drunk Volk about all the new arrivals. Tourists mostly. Within minutes the entire pub is giving out stink about them."

"So, what?" Noid snorted. "Everyone gives out about the newbies. They're a bunch of rich a-holes with more dollars than sense. They come here thinking they'll see a brave new world and end up staring at a giant dome."

"We've all interacted with them in one capacity or another," Smack continued, trying to mask her excitement. "What's the one thing they constantly complain about?"

We looked at one another, knowing the answer.

"They give out about wanting to see more of Big Red rather than being stuck here," I said, as the dots connected in my mind. "You're proposing we find a way of cashing in on that using our skills? How? Walk up to the MOF guards on the parameter and ask them to let us take a bunch of tourists out on a nice little picnic?"

I said that with a laugh, but Smack tapped a finger on her nose and nodded. "Nail on the head, Dub. We take them out as their security. We rent a lander, bribe the guards, and go for an excursion. You need to be rich and connected to book passage to Big Red, that's why it's all businessmen, politicians, and high-ranking ex-military. We can charge them whatever we want, and they'll pay."

"We'll need guns and armour," Noid said, warming to the idea.

"The guns aren't a problem," Big Mo said, stroking his beard, "but if we're going anywhere outside New Berlin, we'll need military-grade equipment, not just something we can pick up in a gun shop. I think I may know a friend of a friend who could help us out, for the right price."

It took time to work out the details and months to save up enough credits, but we eventually found a sympathetic MOF Quarter Master who agreed to sell us outdated surplus equipment under the radar. Of course, outdated by his standards meant that we were getting the exact same type of Exo-suits we wore originally, but it took a lot of work to bring them up to standard. Getting our hands on weapons wasn't an issue at all since, given the nature of Big Red, there were no gun-control policies, even for people like us with criminal records. We heard whispers from a few friendly voices in the MOF that the powers-that-be didn't like what we were up to and had stepped up surveillance on us, but we weren't breaking any laws and we made sure that we didn't pose a threat in any way. At least not yet.

We landed our first contract escorting a Chinese Communist Party official to an area about sixty klicks east of New Berlin to the site where his nephew had been ambushed and killed years ago. It cost us ninety-five percent of the contract fee to bribe the guards to let us out of the colony and we had to dig into our own near-drained funds to rent a suitable lander, but it went off without a hitch and gave us an air of legitimacy. It started as a trickle, but we gradually began building a client list, refined our methods, and turned a profit.

Most of our clients in the early days were ex-military, politicians, and even a few scientists, but they were all wealthy and paid us well to facilitate their safe passage out of the colony. Usually, they had a specific agenda, wanting to visit certain places, but others were here for the novelty because they were rich enough and could afford it. So, for them we organised group tours, taking them around to various historical sites or places of interest.

It wasn't always easy; I dreaded having to shoot at the natives again, but it was inevitable that we would cross each other's path. One in every three excursions involved a firefight, but these were low-level skirmishes and casualties low. Rich, adrenaline-junkie visitors even got a kick out of it, which increased our business by word of mouth. We refused to deliberately put ourselves or the visitors in danger by provoking the natives into a fight, but since they considered all of Big Red as theirs, firefights were unavoidable.

Eventually, Hollow Point Defence—as we called our company—became a part of the social fabric of the colony. The **MOF** top brass made it clear they still didn't like or trust us, but they couldn't do anything about it. We made sure to stay within the confines of the law as much as possible, but it was our professionalism that they grudgingly admired. Our clients loved the services provided, and those who were informed on Martian matters were fascinated at the concept of being protected by cloned 'super' soldiers. We did what Terran law forbade the MOF to do and plugged a gap in the market. The money rolled in, we paid our taxes, and we bought equipment off the **MOF,** which enjoyed earning credits on the side, so everyone was happy.

Smack became our CEO, looking after the business end of things. Although she trained with us daily, as much as she enjoyed being our leader, she'd had her fill of leading soldiers on the ground and the life or death consequences of her decisions. No matter how much I tried to talk to her about it, she still blamed herself for our imprisonment and the deaths of those who fought in our insurrection. Running a business was a welcome reprieve for her.

Big Mo became our 'face guy.' Out of all of us, he was the most eloquent when he wasn't spouting conspiracy theories, so we slapped fancy suits on him, forced him to shave, and made him our point of contact with potential new customers. He even used a refined English accent, making him sound aristocratic, and new clients ate it up.

Noid was enthusiastic about our new operation at first, but after the novelty wore off, she started to lose interest. She began to focus more on local matters and urged us to get more involved in the underworld side of **New Berlin** as a way of making serious money.

The colony didn't have a major crime problem; it was mostly confined to the marginalised German Volk sections of society, but the few German-led crime gangs were small, petty operations. They relied on us for muscle, and Noid suggested we turn that muscle against them and take over.

The majority of us disagreed, but she still took a small cadre of followers and left us one day. I can't say I was heartbroken she abandoned us. I personally never liked her, but she was one of us. Still, it was her decision and, in the end, despite the violent acts she committed, she became an integral part of our later plans.

Intense Dan and I ran the day-to-day operations, leading tours and commanding patrols that escorted clients, but the intensity that earned his nickname had long since faded. After they had let us interact with each other in prison, Dan confessed that his father held a top brass position in the UEAF and he was sure they left us there lingering as an oversight. As the years passed, with no sign of help from his old man, Dan grew more bitter than intense, but he remained a good soldier.

We worked together well as a team, splitting our duties and taking out an equal amount of patrols. Back in our newly-rented company headquarters, we split our other roles, too. Dan looked after the logistics and payroll, making sure we had all the equipment we needed, maintaining it, placing new orders, and ensuring everyone got paid on time. I looked after our soldiers, feeding them and training them on new tactics or equipment we picked up.

Between casualties, injuries, and retirements after Noid and her followers left, our numbers dwindled the first year. Enough soldiers remained to complete our contracts, but we needed replacements if we wanted to expand our operations. Thankfully, a lot of the second batch Hollows—who hadn't taken part in our insurrection but sympathised with us—heard of the high pay and working conditions and swarmed us with applications when we posted the jobs.

We eventually absorbed these in various roles and also began taking on ex-MOF soldiers who, for one reason or another, chose to remain on Big Red after their tour of duties expired. It was inevitable that some of them would be moles spying on us, but we took precautions and, thanks to our own network of informants within the MOF, could easily pay a bribe to find out who was genuine and who wasn't. Even retired Captain Lockhart showed up for an interview. He sported a scraggly, stained beard and reeked of alcohol, but I figured it might be handy having a pilot on the payroll, so I hired him on the condition he kept the singing and music down.

After two years in operation, we posted record profits and even picked up contracts from MARSCORP. The execs we transported were nervous and jittery at the prospect of protection from the same people who had ransacked and destroyed their building over two decades ago, but the MOF remained bound to the UEAF's rules and regulations. More secretive—or frankly, illegal—operations forced them to rely on us. We charged them treble the amount for our services, knowing there wasn't a rival company even remotely capable of carrying out what they wanted, and ferried them across Big Red.

Most of these late-night excursions involved secretive meetings between MARSCORP execs from the other colonies at abandoned outposts, but others were survey missions close to the native's borders. We drove out in force and never lost a single MARSCORP exec, as tempting as it was, although we inevitably took casualties ourselves. It was one of those early morning meetings that would forever crystallise what

I would do, once and for all, to enact my revenge.

It started like any other job. We donned our Exo-suits, checked and stored our equipment on one of our landers, crammed ammunition into every available suit compartment, and waited for Big Mo to bring us the clients. We had renovated one of the landers specifically for MARSCORP personnel, building a dividing wall in the transport compartment, segregating them—apart from one or two guards who sat with them—from the bulk of the patrol. This put the MARSCORP execs at ease and allowed me to brief the team en route. I showed them the holographic map, pointed out our mission location, and explained it was a standard meeting and survey.

The target was a small mining facility located dangerously near the border. It had long since been abandoned due to the frequent skirmishes, and it was our job to secure it, allowing the execs to meet up with MARSCORP top brass from Trump Colony. At the same time, their scientists would take soil samples and drill for the artefacts MARSCORP remained so fixated in finding on Big Red. Due to the proximity to the border, I opted to take a full platoon and gave everyone their individual orders. We moved at night, hoping to use the darkness as cover. The plan was to get in and out without drawing any attention to ourselves.

After a couple of hours spent traveling across planet, we arrived at the location and kicked into action. With my HK-17 at the ready, I led the team into the mining facility and checked it room by room. Thankfully, it had been a small mining operation, so once we were certain no one lurked inside, we secured all the entrances and exits and began moving our heavy weapons into place to form a defensive parameter. With everything locked down tight, we escorted our MARSCORP guests inside to await their colleagues. Outside the base, a patrol protected the scientists who eagerly got to work.

Once the visiting execs from Trump Colony arrived, I took my leave and began doing the rounds on the parameter. Even after years of carrying out missions like this, I always got edgy being so close to the border. The scars of past battles etched onto the walls in the form of particle beam hits did little to soothe me, but I kept my cool and frequently checked in on everyone. I wanted this to be one of those days when everyone got home safely.

The meeting went off without a hitch. A few hours later, as the sun started to rise on Big Red, they wrapped things up. After the Trump colony execs departed, we led our own guests back to the lander and packed our equipment. The scientists were finishing up their work when the first shots rang out.

Everyone dropped at the same time and brought their weapons to bear. We checked to see where the enemy attack came from, but after a few more shots echoed around us and no one saw anything, we realised we weren't the target. Although we were no longer MOF, we had a long-standing relationship with a few bribe-loving officers who allowed us limited access to the MOF satellites (and only when we took fire on a mission), so I quickly relayed my request and within seconds gained access to the satellite feeds. I identified six hostiles moving down a sloping hill to the west of the mining facility. At first, it looked as though they were charging right at it, which didn't make sense. If our sharpshooter still sat on the roof, we could have easily wiped out all six of them in seconds. Even more strangely, a gap existed between the two at the front and the remaining four. The satellite feed recognised them as hostiles most likely due to the Bio-suits they wore, but I had a scary thought they were escaped **MOF** prisoners.

Not wanting to risk leaving a possible ally behind, I ordered the bulk of my platoon to establish a defensive parameter around the lander while I took a two-person team around the far-side of the mining facility to investigate. We moved at full speed but stayed as close to the rusting facility walls as possible for cover. Concealing ourselves in the shadows, we rounded the base of the facility and came into view of the approaching hostiles.

All six wore the make-shift, red-stained Bio-suits the natives used and, as the feed had indicated, two were out front while a group of four closed in on them, wildly firing their particle weapons. I cocked my HK-17 and raised it to take aim but paused when I zoomed in on the visors of the two at the front. One's stature suggested they were a child, and the other was a woman who gripped the youngster's hand tightly as they raced over the rocky Martian terrain. Neither carried weapons. The other four kept their weapons raised as they ran, taking turns firing pot shots in between recharges.

The Voice of God, dormant these days—except for when I found myself under attack—urged me to shoot them all or withdraw completely. For a split second, I thought about following the Voice's advice and withdrawing; this wasn't my concern and all six looked to be natives, so why involve myself and put the lives of my soldiers at risk? But at the last minute, I looked at the two fleeing natives and saw terror engraved on their faces. It made me think of long-faded memories of Kat and Louise, so I decided to act.

After signalling to my comrades, we emerged from the shadows of the mining facility just as two approached. They stopped dead in their tracks, their bodies frozen in terror at the sight of three Exo-suited soldiers with heavy armour. The woman's face exploded into a terrified scream as she dropped to her knees and wrapped her arms protectively around the child. Thankfully, her actions gave us the perfect line of fire to target her pursuers.

"Stand down," I screamed as I pointed my weapon at the lead pursuer.

I know a lot of people would suggest shooting first, but I couldn't bring myself to do it without direct provocation. Even if that meant my life, I owed the natives that much after everything I had done to them. As always, though, they responded by opening fire. Lucky for us, the natives were terrible shots, even at close distance, so every particle blast went wide. We responded in kind, and three of them slammed into the Martian soil with holes blown into their chests. The last one hit the ground for cover and fired, missing again.

My soldiers switched to standard fire to let their own HKs recharge and broke off to flank the attacker while I grabbed the two cowering natives and tried to move them out of harm's way. They shrieked and feebly tried to fight me off. Shouldering my weapon, I grabbed them and pushed them towards the mining facility as fast as I could.

I kept an eye on the action via my rear helmet camera as I ran and watched one of my soldiers take a particle shot to the stomach. At the same time, her colleague killed the last native. A wave of guilt hit me as it always did when one of my soldiers died, but I supressed it. We weren't out of danger, yet—the natives used underground caves and caverns to shield themselves from our satellite detection systems and rarely travelled in groups of less than ten this close to the border. I reached the mining facility, stowed the two terrified natives, and urged my other soldier to hurry. He had picked up the body of his fallen comrade and was rushing back to my position when another series of shots echoed from somewhere to the south. He crashed dead to the ground from a lucky shot with barely enough time to scream as all hell broke loose around us.

I checked the satellite feed and saw at least three dozen hostiles stream out of an undisclosed location to our south and charge the lander parameter. The first volley of shots came dangerously close to the lander. Since it was our only way back, the hostiles wanted to destroy it. Then they would call for reinforcements and break us through sheer weight of numbers. I had seen them use this tactic plenty of times before. Although we were better equipped and armoured, if they had enough soldiers nearby, it could be done. Giving us fifty-fifty in a fight like that, I ordered the lander to withdraw and get the execs back to safety.

I ignored the objections hurled at me from my subordinates and commanded them to pull out. I watched as the last of my soldiers streamed into the lander and beat a hasty retreat into the distance. At around the same time, the natives' jamming signal came online, blocking any chance of communicating with my team or tracking enemy movements. But I knew once the lander was out of range of the jammer, my soldiers would signal for reinforcements. Dan would most likely load up every available soldier onto our refurbished troop transport to spearhead a rescue, but that would take hours. I had more immediate problems.

I turned to my new charges and found them

trembling under my gaze.

"I'm not going to hurt you," I tried to say as calmly as the situation would allow. "Do you understand? I'm not your enemy."

They looked at one another with eyes as large as saucers and gripped each other tighter.

"Terrans kill," the woman replied in heavily-accented English. Her voice shook with fear.

I risked a glance south and saw the hostiles cautiously moving towards the mining facility. "We need to move," I whispered. "Your friends will find us if we don't hide."

"No friends," she replied with venom.

"Okay, but we still need to hide. Follow me."

I extended a hand to help the woman up, and she flinched at the sight of it. After a moment of looking at my hand and face, she extended her own shaky hand and allowed me to pull her up. I nodded towards a nearby entrance, opened the airlock, and led them inside. I still couldn't be sure natives weren't inside the facility, so I moved as quickly as possible towards the lower levels. I had personally inspected the mining station hours ago and remembered the vacant processing centres in the depths of the installation. There were plenty of dark and isolated rooms that we could stash ourselves away in and, if needs be, mount a defence, at least until reinforcements arrived.

We navigated into the heart of the facility, moving down dimly lit stairs and through narrow, darkened corners until I found a room that would serve our needs. Using the night vision filter on my visor to see in the faint light, I created a barricade out of discarded furniture and equipment and bolted the door tight. Confident we were as secure as we could be, I positioned myself in line of sight of the door and listened for the tell-tale signs of approaching enemies.

Hours passed with no sign of friend or foe. I knew

my team would search every inch of this building when they arrived, so when they didn't, I began to fear the worst. I had calculated that even with the range of a jammer and the time to organise and transport a rescue mission, they should have arrived at least an hour ago. Martian night would fall within a few hours, and I certainly didn't relish being this close to the border without backup. To remain undetected by any native search parties, I'd barely spoken to the woman and child since we barricaded ourselves. When I did speak, they flinched.

"I need to go up and check around," I said, gesturing to the higher levels. "Stay here and I'll be back soon."

"No," the woman replied, less fearful than she had sounded earlier. "We go with Terran."

"Darren." I sighed as I shouldered my weapon and stretched my aching muscles. "My name is Darren."

She cocked her head to study me. Even in the dull light I could see she was trying to understand my words. Her enunciation was thick and heavy, unlike anything I had ever heard before, so I assumed my own Irish accent was as difficult for her to understand.

"We go with Terran," she said firmly.

Shrugging, I readied my weapon and gestured for them to be quiet and stay close. Then I unbolted the door and checked the corridor. I didn't like the idea of two unarmed civilians so close to me, but I understood their desire not to be left alone.

I retraced my steps, scanning every room as we passed, and made my way through the upper levels. I listened intently for any hint of noise and continued to switch through the various filters of my helmet to detect any semblance of an enemy or allied presence, but the facility was as sealed up as we had left it. Confident there was no one else inside the compound, I led my guests to the roof and studied the horizon but found no sign of movement. I tried to send an uplink request and a distress signal, but both were blocked by the ongoing signal jamming.

It wasn't unusual for natives to leave jamming devices around places the MOF frequented or after they had pulled out of an area, but it didn't mean they'd departed, either. I moved us into the Command Centre of the mining facility where I could try to rig the communications system to cut through the interference. After re-pressurising the room, I raised my helmet visor and took a deep breath of stale, Martian air. I smiled at the woman and child to show them it was safe. They nervously undid their own decrepit helmets and took in cautious breaths.

Placing as much distance between me and them as possible, they took seats near one of the deactivated consoles and wrapped their arms around each other. I sensed they didn't perceive me as an immediate threat, but they were wary of me and my intentions. I couldn't blame them. Following my release from prison, I started to grasp the nature of the conflict on Big Red and had dived into as many reports and news articles as I could to get a better picture of what was going on. We were the occupiers—the colonisers. My charges probably grew up with horror stories of the Terrans; indeed, they had probably lost people close to them from the actions of people like me. They were right to be wary of me. I was a tool of genocide used against them and their people, no matter how much I tried to deny it or blame someone else for my actions.

Exo-suits contain built-in water and liquid food supplies for long term missions, but we also carry around limited solid food supplies and water canisters just in case, so I opened one of my suit's compartments and pulled out compressed protein bars and a water bottle. The woman and child eyed me suspiciously, so I took a drink from the water canister and nibbled on the protein bar to show that they weren't poison. They accepted them with trepidation. After taking small bites to start, they devoured them. Smiling, I gave them more.

Although I should have thrown myself straight into my work, I couldn't help but study them as I sucked on a liquid protein meal. They looked physically human, but something I couldn't quite place made them come across as unusual to me. The woman, although tall, looked surprisingly thin-faced, which gave me the impression her Bio-suit made her appear bulkier than she was.

She had lightly tanned skin, and her eyes were full and deep. They soaked up everything they saw, and I felt a strange level of discomfort when she looked at me. Although she studied me as I studied her, I sensed she was looking through me rather than at me. From her body language and similar facial traits, I guessed the young girl to be her daughter and placed her at around ten or eleven years old. Like her mother, she too had deep, round eyes that absorbed everything, but rather than the discomfort I experienced from her mother's gaze, a strange, curious fascination emanated from her gaze when she looked at me.

Resting my HK beside me, I started to work on the communications console to see if I could boost its signal. I was by no means an engineer, but we tried to upskill our people in the company as much as possible. I had sat in on plenty of classes, so I hoped I could recollect something of use.

"Why were your people trying to kill you?" I finally said, making sure to keep the two natives within my peripheral vision as I worked.

A long moment of silence ensued before the woman answered. "They are not my people," she responded defensively. "They are outcasts who prey on the vulnerable."

"I admit, I don't know as much about your people as I'd like to," I said, trying to flash a friendly smile as I worked, "but I thought you were all on the same side? You know, united in a common cause..."

I trailed off, unable to finish that sentence. I nearly said "against us." I cursed myself for being stupid enough to point out our differences at the same time as trying to get them to relax around me. The woman eyed me but didn't pick up on it.

"Some of us have discarded the old ways. They forsake the words of those before them and wish to be strong and feared and powerful. They wish to be like Terrans, so they act like Terrans."

I sent a test signal and studied one of the consoles to see if it cut through the interference. After a few seconds, the read-out showed as negative, so I boosted the power before giving it another attempt. I upped the power ever so slightly and sent another signal before turning to face the two natives.

"Where do you come from?" I asked, unsure of what else to say or do in response.

"Why?" the woman asked, cocking her head again. Her eyelids tightened as if to gaze at me with laser focus.

"So I can take you home. Once my friends come back for me, we can take you to wherever you live, back to your people."

"Terran lies," she hissed.

The signal came back as negative again. In a desperate attempt at communication, I upped the bandwidth and sent another.

I faced the woman. "You don't have to trust me, and I don't expect you to, but I helped you when I could have left. I'm offering to take you home safe, but if you would rather go alone, there's the exit. I won't stop you."

I turned in time to see the last signal succumb

to the jamming device. It was either exceptionally powerful or within proximity so that no matter how much I boosted the signal, it wouldn't cut through. That didn't leave me with a lot of choices.

I knew Smack, Dan, and Mo wouldn't leave me out here. Even if they thought I was dead, they would still show up to retrieve my body, but they were long overdue. Night would be approaching in a few hours. Even though I was confident I could secure myself in the Command Centre of the mining facility, it wasn't an ideal location. A few concentrated particle shots would blow a hole in any of the doors, and there was no telling if the natives would return looking for the woman and child. I could hold them off, but if they stormed this position, a single HK-17 wouldn't keep them at bay. As I tried to figure out what to do, the woman broke her silence.

"We live west of this place. On the higher ground."

"Do you have any way of communicating with your people to pick you up?" I asked, pointing at her worn-out Bio-suit.

"No."

"Can you reach your home before dark?"

"Yes."

I took a momentary break from our thrilling conversation and weighed my options again. The logical thing would be to stay in the mining outpost and await rescue, but I didn't have a good feeling about the fact that no one had shown up yet. It would be dangerous moving into hostile territory, but the farther I got away from this place, the better chance I had of escaping the jamming signal and calling for help. Forward Bases resided roughly a hundred klicks to the north and south of our current position. Although the MOF wouldn't be too keen on rescuing a contractor, they'd be obliged to send a pick-up for me, or at least relay a message back to the company.

"What are the chances of running into a hostile patrol on the way back to your home?" I asked the woman.

She squinted as she processed my question. Finally, she answered, "They will have lookouts in the mountains watching for Terrans to come back to this place. They will not be watching the passes."

"Okay," I nodded as I clicked down my helmet visor. "I'll take you back to your people and then call mine. You lead the way."

"Terran lies," the woman spat. "Will not show you where my people live. Would rather die than let Terrans see where we live. Terrans send fire from the sky to kill my people."

For a moment, I considered rubbing my temples in frustration but that wouldn't help.

"Fine. I'll take you as close to your home as you feel comfortable that also doesn't get me clipped in the process. Fair deal?"

The woman gave me a hard stare in response but pulled on her helmet all the same and assisted the child with hers. I scribbled a cryptic message onto the Command Centre walls, knowing Dan and the team could decipher it. Moments later, we exited the mining facility. A lot of flat ground rested between us and the hills to the west, but that was the same in every direction, so I hoped any potential spotter would think we were natives scavenging for supplies. Nevertheless, I still ushered them on as quickly as I could and felt a bit more secure as we trekked over the mountain passes where I was prepared to hurl myself behind a natural barrier the moment we came under fire.

In between checking the satellite feed and trying to get a clear channel, I tried to make small talk, but the woman refused to engage. Nearly every response carried derogatory remarks about Terrans, so I gave up. I made mental notes of the various landmarks we passed as we walked, figuring it would come in handy if I had to bail out in a rush, but nothing appeared too far out of the ordinary. Once you've seen one rock formation on Big Red, you've seen them all.

The natives walked ahead of me, winding through an unseen path which, by luck or design, didn't include any good ambush spots. With every pace I took further into enemy territory, I cursed myself secretly. The natives didn't use living decoys to lure us into traps, mainly because of the MOF's shoot first policy. I hated the thought of being known as the first sucker who got captured that way.

After about an hour, we got outside the jamming signal's range. I was trying to patch another satellite uplink request through when the woman stopped dead in her tracks and faced me. Out of instinct, I raised my weapon and aimed it directly at her, but she shot me a look of pure loathing. Placing her hand on her hips, she glared at me until I lowered my HK.

"This is close enough, Terran," she hissed.

"You're welcome."

She looked me over curiously. When she opened her mouth to speak, a series of particle shots struck the ground around us. I dove behind the nearest cover I could find and took aim at the native woman, expecting her to charge at me as part of an elaborate ruse, but she gripped the child and protectively threw herself over her, crying out in fear from the sudden barrage of shots.

Another volley of particle blasts sent a fountain of copper sand and rock splashing over my visor, but all their shots went wide. I slammed my left arm console, praying for the uplink request to go through and hedged my bets by sending an all-out distress signal, too. Through some miracle, I gained immediate access to the satellite feed. Even though it was slow and patchy, I could make out a small group of hostiles a few hundred metres to the south and closing in fast.

"How far to your home?" I shouted over the din of particle fire. I waited for an opportunity in between weapons blasts to raise my assault rifle and fire a well-aimed shot, taking down one of the approaching attackers.

The woman looked at me with that same expression of absolute terror she wore when I first found her. But despite fearing whoever hunted her, I could tell she feared me and my kind more.

"It's your choice," I called out as I fired and missed. "We're sitting ducks in this position. We need to pull out. That involves either you coming with me or, if you're close enough, making a break for home while I cover you. You don't have time to think this one out."

For emphasis, I fired another particle shot, hitting one of the hostiles in the chest, and then switched to standard ammo while my HK-17 recharged.

"There," the woman finally said and nodded towards a small cave opening roughly two hundred meters east, off the dirt path.

"Stay low," I roared as I fired another shot at our attackers, "and stay behind me. My suit can absorb the particle blasts."

That wasn't necessarily true, but I would have said anything to keep a panicked mother and child from freaking out any more in a firefight.

I reached into one of my Exo-suit's compartments, pulled out three smoke grenades, and tossed them towards the enemy to mask our escape. A few seconds later, dark smoke filled our vision, but my visor homed in on the enemy's body heat. Firing another particle blast, I scored a direct hit. I lifted the woman to her feet and placed my left arm around the child to shepherd her along. Keeping my body between them and our attackers, I shoved them down the path, with my weapon trained on the enemy's direction.

We were about halfway there by the time the ambushers stormed our previous, smoke-screened position. After some confusion, they spotted us and opened fire again.

"Go!" I shouted. Dropping to a knee, I emptied my magazine clip.

Energy blasts erupted around me in response, getting dangerously close to striking me, but I needed to buy the woman and child a few more seconds. I tracked them on my helmet's rear-view camera and watched as they bounded closer to the cave entrance.

At the same time, all hell broke loose.

I dispatched two more of the native attackers just as I lost my satellite feed to interference. Noting at least three more hostiles were out there, I retreated towards a more defendable spot. The woman and the child disappeared into the cave entrance, and I allowed myself a victorious smile before I was hit with a particle blast.

I didn't see who did it or what direction it came from, but a heartbeat later, I found myself lying on my back with a burning sensation across my right side. I lifted my head up enough to see that it wasn't a direct hit, but the particle charge had punctured the right side of my Exo-suit and seared my flesh. As if seeing the damage was enough to trigger the pain, a horrible burning sensation clawed at my flesh and cut deep into my insides.

My suit automatically began repairing the damage to itself with its Smart Fibre technology, quickly sealing the breach, but a massive gap remained in my exterior armour.

I tried to pull myself out of harm's way, knowing the enemy would be upon me soon, but my limbs felt as heavy as lead from the shock, the blood loss, or both. Nor could I find my HK to make my last stand. Condemning myself for my stupidity, I pulled out a plasma grenade and kept it close to my chest as a final present for my captors. My armour could easily absorb the blast, but with my side dangerously exposed, it would finish me off.

I thought of Kat and Louise and knew they would be proud that I saved a mother and child. Resigning myself to my fate, I cursed Big Red one last time and readied myself for the inevitable. Footsteps approached from behind me. I turned to see two Bio-suited natives armed with crude-looking particle weapons taking aim at me. I feebly tried to lift the grenade, but my body refused to act. Light-headed, my vision grew blurry. The sounds of weapons fire and shouting grew distant and faded into the ever-approaching blackness that absorbed me into it. My last thoughts were of how much I hated this damn planet.

When I awoke, I thought I was back in New Berlin, but as the events of the ambush raced through my mind, I doubted the likelihood of that. Remaining perfectly still and keeping my eyes closed to appear unconscious, I trained my ears to see if I could detect anyone. After a minute or two, I opened my eyes enough to get my bearing and tilted my head to the side to look for any tell-tale indications of where I was. I spied a small wooden table and chairs to my right but could see nothing else of interest. Out of my peripheral vision, I did note that I wasn't wearing my Exo-suit, which I took to be a bad sign. No doubt my captors would have fun shredding it to pieces for spare parts.

"There is no need for deception here, Terran. We mean you no harm."

A voice spoke from somewhere at my feet. I contemplated remaining quiet until I could come up with a plan but doubted it would do much good at this point. I needed to find out who I was up against and what sort of fate awaited me.

Slowly, I lifted my aching head and spotted a tall, thin, tanned man with a snow-white beard sitting at the edge of my bed. Behind him, I recognised the native woman perched on a stool, gazing at me with those cool, deep eyes. Both wore long, white tunics and remained as still as statues as they regarded me. I ventured a quick look around at what appeared to be a simple, sparsely-furnished bedroom and saw no one else present. I spotted the door behind them. If needs be, I could grab one of the chairs at the table to fight them off and make a break for it.

"Am I your prisoner?" I asked with a hoarse voice.

The native man reached into a satchel at his feet, pulled out a flask, uncorked it, and took a swig before offering it to me. I was reluctant to take it, but a ferocious thirst overrode any fear of being poisoned, so I took a mouthful and was relieved to taste cool, refreshing water. As I drank, I realised the one-piece body suit I wore under my Exo-suit had been peeled down to my waist. Fresh bandages covered my right side, from hip bone to armpit. I took a deep breath in and, considering the size of the bandaged area, didn't feel even a lingering thread of pain.

"You are our guest," the old man finally replied.

Although he was easier to understand than the native woman, he still bore that strange, unplaceable accent. He continued looking at me as I took another mouthful from the flask, but I observed no tell-tale sign of emotion on that worn, yet chiselled, face.

"Guests can leave whenever they want," I said and moved to get up out of the bed.

"Wounded guests won't last long outside," the old man said and pointed to my bandaged side. "We have begun treatment. To leave before its completion is to invite death."

Firing a curious look at the old native, I paused on the edge of the bed and ran a hand over my bandages. In response, he reached into his satchel again and pulled out a small, transparent glass jar with a light-green paste inside.

"A natural remedy," he said, handing it to me.

I unscrewed it and took a sniff. It didn't have an odour I recognised and looked more like toothpaste than something to heal a wound, but I nodded my thanks as I handed it back to him.

"How long have I been out?" I asked as I stood to stretch my muscles and began pulling on my body suit to cover my exposed chest and arms.

"A full night and half a day," he said and nodded towards the woman. "Nala told me what you did for her. This is the reason you are here, Terran."

The native woman continued to study me in silence, any trace of fear long since erased from her sombre face.

"Thank you," I said to her before stretching my hand out to the old man. "My name is Darren."

The elderly native studied the gesture for a long moment. For a few heartbeats, I thought he would reject my handshake, but he stood up slowly from his stool, raised his hand, and gripped mine.

"Gya," he said as he mechanically shook my hand, trying to mimic my actions. "For what you have done for Nala and Rela, I extend my protection to you while you heal. No hand will strike you. What is ours, is yours. But know the hearts of my people, Terran. You are not wanted here. When you are healed, you will leave."

"Fine by me," I said, relieved that I knew where I stood with my hosts. "My Exo-suit and weapons..."

"Will remain under my eye until you leave."

I didn't like the sound of that, but I couldn't do anything about it until I learned more about my hosts and their intentions. Back on the streets, rumours persisted of the violent retaliation meted out by the hostiles to captured MOF soldiers. It could have been propaganda, but I decided it best to be prudent and go along with everything, until I knew more.

"Come," Gya said and extended his hand. He gripped me by the left elbow and led me towards the door.

He walked me into a well-illuminated corridor with immaculately white-washed, smooth walls. Candles in glass bulbs placed a few feet apart on either side of the wall flickered, guiding us towards the end of the corridor. Two guards outside my room, armed with make-shift particle weapons, fell in behind Nala as we walked.

"We're underground," I said, remembering that the natives dwelled mostly beneath the surface.

"Yes," Gya said as he guided me by my elbow. "This place is old. It is one of the last places we have left that is close to the surface. Our people burrow deeper and deeper when building homes."

"In case of aerial bombardment," I finished for him.

The old man gave me an affirmative nod and remained silent until we reached the end of the corridor. He stepped through first but pulled me close behind him. I found myself in a large hall or common area. It must have been at least two or three times the size of the canteen back at MOF HQ, with a long trencher table running the length of the room. All around us, people were setting food on the table or pulling chairs close to it. Young children laughed and played with one another, and men and women talked loudly as they went about their chores. The room was warm, inviting, and filled with laughter. That all died away as soon as they laid eyes on me.

Every single one of them sported the same look as Nala and Gya. Unusually thin, tall, and tanned, they made me look short and stocky by comparison. Their gazes studied me as intently as Nala's, but the over-riding fear for her daughter had kept her hatred of my kind in check, whereas their mutual anger struck me as strong as a particle blast to the chest.

I spotted various corridors and doorways along the walls on either side of the room. I considered making a break for it, but before I could act, Gya stepped forward and spoke.

"This Terran saved Nala and Rela from the outcasts. He risked his life for them. He will be our guest until he heals, and then we will send him home."

The room remained deathly silent as the young and old looked at one another in shock and surprise. After a tense moment, they went back to their chores, shooting sideways glances at me as they worked. Gya led me towards the head of the table, near a massive open fire, and gestured for me to take a seat. Nala took a seat beside me but made sure to keep a more-than comfortable distance between us. She said something to one of the women near us in a language I didn't recognise and accepted two plates of food and a couple goblets of water. She set mine down in front of me and began nibbling at her own meal.

My plate overflowed with vegetables covered in a gravy-like liquid. They didn't exactly look like anything I recognised back home, but I ate it all the same. It wasn't half bad. More people sat around us, also ensuring to stay as far from my orbit as possible. Within minutes, a full-blown feast erupted. I sat content, taking small bites of my food, studying the natives and keeping an eye on the two-armed guards behind me. So far, they were the only ones who carried weapons that I could see.

After the meal, the dishes were cleared away and another series of goblets were handed to everyone— although mine was set down directly in front of me. Glass bottles of purple and golden liquid were passed around, and all the adults poured themselves generous glasses before breaking off into groups to chat. Nala handed me a half-full golden bottle and nodded at my goblet.

"Drink this. You will like it."

Ever willing to try new things, I poured the golden, syrup-like substance into my goblet, sniffed it, and took a sip. It tasted exactly like honey but with an

272

alcohol bite. I gratefully took another large mouthful and a wave of relaxation cut through my body.

Rela, Nala's daughter, joined her after the meal and jumped playfully on her mother, whispering something to her. It warmed my heart to watch Nala's serious face light up like a sunrise as she interacted with her daughter. After a few moments, that smile faded when she caught my gaze. Rela faced me and smiled shyly.

"My daughter wishes to thank you for getting us home," Nala said reluctantly but less harshly than I expected, "and I want to thank you too, Terran. It is an unexpected kindness."

She patted her daughter away to re-join her friends and refilled my glass. From her body language and physical distance, I could tell she was massively uncomfortable around me and it had taken a lot for her to say that much to me. I thanked her, and we returned to the awkward silence that existed like a canyon between us.

Wanting to keep my head clear, I nursed my drink as I absorbed everything that happened around us. At one stage, Gya returned to apply that toothpaste substance to my wound and fix a new bandage in place. For the most part, though I was surrounded by strangers, I remained alone. Ironically, I didn't feel lonely; it was interesting just to watch such lively people interact. I didn't know if living on Big Red caused their thinness, but they certainly didn't look to be malnourished—everyone appeared happy and healthy. The vibe in this communal hallway was one of safety, peace, and laughter.

As the night wore on, the lights dimmed. Some of the babies and toddlers were taken back through the corridors by the parents. Those children who remained took their places on the smooth stone floor in front of the roaring fire, facing a group of elderly men and woman. Everyone else crowded around them as well, listening intently as one of the old women spoke softly but animatedly in their native tongue.

I had no idea what she was saying, but I found myself lost in the sheer music of her words, the vivid hand gestures that accompanied every sentence and the expressive facial expressions she pulled that breathed life into her story. It was strange, almost hypnotic in a way. Even though I couldn't understand her, I felt as though I knew what she was saying, as if she sang a long-forgotten lullaby from the earliest days of my childhood.

She spoke of the wars that gripped humanity and the wrath of the gods. Her voice filled with despair as the fires rained down from heaven, burning the innocent and guilty alike. She wept when the false gods took slaves of the people and burned their cities. She whispered about the Great War and the stars that blazed and blotted out, never to shine again. Finally, there was the Exodus. Every single person lingered on her words, fascinated and enthralled with each syllable she uttered.

"Do you understand, Terran?" Nala whispered into my left ear.

I turned and found myself centimetres from her. She didn't flinch or pull away; there was no more sadness or anger reflected in her eyes. The old woman's story, as terrible as it was, had washed the walls of anger away. Whatever had happened, had happened to all of us—Terran and Native alike. It happened to all of humanity.

"I think so," I said, surprised at the truthfulness of my words.

"We have always been here," she whispered softly as her eyes peered deep into my own. Her gaze lowered to study my lips.

"We have always been here," I replied without

thinking, knowing for the first time that it made sense in a strange, inexplicable way.

We kissed. I don't know how or why, but we did. The whole room faded away, and everyone around us disappeared. For a moment, I knew peace. I lost myself in her warm lips and soft breath. My heart pounded rapidly as my hand caressed hers, and a tingle of electricity turned into a full electric shock the longer I touched her. The world melted away—all of my guilt and all of her anger disappeared—until we were the only two people who existed in the universe.

When it ended, I felt strange and hollow again. The words of the old woman returned to my ears and snapped me back to the hall. Nala pulled her face away and looked at me with the fondness of someone who had known me for years. My heart skipped a beat as she gazed at me and touched my face with her soft hand.

"We will meet again, Terran. We always have, and we always will."

She said the words with both a joy and a forlorn sadness as she stood to leave. She called for Rela. After her daughter appeared by her side, she gave me one last lingering look before she disappeared into the crowd. As the old woman's story ended, the crowd dispersed and the last of the children were stewarded off to their beds. Teenagers paired off and sat along the walls, holding hands and whispering to one another, while smaller groups of adults continued their hushed conversations, refilling each other's goblets. A part of me hoped Nala would return, even if only for a minute or two, but Gya took the seat beside me.

"Do you understand now?" he asked. His warm eyes probed me.

"I think so. At least, I thought I did when the old woman spoke. It doesn't seem clear anymore."

That was the truth. Even without understanding

her language, her words had painted a vivid picture so real I could make it out as the images changed from one scene to another, but the memory of it faded quickly. Although I knew that I had been on the crevasse of understanding something primal and true, our mutual past continued to slip away.

"I see you," Gya said, without breaking eye contact. "You have two hearts and two minds and two bodies." Technically, that was true. "No one can exist like this. You must choose. Only then will you know peace."

"What if one of those choices is to go home, but there's no way back?" I asked, surprised at how open I was being.

"Making the choice is enough. If you want it, you will find a way."

My gaze strayed towards one of the nearby corridors, and I imagined following it would take me to Nala.

"But what if..."

"It is not meant to be, Terran. Not this time," Gya replied. His words were firm but friendly. "Maybe in the next time or the time thereafter you will be reunited, but not here and not now. Things must come to pass as they should. You will see her again, but not as things are now. Do you understand?"

I didn't, but I told him I did.

Shortly afterwards, I was escorted back to the room I had woken up in and fell into a deep sleep. I had strange dreams of different places and times, of events and things I couldn't comprehend—a tortured boy-soldier who walked with death, a young girl who lived a thousand lives, and a new-born child who held a smouldering, blackened Terra in its tiny, chubby fingers. Although disturbingly intense and vivid, the dreams faded after waking, for which I was grateful.

I spent another two days with the natives until they decided I was healed enough to return home.

Except, I found myself wanting to stay and learn more about them. The hostility I faced when I first saw them had evaporated into a grudging acceptance of my presence. Even so, I enjoyed the peaceful vibes that emanated from their community.

I saw Nala fleetingly over those two days, and only from a distance. When our gazes did meet, I observed that strange, melancholy fondness, but every time I tried to talk to her, someone got in our way. I never even got to say goodbye to her or Rela. That confused me a lot. In all the time I'd lived on Big Red, I had never once cheated on Louise. At the start, especially during the first year, she had constantly been in the forefront of my mind. Even during my prison term, thinking of her and Kat had staved off my darkest thoughts. I had urges just like everyone else, but never acted on them, and yet, out of nowhere, I had kissed a native. More surprisingly, I didn't feel guilty about it. That made me feel bad, but I hadn't seen Louise in decades so, as terrible as it sounds, I tried not to beat myself up about it.

Gya arranged for a patrol to bring me back to the mining outpost and for his people to patch up the wound on my Exo-suit. It wasn't exactly battle-ready but would last long enough for me to get back to New Berlin.

I said my goodbyes and asked for permission to return and visit with my new acquaintances, hoping that we could build a bridge between our people. I expected him to decline, but he consented, and we planned for my safe passage back.

The patrol left me at the hills beside the mining facility. Upon seeing the landers and transports of my colleagues, I felt relieved that after three days they were still searching for me. I called them on the comm as I approached and received a hero's welcome. Smack herself had taken personal charge of the mission to find me and gripped me in a massive bear hug, with tears streaming down her face. When we had all the equipment packed up and the privacy of one of the landers to ourselves, I finally told her of my whereabouts for the last few days.

She was dubious at first, but after I passed all the medical and psychological tests, I filled her, Dan, Big Mo, and a reluctant Tazz in on my experiences. Everyone agreed that going back could be a trap, but I convinced them it was worth the risk. It was a chance to learn about the people we had been killing since we arrived, to uncover the truth of what this conflict was all about or make amends for our past actions.

It took a few weeks, but I eventually convinced my friends to pay a friendly visit to the natives. We listed it as a private recon mission with the MOF authorities and set off for the natives' home on a transport. Flying through the sky as opposed to over land made it a bit trickier to pin-point where the entrance to their subterranean dwelling lay, but I managed to locate it.

We made our way down through the tunnel. The lack of guards to greet us surprised me, but the reason for that became apparent once we reached one of those white-washed corridors cut into the stone. A solitary guard lay at the entrance to the corridor, with his throat slit from ear to ear. Filled with dread, I raced down the corridor with my HK-17 and found the main hall where I had sat and listened and ate and kissed Nala weeks before. All the natives were there—men, women, children. All dead.

I stepped carefully over the carpet of dead bodies, surveying the carnage and searching for survivors, but no one had lived through this. From the spent shell casings, the grouping of the bullet holes on the victim's bodies, and the surgical stab wounds, it was clear that it wasn't the work of the outcasts. This had all the hallmarks of a MOF operation.

I wept when I found Nala and Rela, each with bullet holes to the head—execution style. Even in death, Nala's arms were wrapped tightly around her daughter. I tried to not imagine how terrifying their last moments were. From their fresh wounds, I guessed they had been murdered hours prior to our arrival, so I blamed myself for not insisting that we leave earlier. Maybe we could have stopped it.

I found Gya sprawled on his back in front of the dying fire. His eyes were wide open. A bullet wound marred his chest, but a knife to his throat had finished him off. I hovered over his eyes, as if to glean any last information from him about the truth that had felt so close but was now so far away. His eyes sparkled from the dying embers of the nearby fire. I thought of the words he had spoken to me in the hall and whispered my goodbye to him.

Heartbroken, I carried the bodies of Nala and Rela outside by myself and buried them together. Aware of my pain but unsure of what words to speak to take it away, Smack called for reinforcements to help us lay the massacred population to rest. The sight of so many murdered children broke even the hardest of us, so much so that we stayed the night, lamenting and weeping and drinking to numb the pain of the cruelty of our people. I found Nala's room and spent the night there, sitting and thinking and trying to come to grips with what I had witnessed—the sheer callousness inflicted on them. By the time morning arrived, the frustration and sadness hardened to anger. Remembering Gya's talk with me, I made my choice.

I would return to Terra, and hell would follow close behind.

Consumed with rage and grief, I could think of nothing more than hitting back as hard as I could at the MOF. The murder of the natives in such an indiscriminate and violent fashion had been the final straw, the last act of cruelty to tip me over the edge.

Their abduction of us, their programming of us into cloned killing machines, the way they used us against other humans who were trying to survive, how they lied to us, imprisoned us, tortured us, and forbade us from returning home; it all boiled over. I didn't want to just hurt them, I wanted to deliver one single, decisive strike that would finish the MOF. I wanted Terra to feel the sting for generations to come. But first, I needed a plan.

I didn't know where to begin, but getting information seemed like the best place to start. I decided to find out why those natives had been targeted, in the hopes that I could unravel MARSCORP's overall intentions for Big Red. That didn't strike me as an overly easy plan since no one in New Berlin would be stupid enough to talk openly to us about such things, so I thought about hacking into their systems. Not being a technical person, I approached Tinnie, our de facto IT expert.

Like me, he was a native of Dublin and from the first batch of Hollows. After being wounded in our little insurrection and jailed alongside us, he had turned away from the life of a soldier-mercenary and contented himself with working on the background side of the business. Invaluable as our go-to tech guy, I figured he could tell me what could or couldn't be done.

"You want me to hack into the MARSCORP and MOF data bases?" He tore himself from his split screen monitors to swing around in his swivel chair and look at me. "Sure," he continued with a shrug. Returning to his screens, he typed in a few commands on his keyboard.

"Just like that?" I asked, surprised at his indifference.

"Just like that," he said, typing furiously.

"Will it be difficult?"

"Not really," he said, shrugging again. "I already have a back door installed to get around their security."

The way he said it with such nonchalance caught me off guard, so much so that I placed my hand on his shoulder and swivelled him around to face me. He shot me a confused look as I removed my hand and squatted so that we were at face level.

"What do you mean a 'back door'?"

"I mean a back door," he replied, as if trying to explain something to a four-year-old. "I can access pretty much anything on the colony except for systems to do with defence, power, life support, that type of thing. All of that is kept on a guarded intranet system with no way of connecting to anything without a physical external connection, but databases, records, non-vital communications systems are all kept on an open system with lax security. How do you think we're able to find out who to bribe or who's a mole?" he said, with a cheesy smile planted across his face. "This guy!" He swivelled himself around and returned to his task.

"You make it sound so easy," I said, standing up and trying to make sense of the lines of commands that raced across the screen with each keyboard strike.

"Only if you know what you're doing," he said and paused to take a mouthful of water from a nearby bottle. "Think of it like this: You're still looking at things through the lens of it being 2018, but back on Terra, they're still coming to grips with Y2K. Even with all the advanced technology they have here on Big Red, their computer systems are only a few years more advanced than what they have back home in this time frame, and that's a hell of a lot easier to deal with. I guess the **MOF** didn't anticipate there being any hackers planet-side."

I remained quiet, processing Tinnie's words as I watched him work. After a few minutes, he handed me a MiniDisc and cracked his knuckles in triumph.

"There's everything you requested." He put his hands behind his head and stretched out his legs. "Anything else?" he said.

I smiled. "Yes."

We spent the next few hours talking everything out. I outlined rough versions of plans as they came to me, which he either shot down or told me were possible. This continued until we had something presentable, something I could take to everyone else. It would require a lot of hard work, commitment, risk, and above all patience, but if they shared my desire for revenge, of finally getting even with those who had betrayed and imprisoned us, I would give them the opportunity, no matter how long it took.

Still trying to work out the details in my mind, I studied the reports Tinnie had downloaded for me on my data pad. The first set of documents covered boring business reports and a series of coded memos between various execs, but the second batch caught my eye. The meeting we protected at the mining facility saw the final decision being made to expand operations into that area. The reports indicated that scattered subterranean communities were located around the surrounding areas and implied that the natives needed to be dealt with.

It took a few more minutes of searching and speed-reading until I came across the death blow, the point of no return where all doubt about my new goal faded. They had tracked the location of Nala's home by homing in on the satellite uplink request I had sent before being attacked near the entrance to their underground settlement. An entire community received a death sentence the minute I decided to rescue a mother and child from harm's way.

I spent the rest of that night inconsolably grief-stricken at my stupidity for not realising how ruthless and vicious the MOF and their MARSCORP masters could be. But as the sun rose the next morning on the blood-red sands of this grave-filled planet, my heart hardened again and filled with a new determination to right the many wrongs. I called for a meeting with my friends to lay everything out. I even called Noid, now an established crime figure in the New Berlin underworld.

I waited until Big Mo, Smack, Tazz, Dan, and Noid were all seated and the conference room door was locked before I took them through my plan. A lot of the details needed to be worked out, but this was about selling it to them. I couldn't do this without them. Even if I had all the resources of Hollow Point Defence at my disposal, I needed people I could trust with my life to make everything work.

I finished my presentation and waited anxiously for their response. They looked at me as if I was crazy, but no one rejected it outright, so I took that as a small victory.

"It's ambitious," Big Mo said, rubbing his neatly-shaved chin and avoiding eye contact. "There are a lot of things that could go wrong, though. You're asking a lot of people—people who've finally settled down and made lives for themselves here—to risk it all."

"I agree," Smack said, sounding unconvinced. "Priority has always been about our people's safety. We should be focusing on getting back to Terra, not sabotaging any prospect of going home."

"There's more at stake than our people, Smack. The natives are getting butchered, and we're the only ones who can stop it. I know I'm asking a lot. And it won't be easy, but it's the right thing to do. If we do things my way, we'll keep those people safe and get one up on the MOF. They're never going to let us go home anyway. Our tour ended twenty-three years ago. We're going to die on Big Red. Let's do it knowing we made an entire planet a little bit safer."

"But what you're proposing is to seize control of the one device that will get us home," Smack fired back. "If you've put all this planning into that, then why don't we just use it to send our people home? Or better yet, if you can hack their systems, change the records so they don't hire us in the first place?"

I took a sip of water while I considered my response. Of everyone here, I anticipated Smack being the hardest to convince. Her priority was to look after us, even over her own desires. She didn't want to see us back in prison. That's what made her such a good leader; she put the collective ahead of her own personal feelings and tried to do the best thing for the majority, but it also made it necessary that she signed on. If I didn't win Smack over, this was a no-go.

"If we send people back to the 2018, how long do you think it will be before they hunt us down? We'll be waking up in a heavily-fortified, secret military installation. Even if some of us do escape, that'll put our families in the firing line. As for changing the records, we still don't know what criteria they hired us on. And if we do get ourselves removed, they'll just send another bunch of saps in our place. We'd be condemning another group of people to this life, and the natives would be no better off."

"You don't know that for sure," Big Mo said, wavering.

"You're right, I don't. Maybe this could get us home. Maybe we could take control of the London facility, escape, and go underground. Then what? They'll never let us be free on Terra, not after everything we know, and that still leaves the natives. There's a genocide happening here. The MOF programmed us to see them as hostile aliens and forced us into taking part in killing an indigenous people trying to defend themselves. If we leave and do nothing, they'll be systematically wiped out. We have blood on our hands, and I want to wipe some of it off before I die."

"What about the psychosis thing Doctor Milton talked about," Big Mo pressed. "You're talking about sending us back within twenty minutes of being transported. Won't that scramble our minds?"

I reached into my pocket and pulled out a MiniDisc and slid it across the table to him. "Here's everything MARSCORP has on compression travel and its effects on the human mind. A lot of it is based on research conducted on us and the second batch, but they have made a lot of headway with it. We will be disorientated when we first wake, and we may not remember everything that's going on, but our memories should return gradually. At the same time, our people on Terra will move into position. We'll have people in the London facility to prep us as we go along. Then, using hypnotic suggestions, our minds will be triggered fully awake when the time is right."

The room remained silent for a few more seconds as everyone considered the depth of the plan.

"You sure this isn't over your native crush?" Noid asked, sticking one of those pre-rolled cigarettes the Volk favoured into her mouth and sparking it. She took a drag, leaned back in her seat, and shot a cocky grin in my direction.

"We all saw what the MOF did," I said, focusing my attention on Noid. "We buried men, women, and children. Newborns were shot in their cribs. Mothers were killed in front of their children. This is happening everywhere."

I handed a data pad with records of various covert MOF attacks over the last few weeks to her. It listed in gruesome, methodical detail the body count of the pacified areas. Noid studied it in silence. Saying nothing, she passed it to Big Mo. He did his best to hide his discomfort as he handed it to Smack.

"But for this to work, we need to get the natives and the Volk on board. How are we to convince them to do this? They'll think we're crazy or that it's a trap," Dan chimed in. "And do we really want to get into bed with Nazis? No offence, Noid."

"None taken," Noid said with a cheeky wink to Dan as she tapped cigarette ash onto the floor. "Leave the Volk to me. If we do go ahead with this, you can count on them."

I nodded my grudging thanks to Noid before turning to Dan. "I'll deal with the natives. I'll convince them it's in their best interests to join us."

"How?" he asked.

My thoughts drifted back to the old native woman's story and the cryptic talks I had with Nala and Gya.

"We have something in common with the natives. Some shared history, an event that separated us as a people. I'll share my truth with them the way Gya tried to with me. It will take time, but I know I can reach them. I've never been so confident about anything in my life. I can do it."

"Say we do get everyone on board," Big Mo started, "the natives, the Volk, our people. Then why wait till 2018? That's two decades away, most of us will be in our sixties, if we even live that long."

"There's two reasons for that," I said, suppressing the smile that wanted to curl up on my face. "One, we need time to infiltrate the MOF and gain access to the fleet and the other colonies. We also need to smuggle people back to Terra to infiltrate EISEN. As an organisation, it won't be officially founded in its current format until a few years from now. We need to redact our records after 1976, hiding our operations, rebellion, and incarceration to make them think we're returning from our original tour. It's also vital we have our people in place to seize control of the installation and destroy their Compression Matrix.

"Two, it will give us plenty of time to gain leverage on Doctor Milton and whoever else can grow new Hollow bodies. After we take down the London EISEN facility and return to Mars, we'll have fresh Hollow bodies just as we did when we first woke up on Phobos. We'll also have forty years of memories and experiences. Oh, and an entire planet under our thumbs."

Everyone grinned at the thought of that as they flicked through my proposal.

"I have contacts in the fleet," Dan said. "For the right amount, I should be able to get some of us smuggled aboard long enough to get that computer virus planted."

"Good," I said with a smile. "Start cultivating those contacts. We'll need to get our people aboard to seize control as soon as the colonies and fleet goes dark. If we don't take or at least cripple the fleet, then this will all be for nothing."

"Understood."

Smack, who had been engrossed in the list of MOF atrocities, placed the data pad back on the table and looked me right in the eyes.

"I'll lead the infiltration team back to Terra. You're right, Dub. We need to do something about this."

"Are you sure, Smack?" I said hesitantly. Someone had to do it, but I envisioned myself or maybe Big Mo leading that team.

"I'm sure," Smack said, with iron in her voice. "Dan, do you think your contacts in the fleet can smuggle me and a few volunteers back to Terra?"

"Sure," Dan replied, stroking his chin. "For the right price, that is. But according to the plan, that means you and whoever else leaving ten years before we even arrive via compression. That's ten years of pretending to be someone you're not while trying to not get caught. I'll go instead, if you prefer."

"No, it's my call. You're needed to take the fleet. I won't send someone else when I can do it myself. This decision has been made."

The room fell silent as we absorbed what that meant. In a few years, we would be sending our friend to infiltrate the enemy that had exiled us here. Even worse, when we did meet again, we probably wouldn't even recognise her. At first.

"That will leave a lot of dead natives for the next two decades," Smack said, clearing her throat.

"I'll convince them to pull out of any contested areas. It won't be easy, but I'll make them see that if they can lay low for a while, we'll give them back their planet."

"You sure that last part will work with our families?" Big Mo asked hopefully.

"We'll have Terra hostage and we'll have their people here. They'll give us our families in exchange for not wiping them out."

Big Mo shifted uncomfortably in his seat at that. "Could we do that? Bomb Terra, I mean?"

"We just need to make them think we will, Mo.

Look, this won't be easy, and there will be casualties on both sides, but if we do this my way, we'll keep it to a minimum."

Noid laughed as she read something from my plan. "You want to infiltrate the MARSCORP building by triggering a fire alarm and then posing as firefighters? You are crazy, Dub. But I'm in. Count the Volk in, too. There's a lot of money to be made if this works."

I returned my attention to Big Mo, who appeared to be mulling it over. After a few seconds, he nodded his consent. "In."

I patted him on the back in thanks and finally looked over to Tazz, who had remained silent for the duration of the meeting. She finished reading over my proposal. With those sad eyes, she looked up at me.

"We have always been here," she whispered, "but it's time for us to make a difference. I'll do the last part, that bit at the end."

It took me a few seconds to understand what she was referring to.

"Are you sure?" I asked, trying to mask my surprise.

"I've done it before," she whispered, still unwilling to make eye contact.

We took a few moments to look at one another and let the gravity of what we were planning sink in. We were risking everything. The tinniest, unanticipated detail could be fatal and derail our entire operation. Still, we had the guts of twenty years to work it all out. The UEAF would never know what hit it until it was too late.

"You're doing this for those natives and those in-bred Nazis?" General Barrymore roared at me, practically foaming at the mouth. "You've no idea what you're in for."

"It's not too late to stop and think this through, Darren," Doctor Ling pleaded. She gaped at me with a horrified fascination. "I know you feel hard done to, but we didn't know. We could only access the information that you allowed us. You covered up what you did up there. If we had known..."

"He knew," I replied, nodding at the general. "He knew his son was locked up for twenty years and he did nothing. Even after serving our time, he was content to let us rot on Big Red."

"It's not as simple as that," the general shouted. "I love my son, but you chose to take up arms against your superiors. By all rights, every one of you should have been executed."

I didn't reply to that but let it hang in the air. Even if I was interested in justifying myself to them, I wouldn't be able to change their minds. I could point to the hundreds of massacres carried out by the MOF, but they would hide behind the twin pillars of duty and obligation to the Terran cause rather than face up to the possibility that they were serving a genocidal regime funded by shady conglomerates.

"I have Big Bird online," Smack called out and nodded towards the static-filled viewing screen. Her face lit up with excitement.

"You're going to want to see this." I laughed at the general and doctor. "I know you're going to love talking to Big Bird face to face."

I gestured with my gun for them to stand and waited until they had pulled themselves to their feet before I nodded at Smack. She typed in a series of commands and the main viewing screen flickered to life, revealing a fancy office and desk. Several plaques and framed certificates hung prominently on the office wall in the background, but the names on them lay out of focus.

No one appeared in the camera frame.

"Now we see if everything went according to plan." Trembling with excitement, I picked up a nearby headset and cleared my throat. "New Berlin, New Berlin. This is Echo One-Niner. Sending confirmation code."

It felt a bit redundant considering who I would be speaking, too, but I had to play it safe until I knew for certain. Smack gave me a thumbs-up to indicate the confirmation package was sent and received. Everyone in the room fell silent as we waited. The camera angle shifted, as if something had barely touched off it. A shadow on the desk at the foreground of the frame indicated someone standing nearby. Slowly, a withered face emerged in front of the camera. Greying, straw-like hair was matted to a balding scalp. I watched as a familiar but aged face came into focus, staring directly into the camera lens.

"Doctor Milton," the general seethed through gritted teeth.

As if in response to the general's barely audible utterance, Doctor Milton's head and body slammed into the desk before slumping to the ground with a violent thud. The sound of pained whimpers indicated he still lived, though. The hand that assaulted the doctor remained in view before the body it was attached to shifted in front of the seat behind the desk. It bore the familiar Red'n'Black camouflage colourings of an MOF soldier, but no rank, insignia, or name tag gave any indication of who it belonged to.

With bated breath I waited, terrified that we had failed in our mission. I needed to see that face with my own eyes to know we had been successful, or I'd be forced to destroy the London installation and everyone in it. Slowly, dramatically, the body took a seat and the face came into full view of the camera. Every ex-Second Battalion soldier breathed a mutual sigh of relief.

We had done it.

"Hello, Darren," the voice said. A smile was plastered on the face from ear to ear.

I looked over at Doctor Ling, who tore her gaze off the screen to look directly at me.

"Hello, Darren," I replied victoriously and pumped my fist in triumph.

"This whole-talking-to-myself-from-the-past thing is weirding me out a bit," my Martian doppelganger said with a laugh, "so let's make this quick. Confirmation code Sierra-Tango-Tango-Bravo-Niner-Seven-Three-Three-One-Indigo. Everyone of your... or should that be 'our' team...downloaded from the London complex into their brand-new Hollow bodies approximately twenty-eight minutes ago my time, no casualties. New Berlin, the fleet, and the colonies are all ours. The natives and the Volk send their regards. You did it."

The room erupted into a round of cheers and applause, but I ignored it. I had a promise to keep to an old friend.

"I know what you're going to ask," my counterpart said, cutting me off in anticipation and gestured to someone off camera.

A blonde-haired face that I hadn't seen in what felt

like a lifetime appeared in front of the camera lens.

"Hey, gorgeous." Smack laughed to her aging counterpart standing near me. "Hurry up and get back here. There's one hell of a party planned for tonight." She lifted a bottle of wine to her lips and took a massive gulp before grinning back into the camera. My Smack turned to me and wrapped me in another bear hug; tears welled up in her eyes.

"We did it," she whispered and kissed me on the cheek.

"We're not home yet," I replied, patting her joyfully on the back. "Destroy all communications systems and data bases and initiate a Code Black. Send the emergency evacuation order and have Tazz arm the charges. It's time to move out."

I looked back up at my future self, and Smack fired off a mock salute at them.

"Safe journey home," Darren said as the viewer cut out and faded to black.

Without hesitation, Smack typed in a series of commands, irreparably damaging the current communications system and triggering the evacuation alarm. Sirens wailed as security doors around the building lurched open. An automated voice proclaimed a Code Black emergency and began a steady five-minute countdown before the installation's destruction. Smack signalled to the remaining soldiers to usher our hostages out of the nearest exits before escorting the general and doctor with us to the Compression Matrix. She waited until they had been led away and out of earshot before she spoke.

"You're positive you want to keep them alive?"

"We've made our point, Smack. There's been enough killing today. Let's wrap this up and get back."

Nodding her agreement, she patted Big Mo on the arm. Together, we left C&C, rushed down the stairwell, painfully aware that the clock was ticking, and sprinted through the corridors until we reached the Compression Matrix, located off the room where we had passed out in and awoken only hours and decades ago. Most of the bodies of those who had woken up highly traumatised lay peacefully still; their consciousness already downloaded to their new bodies back on the colony.

The last of my soldiers secured the room and guarded the doctor and general at gunpoint. Tazz sat silently by the Compression Matrix with a series of explosive charges around her and a trigger gripped in her hands.

"What to do with you two," I pondered aloud as the second last batch of soldiers strapped themselves in for transportation home.

"If you're going to kill us, then do it, coward," General Barrymore hissed.

I smiled and pointed my gun right at his face. He remained defiant, but fear flickered in his eyes.

"I don't think your son would mind," I said, giving it serious consideration. But as quickly as I pointed it at him, I lowered it. "No, you can live as a testament to Hollow mercy. I want you to deliver a message for me: Leave Big Red alone. If you interfere with our business in any way, I'll personally pull the trigger to bombard every UEAF facility on Terra, right after I give exclusive interviews to the media from the flagship. You'll receive a list of people you'll transport to Big Red in exchange for your soldiers, top brass, execs, and their families. Failure to comply will result in devastating consequences. Do I make myself clear?"

The general glared at me in response, but Doctor Ling nodded emphatically.

"Cut them loose," I ordered one of the guards. "Throw them out and secure those doors."

Eager to return to the colony, the guards unbound

the prisoners and prodded them with their HKs and forced them out of the doors. Confident that the room was sealed, I nodded for them to connect to the Compression Matrix. Right then, the automated voice counted down past two minutes. Unbeknownst to everyone who fled the London facility, we had disabled the explosive charges that would incinerate the entire building. Having already sabotaged the communications system and data bases, we were also going to destroy the Compression Matrix in its entirety. To prevent any issues with it being destroyed prematurely while the last batch of us were transporting back, it required a manual detonation.

"You sure you want to do this?" I asked Tazz, with only myself, Smack, and Big Mo left to transport.

"No," she said sadly, "but I want this nightmare to end. I can't do it anymore. They took everything from me, and I can't be strong like you. I just want to feel nothing."

For years I had talked to Tazz about her decision. Originally, I planned to use a timer to trigger the explosive, but she had been adamant. She saw it as symbolic; she wanted to destroy the very thing that had snatched her away from her happy life, from any connection she possessed with another person. No matter how much I tried, she wouldn't listen.

Without another word, I leaned in and gripped her tightly in a hug. Squeezing back, she rested her head on my shoulder and whimpered softly.

Smack started the transfer sequence while we each attached headbands and lay back on one of the vacant cots. We said our last goodbyes to Tazz and watched the Compression Matrix begin its automated countdown sequence. Laying back on the folding cot, I looked up at the piercing, white glow of the light above me and exhaled a nervous breath. My head spun and everything turned black as I drifted home.

After speaking with the past version of myself on Terra, I kicked my feet up on the desk in the office back in New Berlin and grinned at Smack again for the millionth time in the last half hour. Of all the nuts and bolts of the overall plan, I was most proud of the idea of sending our consciousness back thirty minutes into the 'past' from the time back on Terra. Who else could we trust to verify that Big Red was truly ours, but ourselves?

Perched on the desk, Smack handed me the half-full bottle of wine, which I gratefully took a swig from, before leaning back in the chair and savouring the moment.

"I feel like I'm in my twenties again," she said, studying her soft, porcelain skin in awe. "I forgot how good it is to be young. So full of energy, you know?"

"It'll take some getting used to," I replied running my free hand over my wrinkle-free face. "I'm a seventy-year-old man, in a young man's body. It's worth the wait, though. I told you I'd get us all our old lives back. We can pick up right where we left off before our tour of duty started."

Grinning, I took another swig and handed her back the wine bottle.

"What should we do with him?" Smack asked, waving at the injured Doctor Milton, who was sprawled in agony on the floor.

For a moment, I considered putting him out of his misery, but not wanting to endanger our people still back on Terra, I decided against it.

"Have him seen to and lock him up," I said to one of the soldiers under my command.

Without hesitation, the soldier lifted the wounded doctor and carried him out of the office.

"They're going to come after us," Smack said, as soon as we had the room to ourselves. "You do know that? They'll never let us get away with this. Even if we do round up all their people, there's bound to be people who'll slip through the net and cause us a lot of problems. We don't have the manpower to hold all the colonies and the fleet, even if we could train up the natives and the Volk. The best and the brightest on a planet with over seven billion people will be working around the clock to find a way to screw us over, Dub."

"I know," I said sombrely. "But we stick to the plan for as long as possible. We need to buy as much time as we can until we can excavate the artefacts. Once we have those, we'll have an insurance policy until the end of days. To think; MARSCORP wasted their time with just one artefact and developed cloning technology. Imagine what we can do with all seven."

Smack took another swig from her wine bottle before offering it to me. I shook my head as my thoughts moved to the hard work and long days that lay ahead.

"Are you sure we'll find them in time?" Smack asked, with an uncharacteristic tinge of nervousness in her voice. "MARSCORP has been searching for over sixty years."

"We'll find them," I replied confidently. "We've done more for the natives in a single day than any Terran has in six decades. We've given them back their planet. They'll come through for us. They have to. If they don't, then all of this will have been for nothing."

Smack stood up and moved to the far side of the

desk, running her hand along the smooth, ebony surface as her thoughts trailed off. I knew this was the part of the plan that bothered her the most. She didn't like the idea of withholding information from people we had served alongside for so long, but I had convinced her it was a necessity. This was our ace-in-the-hole. I couldn't run the risk of anyone finding out, not when we were so close.

"Look at me," I said to her.

After a moment's hesitation, she lifted her gaze to meet mine.

"If they find out, if they figure out we've been lying to them, they'll turn on us in a heartbeat. I can't do this without you, Smack. I need to know I can count on you one hundred percent. Do I have your support?"

"Yes," she replied firmly, without even a moment's hesitation.

"Good. Send word to the Old Man in the tower. Tell him it's time to talk. I need to know everything he knows before he croaks."

Smack sighed as she paced along the side of the desk. "That could be sooner than you think. MARSCORP was keeping him alive till they found all of them. He'll be the first one they take out if they can get close enough. I can't imagine it would be too difficult to kill a one-hundred-and-twenty-eight-year-old man."

"Believe me, I'll sleep better when that old Nazi's dead and buried. But we need him alive. Do what you need to."

Smack shuddered at that. I couldn't say I blamed her. The last time I had been in his room during the Reicher Rebellion, it had sickened me to the core and I hadn't even seen his face. Now, I'd have to sit down and talk to pure evil incarnate to find what would forever alter the balance of power in our favour and keep Big Red free.

Reluctantly, Smack picked up her communicator, switched to a secure channel, and called our Volk liaison.

"Heinrich," she said icily, "the colonies are secure. Everything's locked down."

"Ja," a heavily-German-accented voice responded.

Smack shot me an uncomfortable look before she continued. "We followed through on our part of the bargain, now it's your turn. Set up a meeting as soon as your **führer** awakens. It's time to get to work."

He mumbled something back in German before disconnecting the transmission. Smack flashed me another uneasy look. Then she made her way towards the office door to oversee preparations. As I watched her leave, my mind drifted back to a time when I had been just another face in the crowd; happy with my lot for the most part but still unfulfilled. I wondered, as I sat here as de facto ruler of an entire planet, if I would trade it all to go back to that simple, unremarkable life. I missed it—it would be a lie to say otherwise—but here, I felt as if I was home.

On Big Red—on Mars—my destiny resided. The Hollows, the Volk, and the Natives were all one, united in a common cause against Terra. There would be war soon; that much was unavoidable. Many would die, but what we did here would echo throughout the ages.

After a lifetime of searching, we were so close to finding what each of us secretly desired, buried deep beneath the rational constructs of our minds and the harsh, now-lifeless Martian soil. We would unearth the truth, long suppressed by those in power and forgotten to the mists of time. We would uncover this truth once and for all, and that truth would give us power.

We have always been here.

Always.

About the Author

Damien Larkin is a full-time stay-at-home father of two loud (but happy) young children. He studied to become a social worker but instead spent ten years in the hospitality sector. At seventeen, he joined the Irish Reserve Defence Forces, ending up as a weapons specialist. He holds a black belt in Tae Kwon Do and is an avid reader of history, psychology and science fiction books. Big Red is his debut science fiction novel, based on a disturbingly vivid dream. He currently resides in Dublin, Ireland.

Website:
www.damienlarkinbooks.com
Facebook:
www.facebook.com/DamienLarkinAuthor
Twitter:
www.twitter.com/Damo_Dangerman

CPSIA information can be obtained
at www.ICGtesting.com
Printed in the USA
LVHW110306280519
619246LV00004B/504/P

9 781939 844606